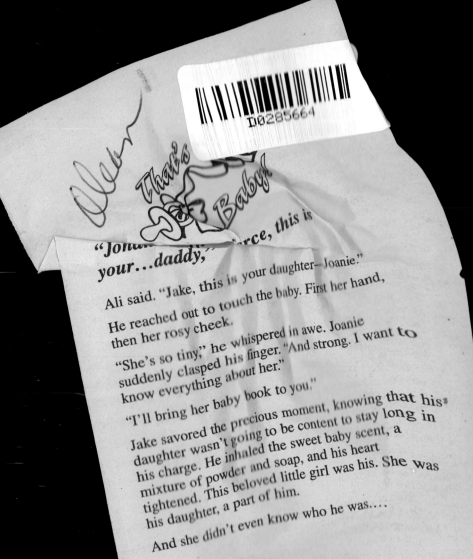

That's My Baby!

"Joh... ...rce, this is your...daddy,"

Ali said. "Jake, this is your daughter—Joanie."

He reached out to touch the baby. First her hand, then her rosy cheek.

"She's so tiny," he whispered in awe. Joanie suddenly clasped his finger. "And strong. I want to know everything about her."

"I'll bring her baby book to you."

Jake savored the precious moment, knowing that his daughter wasn't going to be content to stay long in his charge. He inhaled the sweet baby scent, a mixture of powder and soap, and his heart tightened. This beloved little girl was his. She was his daughter, a part of him.

And she didn't even know who he was....

PATRICIA THAYER
BABY, OUR BABY!

Silhouette®

SPECIAL EDITION®

Published by Silhouette Books
America's Publisher of Contemporary Romance

To Mindy Neff,
You always seem to be there when I need you. Thank
you for your time and talent and especially for
your friendship.
To Joe and Kim Rangel, for sharing your special
love story.
And to Aunt June. We'll miss you.

 SILHOUETTE BOOKS

ISBN 0-373-24225-5

BABY, OUR BABY!

Copyright © 1999 by Patricia Wright

Books by Patricia Thayer

Silhouette Special Edition

Nothing Short of a Miracle # 1116
Baby, Our Baby! #1225

Silhouette Romance

Just Maggie #895
Race to the Altar #1009
The Cowboy's Courtship #1064
Wildcat Wedding #1086
Reilly's Bride #1146
The Cowboy's Convenient Bride #1261

PATRICIA THAYER

Patricia has been writing for eleven years and has published eight books with Silhouette. Her books have been nominated for the National Readers' Choice Award, Virginia Writers of America's Holt Medallion and a prestigious RITA Award. Pat has been a longtime member of the Orange County chapter of RWA, has served on the board and was elected co-president in 1995.

Thanks to the understanding men in her life—her husband, Steve, and three sons—Pat has been able to fulfill her dream of writing romance. She loves to hear from readers. You can write her at P.O. Box 6251, Anaheim, CA 92816-0251.

Dear Reader,

In *Baby, Our Baby!,* hero Jake Hawkins battles death as a woman from his past attempts to draw him from a coma by telling him that he's fathered a child. Jake and Ali Pierce had but one night together, a night full of compassion and love, and their joining created the beautiful baby she now places in his arms.

Having something to live for, Jake fights his way to consciousness, desperate to see his child and the woman who kept her from him.

Ali has always loved Jake, but he'd never been hers…except for that one forbidden night. The next morning he'd left her and the town he hated far behind. Now Jake is back, and their scandal is revealed. Amid gossip and censure, Ali and Jake must find their way to forgiveness and love, if they are ever to create the family they so desperately crave.

I'm excited that my book has been chosen for the THAT'S MY BABY! promotion. Nine-month-old Joanie Pierce will steal your heart as she draws her parents together forever and teaches them the true meaning of love…and coming home.

Enjoy!

Patricia Thayer

Prologue

She knew he'd be here.

Ali Pierce brought her car to a screeching halt next to Jake Hawkins's Porsche with the Just Married sign still on the back. She shut off the engine and jumped out.

She could hardly make out the area surrounding the cottage on this dark, moonless night, but that didn't stop her. Ali picked up the skirt of her long bridesmaid's dress and hurried around the side of the small structure, concentrating on the steep grassy slope as she made her way toward the front porch.

Her concern was Jake. He'd been so angry when he'd left the church, Ali was scared that he'd do something crazy.

Damn you, Darcie, for always leaving messes for me to clean up.

When Ali reached the front of the cottage, she kicked off her satin heels and began climbing the familiar steps that led to the wooden deck. She'd started across the porch when a shadow caught her attention. A tall figure stood motionless at the railing. Ali didn't need any moonlight to recognize Jake Hawkins. Since the age of fourteen, she had all but memorized his physical features, from the slant of his broad shoulders to his tapered waist and slim hips. She also knew he had a coffee-colored birthmark on his left side just below the waist, a scar on his right leg just below the knee and a slightly crooked nose that had been broken by Randy Foster in the eleventh grade.

No one knew more about Jake "Hawk" Hawkins than Ali, except...her sister. And Darcie was gone.

A string of curses suddenly echoed across the silent lake as Jake raised his arm and flung a long-neck beer bottle toward the water. Then, one by one, he shoved the heavy clay pots off the railing, their impact resounding in the night.

Like a caged animal, he paced the deck. His words were mumbled, but Ali could hear the pain in his voice. He was fighting back. Fighting the pain that had started only hours ago when Ali had handed him the letter from Darcie. Ali hadn't read it, but she knew what it said.

Her twin sister had decided that she didn't want to be married to a man with no future. At least not the future Darcie wanted, or that she thought was her right.

And Darcie wanted it all. Not only did her sister have the love of the best man in town, but she also wanted the money, prestige and the big house on the hill to go along with it. And Darcie had waited four patient years for Jake Hawkins to return from his hitch in the army, and for him to take over Hawk Industries to complete the perfect picture.

But Jake had other ideas, and running his father's company wasn't in his plan. Last night, at the rehearsal dinner, he'd told Darcie that he wanted to reenlist. Darcie got hysterical. Even after Ali took their grandmother home, the couple was still arguing. And just as the wedding was about to start, Darcie told Ali that she couldn't go through with it. Ali thought her sister was kidding. But when the wedding dress came off, Ali began to panic. Darcie loved Jake Hawkins. How could she walk out on the biggest wedding in Webster, Minnesota, history? But Ali's older sister by eight minutes handed her a note and begged her to give it to Jake. Ali agreed and watched her identical twin hurry out of the bridal room and drive off.

That had been four hours ago.

Ali watched helplessly as Jake continued choking out his anger. She wanted desperately to hold him...to help him get through this.

Ali swallowed back the threat of fresh tears and walked to the railing.

Jake raised his head, and his eyes widened. "Darcie!"

"No, it's me. Ali." Ali was used to being mistaken for her sister. But it was the first time Jake had done it.

"Oh. Did you come to see the fool?"

She shook her head. "I was worried. You took off before I could talk to you. I've been driving around everywhere."

He turned away from her and stared out at the lake. "Was I supposed to greet the guests in the receiving line...alone?"

No. Ali and her grandmother had been left to explain to everyone why there would be no wedding.

"Oh, Jake." She took a step closer and reached a hand out, then pulled it back. She knew how much he loved Darcie. She also knew how her sister had used Jake. "Maybe it's for the best," she offered.

His hands balled into fists. "Best for who? Not me. Ali, what did I do that was so terrible? She knew I'd been thinking about reenlisting. She wasn't happy about it, but she knew I couldn't come home and work with my dad. I told her that a hundred times.''

Ali didn't know what to say to Jake. Darcie was selfish; she wanted what the Hawkins money could buy her. An army captain's salary wouldn't do. ''Jake, she's probably gone off for a few days to think things through.''

He shook his head. ''I should have realized last night that we want different things. But…we've been together so long. Oh, God, I've loved her forever.''

Ali glanced away. She didn't want Jake to see her true feelings—feelings she'd kept hidden. Even though she was Darcie's twin, Jake had never given her a second look, never thought of her as anything more than a friend. And he never would. Darcie would always be his true love.

''You've had fights before,'' Ali admitted.

Jake walked to the patio table and took another beer from the carton. After twisting off the cap, he took a long pull.

''Yeah, but this was different. This was important enough for her to walk out on our wedding.'' He looked at Ali, and she could see the pain etched in his face. He took another drink of beer and wiped a hand across his mouth. ''My dad is probably having a field day with this.'' His laughter was cold. ''I bet if I went home right now, I'd get an earful of 'I told you so.' ''

''Since when did you care what your father thinks?''

Jake's dark eyes searched her face. ''Oh, Ali-cat.'' He breathed the nickname he'd given her the first day he walked through the door of Gran June's house. She and Darcie had been freshmen and Jake the good-looking senior at Webster High School.

That same day Ali had lost her heart to Jake Hawkins.

''What am I gonna do without her?'' he finished.

You've got me, she wanted to cry. ''You're gonna get through it, Jake.'' She tried to sound wise for twenty-three.

Ali heard Jake's strangled sob. "I can't. Darcie was the only thing..."

She crossed the porch. "Don't, Jake. It's going to be okay." Ali wanted to believe what she was telling him. And as much as she loved her sister, she hoped Darcie stayed away a long time. Jake deserved to be loved by someone other than a selfish woman who only used people. Tears filled her eyes as she looked up at him. "I'm here," she whispered.

Before she knew what was happening, Jake pulled her into his arms. "I hurt so damn bad," he choked out.

They clung to each other in silence.

Then Jake placed a soft kiss against her hair, and a shiver ran through her body. Ali started to pull away, but he refused to release her as his mouth continued to caress her temple. Slowly his lips moved to the side of her face.

Suddenly things began to change. She felt his breath on her cheek, then his tongue traced the corner of her mouth. She stood still in his arms, letting his lips roam her face. They were no longer just consoling each other. There was a desperate urgency in the tightening of his embrace, in his rapid kisses. The need to share their pain, to console each other, took over.

Her gaze rose to meet his. The silent plea in his eyes made her breath catch. He needed her. For the first—and maybe the only—time he needed her. Was there anything wrong with answering his need? She had loved Jake for years. If only for one night, she wanted to pretend that he loved her.

"Oh, Ali-cat, I shouldn't be doing this." He started to pull away.

With a shaky smile, she moved her hands up his chest to circle his neck, refusing to let him go. "You need me, Jake," she said, her voice trembling. "As much as I need you."

Jake hesitated a second as if trying to rationalize what was happening. Then finally his head lowered, and his mouth captured hers. The second their lips touched, Ali's blood turned to liquid fire. Jake's kiss was demanding, hungry, and when Ali opened her mouth, his tongue moved inside, stroking and caressing until her legs nearly gave out. He pulled back and planted kisses along her jaw. She almost cried for the loss, but he quickly found his way back to her waiting mouth.

Then he raised his head, his expression one of shock and disbelief. She was afraid that he would push her away. Instead, his mouth closed over hers again in another heated kiss, then he moved back and murmured, "Ah, Ali-cat, we shouldn't be doing this. Damn, you taste so sweet...." He kissed her again and pulled her against his body.

Ali was light-headed by the time he broke off the kiss.

"Tell me to stop." His breathing was labored. "Before it's too late to make you leave."

Ali had never expected to hear those words. Though she knew she looked enough like her sister to be a substitute for Darcie, she didn't care. "I don't want to leave, Jake."

He released a groan and kissed her again, then led her through the French doors into the cottage. Instead of going to one of the bedrooms upstairs, he guided her to the sofa in front of the fireplace. She trembled as his mouth found hers again, as he lowered the zipper of her royal blue taffeta bridesmaid's dress, then slowly pushed the fabric off her shoulders.

Ali pulled his T-shirt off, and her fingertips traced the solid wall of his chest. His hands were busy, too, removing her bra and freeing her breasts. She cried out in pleasure as his mouth closed over her nipple. Then he trailed kisses down her stomach until he reached the barrier of her panties. He raised his head. Their gazes locked in the dim light, and she could see the questioning look in his eyes. The next move was hers.

The silence seemed to stretch out forever as he stared at her. The guilt ate at her, knowing his heart belonged to Darcie. Jake would never be hers. But she didn't care; she wanted this one night to remember. To feel what it was like to be loved by Jake Hawkins.

Leaning forward, Ali pressed her mouth against his. He kissed her gently, then with a low groan he pulled her to him, his body hard and demanding as he claimed her. And for a little while, in Jake's arms, the rest of the world seemed to disappear. There were no promises or words of love shared, only desperate need as they reached out for each other again and again.

Finally he slept and Ali watched him.

Sometime in the night, she heard him murmur Darcie's name. Her heart ached with love for this man, but she knew he could never return it. Jake Hawkins belonged to another.

Her sister.

Ali huddled close to his warm body, dreading the dawn. It came anyway.

The sun rose over the lake, its soft light wakening her. Alone, she sat up clinging to the blanket that Jake had pulled over them during the night. Jake stood in the doorway, dressed, his expression closed—or was that regret?

Oh, no. Don't say anything, Jake. Don't take last night away from me.

Jake combed his fingers through his hair. "I'm sorry, Ali. I had too much to drink and…"

Pulling the woolen blanket up like a shield, she struggled to hide the pain tearing her apart. "It's okay, Jake," she lied, her heart aching. Had she been so stupidly naive to think he could care for her once his immediate pain had passed?

He took a step closer to the sofa, but stopped. "No, what I did last night was not okay. I used you. I had no right."

Her heart pounded in her chest, and she fought back her tears. Please, Jake, just hold me. But the look in his eyes told her he wanted to disappear, to run from the shame he believed he'd caused her.

"I'd better go. Are you going to be okay?"

No. She was never going to be okay again. She'd lost her best friend. She'd lost Jake. Things between them could never be the same. "I'm fine."

He stared at her. "You sure?"

Ali nodded, praying he'd leave before she broke down and begged him not to.

He started through the door, then paused and looked back at her. "Ali, I never meant for anything to happen."

"I know," she whispered.

"I'm sorry, Ali." He disappeared through the door.

She sat unmoving, frozen with emptiness. She heard his car start, then the grinding of the transmission as he slammed it into gear. She closed her eyes against the angry sound.

He drove away, taking her heart and hopes with him. She got to her feet, then walked through the door to the porch railing. On the ground below were the clay pots, broken and scattered like the pieces of her heart. She lifted her gaze. The lake appeared cold and blue in the growing light of day. Clutching the blanket to her chest, she breathed in Jake's elusive scent trapped within the weave. A tear trailed down her cheek, a hot, stinging reminder that she'd been a fool to wish for miracles.

"Goodbye, Jake," she whispered, knowing he'd never return to a town he hated, a father he despised or a woman he would never love.

Chapter One

Jake Hawkins was back.

The nearly two, long years since she'd last seen him faded away as Allison Pierce leaned against the railing in the elevator and sucked in a long, slow breath, trying to fight off the claustrophobic feeling that threatened to engulf her. It didn't work. Although the temperature outside was in the thirties, sweat beaded her upper lip, and her heart pounded in her chest.

Finally the bell chimed for the fourth floor, and as soon as the door opened, she quickly stepped out into the ICU unit of Webster Memorial Hospital. Her gaze darted around the quiet, ecru-colored corridor as she walked across the teal carpeting toward the nurses' station. There were several nurses bustling around, but none were Margo.

Good. She could leave and her friend wouldn't be angry. Margo was the one who hadn't shown up. Ali started back to the elevator when she heard a voice. She turned to find

Margo Wells hurrying toward her. The short brunette hadn't changed much since high school. She was still shapely and cute.

Not like Ali, who was tall and thin, with too curly red hair and freckles, and looked about eighteen.

"Oh, no, you don't, Ali Pierce," Margo cried. "You're not running away from this."

"I shouldn't be here in the first place," Ali argued.

"Wrong," Margo said. "You should have been here two days ago when they brought Jake in."

At the mention of Jake, the fight went out of Ali. "Has there been any change?"

"No, that's why I wanted you here. He's been through a lot the last forty-eight hours. The crash. Being pinned in his car. Exposure to the elements in a freak October snowstorm." Her friend gave her a penetrating look. "And even after all that, he managed to say Ali-cat before losing consciousness."

"An old nickname," Ali murmured, memories flooding her. "Maybe you misunderstood."

The nurse shook her head stubbornly.

"C'mon, Margo. It's been nearly two years," Ali said, more frustrated than before. She wasn't ready to face Jake. Not after all that had happened... "He couldn't possibly want to see me."

The elevator doors opened again, and more people exited. Margo pulled her aside. "Look, Ali. It's only been eighteen months, but that's beside the point. The man has been in a terrible automobile accident, one he probably shouldn't have survived, but he did. He's in a coma, but before he drifted off he said your name, and not just once."

Ali blinked back tears. Darn, she didn't want to cry. She'd shed gallons of tears after Jake left. It had taken her a long time to get over his not coming back to her, but she had. At least she had told herself she had.

"You need to do this, Ali. If not for yourself, then you need to see him for Joanie's sake. He's her father."

Ali glanced around to see if anyone had heard. Margo was the only person who knew the true paternity of her little girl. "Everything I've done this past year has been for Joanie."

"And if you're lucky, you can give her what she needs— a daddy."

"And what will it cost me?" Ali blinked back more tears. Keeping the identity of her daughter's father a secret hadn't been Ali's choice. Jake had left town. Maybe it was her pride, but she didn't want a man who obviously didn't want her. A man who hadn't stuck around long enough to learn the consequence of their night together. Her daughter deserved better.

Margo shrugged. "You'll never know unless you go and see Jake."

Ali gazed down the hall. What would Jake do when he found out about Joanie? "What if he has a wife some-where?" Darcie was supposed to be married to Jake. The guilt over what happened that long-ago night still haunted Ali.

Margo shook her head again. "Besides his father, you and Joanie are the closest family he has."

"But I'm not family. I can't go in ICU."

"Yes, you can. C'mon, I'll keep watch." Margo started down the hall.

Ali relented and followed. Fear dogged her every step. It would be simpler just to leave things as they were. But she knew nothing was simple for Jake now. She had to do everything possible to help him—if only for Joanie's sake.

When Ali finally entered the dimly lit room, she stopped dead. Her heartbeat was erratic, a stark contrast to the steady rhythm of the machines. She gazed at the metal bed where Jake Hawkins lay. Her feet felt like lead weights when she made her way across the tiled floor. Her pulse pounded in her ears as she reached his bedside.

Managing to fight back her shock, Ali stared down at Jake's still, bruised body. Oh, God, she'd pictured seeing him again in a thousand different ways, but she'd never envisioned him lying so lifeless.

Anguish overwhelmed her. "Oh, Jake!" Her gaze swept over him, noting the ugly lacerations, the bruises on his skin and the bandages that encased his ribs and chest. His left leg was also heavily bandaged, and was elevated by a pulley hooked to the end of the bed. An IV drip sent medication into his veins, and a clear oxygen tube into his nose helped him breathe.

He looked pale, so different from the tan, vibrant man she remembered. She gently touched his jaw, which was swollen on one side where it had taken four stitches to close the gash in his chin.

He appeared shattered and defenseless. Her hand moved to smooth back the short curls that brushed his bandaged forehead. Silk. Black silk. That was what it had felt like between her fingers when she'd held him to her breast. Almost forgotten longing clenched tight in her belly, shocking Ali back to the present.

What was she doing? Fighting a sense of panic, Ali reached for his hand. Don't get caught up in fantasies. Do what you came to do.

"Hey, Jake, it's Ali. Wake up and talk to me. I hear you got caught in a blizzard."

Each word became harder to force past her lips. "C'mon, Hawk." She choked on the nickname he'd gone by in the days when life had been fun and she'd been innocent.

"You have some worried people here, praying for you to wake up. I hear your father's hardly left the hospital at all since the ambulance brought you in. Please don't make him wait any longer."

No response, only the incessant beeping of the monitor, its presence reminding her how close Jake was to dying.

A sob escaped her throat. "Damn it, Jake, wake up." Willing herself to touch him again, Ali gently traced his mouth with her fingertip, hoping for a tactile response. "Do you remember the night we spent together?" She drew her finger slowly across his lower lip. "I've never forgotten how incredible it was between us."

No response.

"Please, Jake. Open your eyes. Do it for your father," she whispered. "And for me." Her hands shook. "Do it for your daughter."

No sooner had Ali stepped out of Jake's room than she saw Clifton Hawkins. Surprisingly he looked much the same as she remembered. He was in his midfifties, and his hair was still coal black, though now streaked with gray. There were a few more lines around his eyes and mouth, and he was leaning on a cane.

He seemed shocked to see her at first, then he smiled. "Darcie? Darcie Pierce? Is that you?"

His innocent mistake let her know that she didn't belong here. "Hello, Mr. Hawkins. I'm not Darcie. I'm Ali."

"Of course. I'm sorry, Ali."

"It's all right." She glanced back at the hospital room she'd just come from. "I hope you don't mind...I heard about Jake and I came by to see..." There was a tremor in her voice. What must Jake's father think? "I'm sorry. If there is anything I can do..."

Mr. Hawkins nodded. "Thank you, Ali. Since you've already seen him, you know he's in bad shape." The older Hawkins shook his head. "It's funny. All these years, I've tried to get Jake to come home, and now..." His voice broke. "I had to have hip surgery to do it. Jake took a month leave from the army to come home and run the plant while I recuperate. Now, because of this senseless accident, he might not make it.'' Jake's father blinked and looked away.

''Sure, he will,'' Ali assured him, forcing herself to believe her own words. ''Jake's strong and healthy. He'll pull through this.''

Cliff Hawkins's eyes found hers. ''You think so?''

Ali nodded, wondering if she was crazy. Years ago she'd thought Jake invincible. Maybe she still believed it.

The older man took her hand in his. ''Please come back, Ali. Jake and I need all the encouragement we can get.''

Ali knew that if she agreed, there was no turning back. Not for her. Not for Jake. And not for their daughter.

Darkness surrounded him. Jake tried to move and realized he was unable to, but he could still feel the teeth-clenching pain that tortured his body. A lead weight seemed to press on his rib cage, pinning him down. His leg throbbed. But at least the pain let him know he was alive. He was hurt. Bad.

How had it happened? How had he ended up here? Where was here?

Voices penetrated the pounding pain in his head, fading in and out as he fought to speak but couldn't. When he heard his dad, Jake wanted to cry out, but his mouth refused to obey the command. He tried with all his strength to talk, but he lost. Finally he let the drugging oblivion take him.

Later the voices came again, tugging and pulling him to the surface. It was a woman's voice this time. Her soft, caressing tone lulled him, just as her touch soothed his body. Who was she? Why did her voice, her hands seem so…familiar?

* * *

"Well, how did it go?" Margo asked as she joined Ali at the cafeteria table on her break.

Ali pushed back her hair. "Terrible." She looked at her friend. "Tell me the truth, Margo. Is Jake going to make it?"

Margo sent her a concerned look. "I won't lie to you, Ali. It could go either way. That's why it's so important for you to be here. I know it sounds crazy, but you may have the power to bring him back, to give him the will to fight."

Margo was right; Ali did think she was crazy. Jake hadn't been part of her life, except for their one night together. After that, she'd stopped believing in silly dreams and concentrated instead on raising her child…alone.

But if there was a chance she could help bring Jake out of the coma, she couldn't walk away. A familiar pain gripped her as she thought about Darcie.

Although her sister telephoned almost every week, and despite the fact that Ali had gotten pregnant and had a baby, Darcie hadn't returned home since she left Jake at the altar. She'd gone to New York to build a career. "Maybe we should call Darcie.…"

Margo blinked, then reached for Ali's hand. "I'm not a good person to ask about that. You know I've never cared much for your sister. She was self-centered and spoiled. It's unbelievable to me that you two are twins."

It was equally hard for Ali to believe. Darcie had always been the glamorous one. Though they shared the same green eye color, Darcie's eyes looked richer, larger. Her sister had always known how to do her hair and makeup so she looked as though she'd just stepped out of a photo session. Ali had been plain by comparison. And Darcie's hair wasn't just red, but a beautiful auburn—with the help of a rinse.

There was more of a difference now in their builds, too.

Though both twins had always been slender, since Joanie, Ali's hips and breasts were fuller. From pictures she sent, Darcie still appeared model thin.

"The only good thing Darcie ever did in her life was *not* marry Jake," Margo said.

"But...he's always loved her."

"If that's true, why did Jake call for you? Why did he ask for Ali-cat?"

Three days later, there was still no change in Jake's condition, but he was able to breathe on his own, and was moved from ICU to a private room. At least now Cliff and Ali didn't have to worry about keeping their visits down to only ten minutes. In fact, the doctors encouraged friends and family to spend time with Jake. They thought that having people around, talking to him, might help bring him out of his coma.

Ali had been coming on her lunch hour from her dispatcher job at the sheriff's office. When she'd arrived this afternoon, she scooted her chair closer to Jake's bed. She fussed with him, touching his arm, brushing his hair off his forehead.

"How do you like your new room?" she asked, glancing around at the peach-colored walls. There was a television high on the wall across from the bed. She glanced back at Jake. "Pretty classy place you got here. Of course, I remember you were a classy guy."

No response.

She didn't give up. "Jake, do you remember that time...on the Fourth of July, when a bunch of us kids took off for the lake to watch fireworks? Darcie and I were seniors that year and thought we knew everything. I think Darcie wanted to be alone with you, but you talked her into making a party out of it." Jake had always included her.

That had been one of the reasons Ali had loved him so much.

"Anyway, when we got there, that jerk, Jerry—what's his name?—Huddleston. He suggested we all go skinny-dipping."

Ali had been in shock, more frightened than anything else. Flat chested at the time, she hadn't been about to strip and have everyone laugh at her. She looked down at herself now, thankful she'd filled out some since she gave birth to Joanie.

She leaned close to Jake. "Darcie was so mad when I spoke up and dared you boys to go in the water first. Until I got the other girls behind the bushes and told them my plans to trick you guys. And you all fell for it hook, line and sinker."

She rose from the chair and sat down on the edge of the bed, feeling her face heating up as she recalled what had taken place that night. The room was silent except for the monitor beeping overhead, which echoed the pounding of her own heart.

"Jake, I have a confession." She studied his features for a moment, noticing that some of the swelling had gone down. She reached out and touched his jaw. "When the guys were finally all in the water, I was elected to sneak out and steal their clothes while the other girls distracted them by pretending to be getting undressed. Well…I made it to the tree closest to the water when I discovered not all of the guys had gone in. You hadn't. You were still getting undressed." She drew a long breath and released it. "And I stood behind the big maple and watched you take off your clothes."

Ali's body grew warm as she remembered how the moonlight had made it possible for her to see Jake's broad chest after he stripped off his T-shirt. She swallowed, recalling how he'd popped each button open on his Levi's, how her mouth had gone dry as he'd slid the worn jeans down his long legs. His white briefs had followed, and he stood before her, naked and beautiful.

"You were the first man I ever saw naked," she whispered. "And the last…"

Ali remained on the bed for a long time. How she had missed him. She'd give anything to have him open his eyes. She picked up Jake's hand, rubbing it between hers as she studied his face. He'd always been great looking, and now at nearly twenty-nine, there was a ruggedness about him that was breathtaking, bruises and all. Her blood pulsed through her body, making her warm all over as she inhaled his familiar scent. Oh, God. She couldn't let him get to her again.

She released his hand and averted her gaze, remembering how hard she had tried to forget him, to move on with her life. But it seemed no man could compare. The guys she'd dated in high school certainly couldn't compete with Jake Hawkins, captain of the football team, star quarterback and valedictorian of his class. To make it worse, he was a nice guy.

And he had been totally in love with her twin sister.

She looked down at Jake's face again. The one man she wanted had never been hers to have. He was Darcie's. Even when her sister had left him at the altar, Jake still loved her. Ali told herself she should call Darcie home. Jake might wake up for *her*.

Ali got up and moved across the room as the familiar feeling of jealousy tightened her stomach. Even when Darcie was little, she had to have all the attention. She'd demanded it. Maybe because they had been abandoned by their mother so many times, Darcie was afraid to be left alone. And whatever Ali had, Darcie wanted.

But there was one thing that her sister could never take

from her. That one wonderful night when Jake had made love with her, and they had created a child.

Ali walked back to the bed. Jake was Joanie's father, and no matter how uncomfortable the situation was, she had to remember that.

"Wake up, Jake," she whispered. "There are things I need to tell you. Things I should have told you a long time ago."

She brushed his hair back off his forehead. "Please, you've got to get better. So many people love you. And, Jake, your daughter, Joanie, needs you." Ali bit her trembling lip, trying to stay strong, but the fear was getting to her. What if Jake never came out of the coma?

No! She had to stay positive. "You will wake up, and I'll tell you all about Joanie." She leaned down and pressed her lips against his. A tremor raced through her. "Good night, Jake. See you tomorrow."

Jake felt the warmth of her lips on his, then she pulled away. Don't go, he tried to call to her. Please don't go. He willed the words to come, but they never did. The room grew silent, with just the memory of her sweet voice lingering in the air. When she'd spoken, he'd been mesmerized. He'd tried to listen, but her words got all scrambled in his head. He'd been able to pick out a few, but nothing that told him who she was. And who was Joanie?

A few days later, Ali sat and watched as Cliff Hawkins limped back and forth across his son's hospital room.

"I hate this—I should be able to do something. Anything. All this waiting is making me crazy. Damn those doctors. I'm paying them enough they should have figured out a way to bring my son out of this coma." Cliff's gaze went to the bed, and a sob racked his body. "Oh, hell. I can't stand it."

Ali went to him. "Mr. Hawkins, please. The doctors are doing everything they can. Jake is strong. He's in top physical condition from his years in the military, and we all know how determined your son is. He's going to come out of this."

For the first time in days, Cliff Hawkins looked hopeful. He patted her hand. "Thank you, Ali. You've been such a help." He blinked back tears. "It's just that I feel responsible—"

"But you're not responsible. The sheriff said it was an accident. Jake lost control of his car in the blizzard."

"But if we hadn't argued that day... All I wanted was to help my son. He thinks I'm a stubborn old man."

Ali assisted Cliff to the edge of the bed. "Sometimes we have to let people find their own way," she began. "My grandmother always says, 'To love is to let go, and let God.'"

His hand was trembling, and she wondered how much sleep the man had had in the past week. "I can't seem to do that. Where I came from, Ali, life was tough. My own dad took off when I was only ten. I had to help support my mom."

Ali saw him cringe, and he raised his head to make eye contact with her.

"I bet you thought I always had a good life. Well, I didn't." He sighed. "My childhood was so rotten that I want to forget it completely, to bury the past. I swore that no child of mine would ever know what I had to go through."

Ali remained silent. Cliff Hawkins obviously needed to vent his feelings, and she seemed to be the only one around.

"I made it out of the slums, and made a name for myself. But it cost me."

He glanced over at her, and Ali saw his eyes well up.

"I built a thriving business, but in the process I lost my

wife to the bottle before I realized she needed help. By the time I got her into a rehab clinic, she didn't care to live. She died a year later.

"Now I stand to lose my only son…a son who can barely tolerate me." He swallowed and reached out to touch Jake's battered face.

"He doesn't exactly look like the big strapping kid who played quarterback in high school, or the soldier with a chest full of medals, does he?"

Ali felt her own tears form at the fear and sadness she saw in Cliff Hawkins's eyes.

"Ah, Jake, you need to wake up," he choked. "There are so many things I need to tell you. For one, how proud I always was of you. Funny, I told the whole world, but I guess I never got around to telling you. I am proud of you, son. So damn proud," he whispered hoarsely.

He lifted Jake's hand, held it between his palms, then rubbed it gently. "I never told you that the day you were born was the best day of my life. I know I did a lousy job as a father. I'd give anything to change the past and make things different between you and me. Damn it, Jake, I love you. You've got to give me another chance. Please come back, son. Please."

Cliff Hawkins pinched the tears from his eyes and laid Jake's hand down on the bed. "I'm not giving up, Jake. I just got you back into my life…and I'm not about to let you go."

He stood and looked at Ali. "I'm sure Jake would rather wake up to see your big green eyes than these tired old blinkers."

"I can't stay much longer, Mr. Hawkins. I have to get back to work."

"I understand, Ali. You've already spent a lot of time here. I know it's hard on you, but I think your daily visits are helping Jake."

"That's what I need to tell you, Mr. Hawkins—"

"Please, I told you to call me Cliff."

She nodded. "Cliff. I can't come tomorrow."

Ali could see his panic.

"But why?" he asked. "You know that Jake needs you."

"Yes, but I have to take my daughter to her doctor's appointment."

He looked confused. "I didn't know you were married."

It was a question Ali had been asked a lot. This was the one time she wished she could lie. "I'm not."

Jake heard her voice again. It seemed to float around him, all sweet and cheerful. And this time, he could understand more of what she was saying. It was as if her voice were coming through a tunnel. It was something about a beautiful day and that he should see the morning sun shining off the snow.

She came closer and touched him. First she picked up his hand, then she brushed the hair off his forehead. All the time talking about how she was going to stay until he woke up.

Who was she? Half-formed images flowed through his mind. A woman. The picture blurred again, retreating into darkness. A woman.

Her soft voice called his name again. "Jake, please..."

He felt the tender caress of her hand on his skin.

He knew it had been a long time since anyone had given him comfort in his life. Not since...Ali.

Two days later, when Ali walked into the private hospital room, Margo was busy at Jake's bed, changing the IV.

"Hi, Margo. How's he doing?"

Her friend smiled as she smoothed out the bedsheets.

"Well, his vital signs are steadily improving. And according to his chart, Jake had a restless night."

"And that's a good sign?" Ali asked, confused.

"It's a very good sign. Hopefully it means he's fighting the coma."

After Margo left, Ali walked across the room to the bed. "Jake. Why don't you wake up?" She fought to make her voice upbeat and steeled herself against another day of false hope. What if he never woke up? she thought again. No. She wouldn't let herself believe that could happen. How could she live with the fact that she'd kept her daughter from ever knowing her father?

"It's such a pretty day today," she said. "The sun is out, the temperature is in the thirties. Not too bad for southern Minnesota."

She pulled off her coat and placed it on the chair. Each day she had been careful to look her best. She'd never been vain, but she wanted to be at her best when Jake woke up. She'd tied her hair back today, away from her face. She'd even trimmed her bangs. She wore a green sweater and her favorite black wool slacks. Even her grandmother had asked why she was so dressed up. For Jake, Ali had admitted truthfully, but only to herself.

She glanced down at the man in the bed. The bruises on his face had faded. Now it was easy to recognize the handsome man he'd always been. But it hadn't been his good looks that attracted Ali to him. It had been his big heart. He'd been kind to everyone. And he'd tried to be like a big brother to her. It wasn't his fault she'd fallen head over heels in love with him.

Ali walked around the room. "Oh, Jake," she whispered. "I had a crush on you since the first day Darcie brought you home. Some of my fantasies were pretty advanced for a fourteen-year-old." She felt the heat rise in her cheeks. "It wasn't so much that you had to return my feelings. I just thought you deserved someone nicer than Darcie. Sometimes I hated the way she treated you.''

Ali returned to the bed and sat on the edge. ''I wanted to tell you that Darcie would end up hurting you, but I couldn't. She'd nearly convinced me that she loved you, but I *knew* her, I read the signs. Maybe if I had told you...given you some warning...''

Ali picked up Jake's hand. His palms were rough. A man's hand. A hand that had touched her, and pleasured her beyond her wildest dreams.

''When I came after you at the cottage, I only wanted to see if you were all right. But when you kissed me...it was like a dream come true. I have never regretted what happened between us that night. I never could. That night was so special. We made a child together, Jake.'' Ali smiled proudly. ''Joanie's so beautiful...and so like you.''

Ali stared at him, hoping to see some response. ''You should see your daughter. She's got your coloring, your hair and eyes. She's even inherited the Hawkins stubbornness. I've shown her your picture, but she needs more. She needs you in her life, Jake.'' Ali wiped away her tears.

''I know you'll be angry with me for not telling you, but I'll deal with it. Just wake up. Please. For Joanie. For me,'' Ali whispered.

She leaned toward him and placed her lips gently against his.

Suddenly his mouth began to move slowly beneath hers.

Panic surged through her, but she continued the kiss, and to her shock and joy, she soon realized that she hadn't imagined his response. She couldn't move, didn't want to. Oh, God, it had been so long. Ali jerked back to look at his face, praying that he had opened his eyes. But he hadn't.

''C'mon, Jake.'' She cradled his face with trembling hands. ''It's Ali. You know it's me, don't you? It's okay.

You're going to be all right.'' She hugged him, then went running out the door.

Her heart racing, she somehow made it to the nurses' station and found Margo. ''Jake is waking up.''

Chapter Two

It was Ali. Ali's voice. Ali's lips on his. Jake felt as if he were drowning in the softness of her voice, her sweet scent. He was on the edge of heaven, and it was costing him all his strength just to return the kiss.

Suddenly she was gone. He didn't know where. He tried to move, to call her back, but it was useless. Loneliness pressed in all around him.

For now, he'd be patient and concentrate on getting stronger. Patience was something he'd never been good at, but never had there been so much at stake before.

If only he could remember what had happened to him. Whatever it was had put him in the hospital. He struggled to sort out Ali's words. He had a child? A baby daughter.

A different kind of pain tore through his heart. Why didn't you tell me, Ali? Why in God's name didn't anyone tell me?

Ali stood at the window in Jake's room the next day, rubbing her tired eyes. She had spent almost three hours talking to Jake, touching him, hoping for another reaction. But nothing happened.

The doctor had told her not to give up. Coming completely out of a coma could be a slow process.

Well, she wasn't giving up, but she had to go home. She'd already worked the morning shift at the sheriff's office. Her grandmother was expecting her, and Ali knew there would be questions. It was impossible to keep spending so much time at the hospital without telling Gran June the whole story. They lived in the same house, after all.

Ali glanced at the subject of her thoughts. "I'm tired, Jake. You'd solve a lot of problems if you'd just wake up." She walked from the window to his bedside. She had to tell him about Joanie again, whether he could understand or not.

"There's a little girl waiting to meet you. She's just nine months old, but I've told her all about you." Ali eased next to Jake, careful not to disturb his elevated leg.

"I told her you were a quarterback on the football team and how you went to the state championship. I remember the newspaper headlines, The Hawk Leads Webster Tigers To Victory." She smiled. "When you wake up, you can have the pleasure of telling her about your football days."

Ali studied his freshly shaved face, then laced her fingers through his and gently squeezed his hand. There was no reaction, but she'd noticed subtle changes in him over the past few days. His color was better. The doctor said Jake's vital signs had improved, and his tests showed more brain activity. That afternoon, when she'd come by, she had noticed frown creases along his forehead, but when she sang to him, he seemed to relax and they faded away.

"Oh, Jake." She sighed. "I know you're going to be upset because I didn't tell you about Joanie, but I can take it. Just come back to us."

She reached out her other hand and stroked his arm, wondering if the kiss they'd shared had been some kind of muscle reaction. Deep inside, she knew it wasn't. Just as she knew that somehow Jake sensed her presence.

So she had to go with what worked. Ali leaned toward his mouth and whispered, "Okay, Jake, show me your stuff, fella." She placed a soft kiss on his jaw in the hope of stimulating something. Anything.

She trembled as she braced her hands on either side of his head as her mouth met his. The kiss started slow and easy. She wasn't expecting much, but she wanted everything. Suddenly but subtly, the kiss began to change. Jake's lips became firmer, and...yes, they were moving against hers. Frozen, Ali opened her eyes, but she didn't pull away. She wanted Jake to continue the kiss. He did, so sweetly it brought tears to her eyes.

Ali choked back a sob and sat back. A minute later, she laughed. "If I didn't know better, Jake Hawkins, I'd say you were faking it. Most men can't bring a woman to tears with a kiss when they're awake, and you're supposed to be out of it. No wonder I fell so hard for you."

The hospital-room door swung open, and Cliff Hawkins walked in. "How's it going?"

Startled, Ali jumped off the bed and wiped the tears from her face. "Ah...I was about to leave, and I...kissed Jake goodbye." Her cheeks heated up. "He kissed me back again."

"He did? That's great." Cliff took off his coat and tossed it on the vinyl chair in the corner. "Was it like before?"

Ali looked at him in confusion. "You mean...like yesterday?"

"No. Like...the last time he was home."

Ali's pulse raced. Oh, Lord! He couldn't know, could

he? No. There was no way. She met his gaze, waiting for his next move.

"Does he know about the baby?" Cliff asked. "Is she the reason he came home?"

Ali gasped and took a step backward, then she quickly regained her calm. "How did you…?"

"Find out?" he finished. "Wasn't too hard to put together. My son called out your name instead of Darcie's. And yesterday, when I went to my doctor's appointment, I saw you carrying your baby into the clinic. I called to you, but I guess you didn't hear me. I did get close enough to catch a good look at your daughter." He smiled. "The resemblance between her and Jake is remarkable. She looks just like he did as a child."

He reached into his suit-coat pocket. "If you need pictures to prove—"

Ali raised a hand to stop him. She couldn't look at baby pictures, not now. "Okay, yes, Joanie is Jake's daughter." *Your granddaughter,* she silently added.

Cliff seemed relieved at her answer. "Does my son know he's a father?"

Ali's heart raced a hundred miles per hour at the thought of answering the questions she had known would come some day. But not now. She wasn't ready. Jake should be told first.

"No, he doesn't know." She spoke barely above a whisper. "He left town before I could tell him."

"Why didn't you call me, Ali?" he asked. "I was here. I would do anything to bring Jake back."

"But I wouldn't." Ali squared her shoulders. "If Jake cared, he would have stayed around."

She looked up to examine Cliff Hawkins's unreadable face.

"I take it this happened between you two…after Darcie left him?"

"Of course. I would never..." Ali couldn't finish. She didn't want to go into any details. "Jake loved Darcie. That's the reason I didn't try to contact him. I couldn't trap him." She shuddered as she took a long look at Jake. "But what if he doesn't come out of this? He'll never know...."

Cliff was the one to comfort her this time. "Hey, who's been telling me everything is going to be okay? You've been the one who has been here every day getting him to respond. So don't give up now."

"I've been telling him all about Joanie, but I'm not sure he hears me, or...if he'll ever hear anything. What if he never wakes up?"

"I think he does hear you, Ali," Cliff offered as he looked over at his son lying in the bed. "I think his kiss was a way of communicating with you. But maybe we should try something else."

Ali went to Jake's side and picked up his hand. "Like what?"

"Maybe you should bring Joanie in."

Ali gasped. "I can't. She's just a baby."

"But she's Jake's daughter. Her being here could be just the thing to bring him around."

Ali drew a long breath. "I don't know...."

"What if it helps Jake?"

Ali studied Jake's lifeless hand. "But the hospital has rules. How could I get them to let her in?"

Cliff began to smile, reminding her so much of his son. "Let me worry about that."

She nodded. And somehow she knew that her and Joanie's lives were about to change...forever. "I want you to know, Cliff, that I'm a good mother. I'm doing my best to provide a secure, loving home for my daughter. I'd do anything for her."

"I know, Ali. And I can't thank you enough for what you're doing for my son. After he comes out of the coma, he'll still be facing surgery on his leg. So as his father, it's Jake's welfare I'm thinking about now, and he needs his daughter.''

Ali tensed. Ever since she found out she was pregnant, this child had been hers…alone. Now Joanie would belong to her father, too. She glanced at the hospital bed where Jake lay half-alive. She had no choice. Her daughter might be the one to help him. She drew a long breath and released it. ''When do you want to do this?''

''As soon as possible.''

It was worse when Ali was gone. He missed her touch. Without her encouraging words, the darkness surrounded him, drawing away the warmth, the hint of light. He needed her.

Don't leave me, Ali.

His heart started to race as he fought to speak, to bring her back to him. He didn't want to be alone. He tried to cry out, but all he managed was a garbled sound, then the darkness pulled him back in.

The next evening, Ali returned to the hospital with Joanie held protectively against her chest.

Once the elevator reached the fourth floor, she stepped out and started down the hallway toward Jake's room, her heart pounding in her chest. Luckily her friend was waiting for her.

''Margo,'' Ali whispered.

The nurse quickly glanced around, then hurried toward Ali. ''Hurry, the head nurse, Brenda, is on her dinner break,'' she said as they ducked into Jake's room. ''I figure you have about thirty minutes before she returns.''

Ali opened her coat to reveal her sleeping daughter. Margo smiled at her goddaughter as she caressed Joanie's head, which was covered in a red knit hat. The baby's heart-shaped face was fringed with strands of silky black hair. Her little mouth puckered as she made sucking sounds.

"If this precious cargo doesn't bring Jake out of his coma, nothing will," Margo said. "Go get 'em, kid." She kissed the baby's head and left.

Ali glanced around the quiet room, and a shiver of panic sliced through her. She looked down at her daughter and stroked the baby's back. "It's time to meet your daddy, sweetheart."

After taking Joanie from the sling carrier she'd outgrown months ago, Ali gently removed her daughter's coat and hat. Joanie usually woke up cheerful. Ali hoped this was one of those times.

A little dazed, Joanie blinked her big brown eyes, then gave her mother a sleepy grin and cooed softly.

Ali's heart tightened. "That's my girl." She hugged her baby as she carried her toward the bed.

"Hello, Jake. It's me again. Ali. I guess you know my voice by now without me telling you." Why was she rambling? She drew a deep breath, reached down and touched his arm.

"I stopped by tonight to introduce someone to you." She studied Jake's face as she balanced Joanie in her arms. "I brought your daughter. Your dad and I thought that her visiting you might help."

Ali sat on the edge of the bed and placed her daughter on her lap. Joanie raised her arm and pointed, chatting something unrecognizable.

"Yes, sweetheart. This is Daddy." She looked at Jake. "This is your daughter, Jake. Johanna June Pierce. She was born February 16, at 3:06 a.m., weighing in at seven pounds eleven ounces. I know I'm a little prejudiced, but when she was born she was the most beautiful baby in the nursery. She still is, for that matter. When you wake up, I know you'll feel the same way.'' She kept her gaze glued to Jake's expressionless face. There was no change.

Tears formed in Ali's eyes. ''Joanie has your dark hair and beautiful brown eyes. She's smart, too. She learned to crawl at five months, can play pat-a-cake and loves to sing along with *Sesame Street.* She even talks. We don't know what she's saying, but she tries.'' Ali kissed her daughter's head. ''Gran June and I have tried to give her a secure home and lots of love. Joanie has a lot going for her, but there is a big void in her life.''

Ali wiped the tears from her eyes. ''She needs a father, Jake. She needs you. Please come back to her.''

Ali took hold of Jake's hand and scooted closer so Joanie could touch him. Her daughter immediately grasped on to her daddy's fingers and tugged. Ali listened to her daughter's gentle chatter and watched as she patted Jake's large callused hand. Anguished, Ali prayed Joanie's touch might trigger some reaction.

''Daddy's hurt, baby,'' Ali whispered. ''He can't talk yet, but I'm sure he knows you're here.'' The words choked off in her throat.

To Ali's surprise, Joanie climbed off her lap and crawled up beside Jake, still cooing her sweet nonsense syllables.

''Daddy's taking a nap, sweetie.'' Ali rubbed the baby's back as guilt and sadness swept through her. How could she have kept father and daughter apart?

Joanie looked at her mother, then cuddled next to Jake, her tiny fists rubbing her eyes in an obvious display of sleepiness. Ali swallowed back the emotions. ''You want to take a nap with Daddy?''

The small child's chubby arm stretched over Jake's bandaged chest. She smiled, showing off four tiny teeth. Then her daughter puckered her mouth and made a smacking sound against Jake's chest.

Ali tucked Joanie's favorite blanket over them, unable to

ignore the resemblance between father and daughter. The whole town would know now who had fathered her child. But for once, Ali didn't care. Her only concern was giving Joanie a father.

And giving Jake the will to live.

Jake could hear her voice again. He tried so hard to wake up, but something seemed to be holding him down. If he could only open his eyes. But it was so hard…to move. Then he felt Ali's hand on him, soothing him, telling him he would be okay. But he knew he wouldn't be okay until he was awake.

Suddenly there was someone else. A baby! His baby. He could smell her powdery fragrance, hear the soft sound of her voice. When he felt the tiny weight against him, it was pure heaven….

Please, God. Let me live. Let me see my daughter.

Ali closed the door to her compact car and started toward the house, careful not to wake Joanie. Her boots made a crunching sound in the three inches of snow piled on either side of the cleared walkway. She stopped on the top porch step of the big brick home with the gabled roof. The house had been in the Pierce family for three generations.

The streetlights glowed overhead, illuminating the quiet residential area. It was nearly nine o'clock, and everyone had been home and eaten supper hours ago. She'd always loved living on Mulberry Street. As a child, she'd felt safe in the small community where everyone knew everyone else. Never had she been afraid to go out and play in the park with her childhood friends.

Now what would the townspeople think of her when they discovered that her child had been fathered by Webster's favorite son? That Ali had lain with Jake the very night her sister—Jake's bride-to-be—had left him standing at the altar?

That was the reason Ali had chosen to live in St. Cloud during her pregnancy, letting everyone think Joanie's father was someone she had gone to college with. The town was only sixty miles away, but even that short distance had kept so many questions at bay—questions that her grandmother had had to face without having answers. Now it was time to tell the truth.

Clutching the railing, Ali climbed the steps to the big house she'd lived in since her mother abandoned Darcie and her. Their mother had decided that seven-year-old twins were just too much to handle, and didn't fit in to her "free-spirit" life-style. Their father didn't want to handle them, either, so Grandma and Grandpa Pierce got custody.

Upon learning she was pregnant, one of the things Ali had vowed was that no matter what, Joanie was going to have a stable home. No moving around the country looking for a better life or another man to latch on to. Webster, Minnesota, was going to be a permanent home for these two Pierce women. Which meant that Jake Hawkins probably wouldn't be around for long. Ali had known that for as long as she had known Jake. He had always wanted out of this town.

He had a wanderlust that drove him to other places—more exciting places. For as long as she'd known Jake, he wanted to go somewhere else. Somewhere that had more to offer than a small town in Minnesota. Ali doubted that even his child would keep Jake in Webster.

Ali unlocked the front door, went inside the large entry and was greeted by her grandmother.

Smiling, the tall, graceful woman pulled her sweater together and folded her arms across her chest when the icy breeze hit her. "Gracious, child. What are you doing with the baby out in this weather? It's nearly zero out there."

"It's not that cold." Ali opened the closet door and hung up her coat.

"Not if you're an Eskimo or a polar bear." Gran June looked at her great-granddaughter. "I can see this little one is unaffected by the cold, too."

Ali unhooked the baby carrier, careful not to wake her daughter. "What can I say—she's a winter baby."

Ali studied her grandmother. At sixty-eight, June Pierce was still a handsome woman. Her fair skin was flawless, except for a spattering of freckles across her nose. Her hair, once rust colored, was now completely white. The mild stroke she'd suffered last year hadn't seemed to leave any lasting effects. But that didn't keep Ali from worrying about her. Every day Joanie was getting bigger and more active. How soon before Gran June wouldn't be able to care for her anymore? How could Ali keep working? She couldn't afford child care.

Her grandmother smiled. "I worry about you driving in the snow."

"I'm a big girl, Gran," she said.

"I guess I'll always think of you and Darcie as my little girls." There was sadness in her voice. "Now I have this precious one."

Ali's throat felt raw. She went to her grandmother and placed a kiss on her cheek, careful not to disturb the baby. "Oh, Gran, you have been so good to me and Joanie. I love you."

"I love you, too," her grandmother answered with her arm across Ali's shoulder. "And as long as I live, you can count on my being here for you two."

I hope you'll always feel that way, Ali prayed silently. She pulled back. "There's something I need to talk to you about."

Gran June frowned. "Sure, honey. Is there a problem?"

Ali hesitated. "No, just something I should have told you long ago. Come with me while I put Joanie to bed."

Ali climbed the winding dark oak staircase to the second floor. The hardwood floors of the old house creaked as they made their way down the hall toward Joanie's room.

Ali opened the door and went inside the pink-colored nursery. An animal lamp on the dresser cast a soft glow in the room. Ali went to the dressing table and removed her daughter's jacket and hat. Already the little one was in her pj's, and she'd just had a diaper change before leaving the hospital. Ali placed Joanie in the crib and gently patted her back until the baby reached for her favorite blanket and quickly dozed off.

"It's amazing how she manages to fall asleep without so much as a fuss," Gran June said. "You were like that. Now, Darcie would let you know how she hated bedtime."

For a long time, they both stood by the crib and watched Joanie sleep until finally Ali spoke. "I took Joanie to the hospital tonight to see Jake."

Gran June took Ali by the arm, and they walked out of the nursery. She didn't say another word until they were downstairs in the kitchen.

"I had a feeling that's where you went," Gran said. "A baby should know her father."

Ali stared in shock. "You *knew* Jake was…Joanie's father?"

Seeing her grandmother's nod, Ali collapsed into a chair at the table.

"I didn't at first," Gran June verified. She went to the stove, picked up the kettle and filled two mugs with hot water, then dropped tea bags into the cups and returned to the table.

"You didn't come home the night Darcie left Jake at the church. When Joanie was born with all that dark hair, I figured out what must have happened." Gran sat down. "I knew you were never promiscuous. I also knew how much you loved Jake Hawkins.''

Ali gasped. ''Was it that obvious?''

''No, honey.'' The older woman reached across the table and took Ali's hand. ''But as much as Jake hung out at this house, I could see how you looked at him, and how you'd hang on his every word.'' She smiled. ''There's nothing wrong with having a crush on a boy.''

''Yeah, sure, especially when he's your twin sister's boyfriend.''

''I'm not condoning what you did, Ali. But Darcie did leave Jake on their wedding day. Jake wasn't anyone's boyfriend that night. I was just worried that he talked you into something—''

''No! Jake was never out of line. I was naive, but I knew what I was doing that night. I wanted to love him, and I can't regret what happened, Gran June. Because of Jake, I have a beautiful baby daughter.''

''Have you given any thought as to what will happen when everyone finds out about you and Jake?''

''I haven't thought of much else. And what about Darcie? I was going to tell her, but she hasn't been home since that day. I can't tell her over the phone. She'll hate me. She'll claim that I stole Jake.''

''The only claim anyone can make now is that Jake Hawkins is Joanie's father. Darcie made her choice. She'll have to live with that. The only two people you have to worry about are Jake and your daughter.''

Ali went to the hospital before work the next morning. She liked the peaceful time she shared with Jake. As much as she wanted him to wake up, she knew there was a possibility that he would hate her. Would he understand that she hadn't known what to do when she'd found out about her pregnancy? That she'd been terrified over facing the community's censure, when everyone in town learned she'd slept with her sister's man?

A garbled sound made her whirl around and stare at the man in the bed.

Jake groaned, his breathing harsh.

She rushed to the bed. "Oh, God, Jake. You're waking up." Reaching for his arm, she shook it. "C'mon, Jake, wake up. It's Ali."

She began to pray silently. Please, Jake, open your eyes. Even if it means you take one look at me and tell me to get lost. I don't care. Just please wake up. Her throat tight, she leaned closer and managed to whisper, "Jake. It's me. Ali. You can do it. Wake up."

Jake groaned again and moved his head, as if trying to hear her voice better.

Ali's heart drummed in her chest as she sat down on the edge of the bed and picked up Jake's hand. She rubbed the back, then the palm, before lacing her trembling fingers through his.

"C'mon, Jake. You can do it. So many people need you. Your father has been camped out here for days. But the most important of all is your daughter. Don't make her wait any longer. She needs her daddy," Ali whispered, staring at his face, hoping for a reaction. None.

Tears crowded Ali's eyes, but she refused to let them fall. She had to concentrate on Jake. She had to bring him back. Leaning closer to the man she'd never stopped thinking about during the past eighteen months, she spoke softly. "I need you, Jake. I need you so much." She pressed his hand against her mouth and kissed his fingertips. "You've got to wake up."

Suddenly she felt a slight movement where her lips touched Jake's fingers. She gasped, then covered his hand with hers. "Jake?"

His long slender fingers twitched again. A jerk of his jaw

had her holding her breath. "C'mon, Jake. You can do it. Come back to us."

Another groan, and her gaze shot up to discover a pair of dazed midnight eyes staring back at her. Her tears pooled, then dashed down her cheeks. "Oh, thank God!"

Jake blinked several times and silently looked around the room, as if to orientate himself to the strange surroundings. "Jake, you're in the hospital." Her voice cracked with emotion. "There was an accident. We've been so worried about you. Oh, Jake. You're back. You came back to us."

Jake opened his mouth, as if to speak, but he only managed a hoarse gasp.

"Here, let me get you some water." Shaking like crazy, Ali managed to pour water into a glass, then helped him take a drink.

Jake rested his head back on the pillow and stared at Ali. He couldn't believe his eyes. Although he hurt like hell, the pain seemed to dissipate as her hands stroked him. So many times he'd thought about Ali, and wondered what happened after that night....

Now he knew.

His gaze fixed on her face, her beautiful face. Gentleness shone in her green eyes, and he wondered how she could have kept his child from him.

"Ali?" The words came haltingly past his parched lips. "Where...where's my...daughter?"

Then the darkness claimed him once again.

Chapter Three

Jake heard her voice again, soft and soothing, willing him from the darkness. But it was so hard to wake up. Damn, not again.

Suddenly there was a different voice. A man's. His father? Jake began to fight the weakness, refusing to give in.

"Wake up, son," his father called out. "Wake up."

"Cliff, maybe we should wait," Ali said. "Remember what the doctor told us. He needs rest."

"I know, but I can't be at peace until I see for myself that he's out of the coma," Cliff insisted. "I want him to know I'm here. That I care."

"He knows you're here. But he needs sleep," Ali said.

Jake groaned.

Cliff's voice grew more insistent. "Jake?"

Jake blinked his eyes open and tried to focus. Relief rushed through him as he glanced around the familiar room. Thank God. He'd been able to wake from his dream.

Slowly he turned his gaze to the man by his bed. His father. The man who had raised him. The man he'd never really known. Jake's chest tightened at the sight of the deep lines on his old man's face.

"How you doin' son?"

Jake blinked and moved his head. He felt like hell, but he didn't care. "H-hurt," he said hoarsely, unfamiliar emotions tightening his throat as he looked up at Ali. "Water, please."

"Sure." Ali poured water into a glass from the pitcher on the table.

Jake watched her closely. Her nervousness was apparent as she tried hard to avoid eye contact. But he couldn't stop gazing at her. He'd thought a lot about Ali over the past months, but still he hadn't been prepared to see her. He remembered her as the quiet sister, but he had never expected to find the beautiful woman standing before him.

She had golden red curls pulled back from her oval face, the silky strands draping to her delicate shoulders. Her clear green eyes were large and mesmerizing, but there was a hint of shyness in their depths.

His gaze moved down her body, triggering his memory of their night together. Once, he'd thought, she'd been too slender, but not anymore. Her figure had blossomed into nicely rounded curves. Was that because of the child she'd carried? His child? Damn, he still couldn't get used to the idea.

Ali slipped her hand around the back of Jake's neck and helped him raise his head. Surprised by the surge of awareness that shot through him, Jake had to concentrate on getting the straw between his lips. He finally managed the simple task. Exhausted by his efforts, he dropped back to the pillow.

"Maybe I should leave," Ali said as she looked at his dad. "Jake's pretty tired."

"No," Jake protested. "Don't go." He'd be damned if he'd let her leave him alone with his father. "H-help me…sit up."

Ali resisted. "Maybe you shouldn't, Jake."

"Yes. We need to talk…our daughter. Please, Ali…"

She nodded stiffly, then reached for the bed control. She brought Jake to an almost sitting position. He thanked her.

"I want to see…my daughter?"

Ali shot a glance at Cliff. "I don't know. Since you're in the hospital…"

Jake also looked at his father. "The Hawkins name can open some doors. Right?"

"Sure, son. You want to see your daughter, you'll see your daughter."

"Today," he insisted. "I want to see her today."

"Look, son. You've just come out of a long coma. You had us worried to death." His voice was shaky. "I think you need rest."

Jake grimaced as he tried to shift his body. No one was going to keep his child from him. A child who was a part of him, who would give him unconditional love. "I need…my child."

Cliff started to argue, then changed his mind. "I'll arrange it." Relying on his cane, Cliff left the room.

Ali didn't say anything until they were alone. "It might be better if you wait to see her."

"For whom, Ali? Not me. You've kept my child from me all these months. It's been too long as it is. I want to see her now."

Before Ali could answer, the door opened and Jake's doctor came into the room. "I hate to break this up," he said, smiling, "but we need to run some more tests on our patient here."

Jake didn't want any tests. "Doc, can't they wait?"

"I'm afraid not," Dr. Walters said sternly. "I have you

scheduled for an MRI in fifteen minutes." He smiled again.
"Count yourself lucky, Jake. It's a miracle you came out
of the coma. You must have a guardian angel looking after
you."

Jake met Ali's gaze, and awareness surged through his
battered body. "Yeah, she had a heavenly voice that kept
calling me back. I'll always be thankful." He pulled his
attention back to the doctor. "Just tell me that my daughter
can visit me."

The older man hesitated, then nodded. "There shouldn't
be any problem as long as she doesn't have a cold or anything contagious. You need all your strength to heal. As
much as your case has been the talk of the hospital, we like
to see our patients get well enough to leave. You, Jake, still
have a long recovery ahead of you."

Jake shifted in bed, feeling every ache and pain. He knew
it was going to be a long time before he was back to normal. The apparatus that held his leg motionless above the
bed indicated he was going to take quite a while to heal.
He'd use the time to think about his future. And his daughter's.

"I really better leave now," Ali said as she backed toward the door. "I have to go to work."

"Ali." Jake had to struggle to call her name.

She stopped.

"I mean it. I want you to bring our daughter as soon as
possible."

Ali regarded Jake for a long time. "I'll be back with
Joanie tomorrow."

Ali hadn't realized her hands were shaking until she
stepped outside the hospital room. She leaned against the
wall and drew a deep breath as the scene with Jake replayed
in her head. He'd had an angry look that was unfamiliar to
her. His eyes had been cold, distant, and deep lines etched

his ridged jaw. He was so unlike the Jake she'd remembered. This Jake would never forgive her for not telling him about Joanie's existence.

She walked to the elevators, stepped inside and pushed the button for the ground floor. A sudden tautness banded her chest as the car began its descent. Joanie wasn't going to be just her little girl anymore. From this day forward, she'd be sharing her with Jake…and her grandfather.

Once on the first floor, Ali walked to the cafeteria where Margo had been waiting for her at a table in the corner.

"Well, how'd it go?" Just off her morning shift, Margo was still in her nurse's uniform.

Ali sank into a chair with a tired sigh. "He's awake and talking."

Margo squeezed Ali's hand. "That's wonderful. Everyone is talking about the miracle in room 408." Her friend waved her hand in the air. "What did Jake say?"

Ali shrugged. "He asked to see Joanie. He seems happy about having a daughter…."

"I hear a 'but' in there," her friend said.

"Oh, Margo, the looks he gave me…" Ali ran her hand through her hair. "I think he hates me. What if he tries to get back at me for keeping her a secret?"

"What can he do?"

Ali shook her head and drew a calming breath. "I'm not sure. But he told me before I left that he wanted to talk with me about Joanie."

"Of course he wants to talk to you. You're his child's mother."

"I'm also the one who kept her from him the past eighteen months. What if Jake wants to take her away? Oh, God, Margo. I couldn't stand it if—"

"Stop it!" her friend insisted. "You'll worry yourself sick. Jake's been in a bad accident, Ali. He just woke up from a coma, and to top it off he just discovered he's a father. That's a lot to take in. I'd say the man is in a lot of pain, both physical and emotional, and he's going to need time to sort everything out.''

Ali studied the brunette sitting across from her. They'd been friends since junior high school. Margo had been there to help her through all the rough times. When Ali had discovered she was pregnant as a result of her night with Jake, Margo was the friend who hadn't judged her. She'd listened and stood by Ali's decision not to reveal the identity of Joanie's father. She had even been Ali's labor coach, and after her daughter's arrival, Margo had moved in with Ali and helped her through the first two weeks of her child's life.

Being godmother didn't cover all that her friend had done. Ali knew that if anything happened to her, Margo would love Joanie as if she were her own child. But now things had changed. Jake was home.

''Am I going to lose Joanie?''

Margo smiled. ''Of course not. But you are going to have to allow Jake to get to know his daughter.''

Guilt plagued Ali, as it had since the day she'd discovered she was pregnant. This was her fault. She was the one who had kept father and daughter apart. She wouldn't be surprised if Jake did hate her. Sometimes she hated herself.

The next morning, Ali awoke to gray snow clouds threatening overhead. She hurried down the stairs and into the kitchen, where Gran June was fixing breakfast. Since her grandmother's stroke, Ali had tried to take over most of the household chores. Her grandmother had relented on all but the cooking.

Thank goodness, because Ali couldn't quite get it together in the mornings. She sat down next to her daughter, who was seated in a high chair, and took a long sip of orange juice. "Morning, sweetie." She leaned over and kissed the baby's cheek.

"What time are you taking Joanie to the hospital?"

"About ten. Why? How many times has Jake called?"

Gran June put a plate of bacon and eggs in front of Ali and smiled. "He hasn't. Cliff phoned while you were in the shower. Jake was pretty upset you couldn't make it last night."

"With the snowstorm warnings, I thought it best not to take Joanie out."

"Jake understands. He's just anxious to see his daughter." Gran June turned to her granddaughter. "There's another person who should know about Joanie. Darcie needs to be told."

Ali lifted her fork to her mouth, but changed her mind. Her grandmother's words caused her appetite to disappear. She didn't want to think about her sister now. She glanced at her daughter, who was busy stuffing her mouth with scrambled eggs. "Nothing wrong with *your* stomach, huh?"

Joanie let out a happy cry and kicked her feet.

"We're going to see your daddy today. I want you to be on your best behavior."

Joanie smiled sweetly, as if she'd understood her mother's words.

"That'll do it," Ali said. "Your daddy won't stand a chance."

"Stop worrying," Gran June soothed. "Jake is going to love her. And all girls are crazy about their daddies. I know your father disappeared from your life when you and Darcie were young, but at least you had your grandfather. You used to follow him around all the time, dog his steps. You would even go fishing with him."

The older woman took another swallow of her coffee. "The relationship between a father and daughter is special,

Ali. Don't deny either Jake or Joanie the chance to form one.''

Ali thought back to how wonderful her grandparents had been to her and Darcie. Ali still remembered the years she'd felt abandoned by her parents—parents who had cared more about themselves than their daughters. After their parents' divorce, it had been her grandparents—her dad's parents—who had given her and her sister a loving, secure home. But the emotional scars were still there. Darcie seemed unable to settle down, always seeking the next thrill, needing attention like an addict craving drugs.

All Ali wanted was a home and a family. A town where she knew everyone and the man she loved, loved her back and cherished the children they created.

She wanted it for herself—and for Joanie. Joanie would never know the agony of being left behind. Ali would make sure of that.

The hospital was quiet when Ali carried Joanie into Jake's room. She stood back while Jake and his father finished their conversation—or, rather their heated discussion. She heard Darcie's name mentioned just as Joanie let out a loud cry that immediately got everyone's attention.

Both Hawkins men looked at her. Ali's heart thumped in her chest as she moved across the room. ''I'm sorry to disturb you.''

''Heavens, no,'' Cliff said as he limped to her. ''Jake's been waiting all morning for this little one to arrive.''. He touched his granddaughter's hand, and Joanie turned and hugged her mother.

Cliff started to touch the child, but slowly drew his hand back. Ali reached out, took the older man's hand and held it in front of her daughter. ''Joanie, this is your grandpa.'' The baby smiled shyly at Cliff.

"I'll get to know my granddaughter later," he promised, and silently left them alone.

Jake was sitting up, his gaze riveted on the child in her arms. "She's beautiful," he breathed.

"Thank you. I've always thought so." Ali made her way to the bed. "Johanna June Pierce, this is your...daddy. Jake, this is your daughter—Joanie."

Ali noticed the tears in his eyes, and her chest tightened. Her daughter leaned forward, obviously recognizing Jake from her first visit.

He reached out to touch her. First her hand, then her rosy cheek. "She's so tiny," he whispered in awe.

"Not if you're carrying her around all the time. May I sit down?"

Never taking his gaze off his daughter, Jake nodded toward the side of the bed. "Sure."

Ali sat and Joanie clasped his finger.

"She's so strong. I want to know everything about her."

"As you can see, Joanie has your hair and eyes. Your dad said that she looks just like you did as a child. I kept a baby book. I'll bring it in next time."

Joanie pointed at something on the wall and began to babble. Ali laughed and Jake smiled as he held his bandaged ribs. The child liked the attention and let out a joyous squeal, then pulled Jake's finger toward her mouth and tried to nibble.

"No, Joanie." Ali shook her head. "Don't bite."

"Maybe she's hungry," he suggested.

"She's always hungry. But believe me, Joanie ate a hearty breakfast."

"Do you breast-feed her?"

Ali's face turned hot, but she couldn't pull away from Jake's penetrating gaze. Her breasts tingled at the very thought of his watching her feed their child. "I did—I stopped three months ago. She still takes a bottle at night. But she is attempting to drink from a cup.''

Jake moved his hand, and Joanie latched on to it again. ''You brought Joanie in to see me while I was still in the coma, didn't you?''

''You knew she was here?''

His dark eyes captured hers, refusing to free her. ''Ali, I remember almost everything you said to me. Your voice was just about all that kept me going. Then when I felt Joanie against me, I knew I had to fight harder to wake up.'' He stroked his daughter's head as tears filled his eyes. ''I couldn't leave her.''

Joanie cooed at him.

Jake smiled. ''Joanie, do you think you can give your old man a hug?''

Ali's stomach ached at the tenderness in his voice. He was asking for so little. She carefully placed her daughter next to Jake. ''Give Daddy a hug.'' The nine-month-old moved up to Jake's side, her small arm resting against his bandaged chest.

''Daddy…I never realized how wonderful that word sounded.''

Jake savored the precious moment, knowing that his daughter wasn't going to be content to stay long in his charge. He inhaled the sweet baby scent, a mixture of powder and soap, and his heart tightened. This beloved little girl was his. She was his daughter, a part of him. Hell, she even looked like him. And as the moments passed, he found himself falling in love with Johanna June.

A protectiveness filled him, and a strange feeling came over him. He knew, without a doubt, he would give his life for this child. He'd always wanted a family. A family he'd never had himself, but he never realized one small human being could steal his heart so easily. And she didn't even know who he was. ''I'm your daddy, sweet girl.''

Joanie seemed to lose interest as her feet kicked against the bed and she shrieked in delight. Ali helped hold her up, then finally took her in her arms. Jake fell against the pillow, exhausted.

"I should have warned you," Ali said. "She can really sap your energy."

"So how do you handle her?"

"That's different. Remember, you've just come out of a coma."

Yes, but he wanted to be her father, Jake thought. And a father was a man who was around all the time to protect her, to hug her and love her. He'd been gone, playing soldier, not giving a damn about anyone other than himself and his pain. He'd submerged his regrets about the woman he'd made love to that night. Never gave a thought about his responsibility to see if she'd been protected. He glanced at his little girl and felt a sudden tug on his heart. No regrets. How could anyone regret this beautiful child's existence?

His regrets were for Ali, and for how he'd hurt her. She had been a mother to Joanie, but he knew from experience that one parent wasn't enough. Joanie deserved more, and he was going to see she got it.

That night, Ali returned to the hospital. Jake had asked her to stop by after she got off work. This was it, she thought. He was angry with her for keeping the baby a secret. He was going to tell her that he intended to fight for custody of Joanie.

Didn't he know that she hadn't had a choice? She couldn't force him to come home and marry her, especially when he'd still been in love with her sister. Ali had more pride than that. She'd watched her own parents' marriage succumb to bitterness and hatred, and she wouldn't subject Joanie or herself to a lifetime without love.

Steeling herself, Ali knocked and heard Jake call out to come in. She pushed open the door and was surprised to find her boss, Sheriff Ray Benson, next to Jake's bed.

"Ray, I didn't know you'd be here."

"Hi, Ali. Just needed to finish up the accident report."

Ray Benson was a big man with warm hazel eyes. He'd been the sheriff of Webster for over thirty years, and he could intimidate any kid in town if he had to. Mostly he was everyone's friend.

"I can wait outside," she offered.

Ray smiled. "You work for me. I doubt you're a security risk, Ali. I was just asking Jake about the accident, but he doesn't remember anything."

Ali looked at Jake. "Nothing?"

"Not even what I was doing on the road," Jake said, sounding frustrated. "Why the hell would I be out in a blizzard?"

"Easy, son," the sheriff said. "A lot of people who suffer head injuries can't remember, and block things out for a while. You're doing great to have even survived that accident."

Ali shivered, remembering how close Jake had come to death. The familiar feeling of guilt washed over her, knowing how close her daughter had come to not having her father.

"The report showed that the car hit a patch of ice on the highway, leading to your apparent loss of control," the sheriff began. "There were no signs of anyone else around. But you were traveling at an excessive rate of speed for the weather conditions." He sighed, but gave no lecture on safety. "Well, folks, I guess that about does it." He checked his watch. "I'm late for supper, so I'll be headin' home." He shook Jake's hand, then waved goodbye to Ali. "I'll see you at work tomorrow."

Ali had trouble breathing as she watched the sheriff leave

the room. The quiet click of the door closing nearly caused her to panic and run after him. Even though she had known this time with Jake was coming, she wasn't ready for it.

A long silence stretched between them until finally Jake spoke. "Were you ever going to tell me about Joanie?"

Ali's gaze shot to his. She saw anger in his dark eyes. "I'm not sure. You left town so fast."

"But my father lives here and could have gotten in touch with me."

"Maybe I should have contacted him, Jake, but given the circumstances of our child's conception, I...I couldn't."

"You should have tried, Ali. I deserved to know about my daughter."

"Don't you think I know that, Jake? I wasn't exactly thinking clearly when I found out I was pregnant. I did what I thought was best." Her voice and anger rose. "The last thing I wanted to do was drag you back to a town you hated and force you into marrying a woman you didn't love. I couldn't do that to you...or to myself."

"How do you know you would have been forcing me to marry you? What if...?" His glare softened, then he quickly masked the tenderness. "Never mind. All that's beside the point. You never gave me the chance to decide. Does...Darcie know?"

Ali shook her head. How dare he ask about Darcie? "If you wanted to play father so bad, Jake, you should have stuck around to find out if I got pregnant." She watched him flinch and wished it made her feel better, but it didn't. "The next morning, you told me that our lovemaking was a mistake. You couldn't get away from me fast enough, and you never contacted me again. I didn't need to be hit over the head to realize you didn't want anything to do with me. You made it perfectly clear."

"Well, the situation has changed. Get used to having me

around now, because I'm not leaving my daughter. In fact, I've been doing some thinking and there's only one solution."

Ali was almost afraid to ask. "What?"

"We get married."

Chapter Four

Ali felt the blood drain from her face. Her legs suddenly went weak, and she had to sit down. Sinking into the chair beside the bed, she struggled to compose herself.

"Get married...?"

Jake Hawkins was proposing marriage? To *her?*

"I didn't think the idea of marrying me was so offensive," Jake began. "I know I got pretty banged up in the accident—"

"No, Jake," Ali interrupted. "It isn't that. It's just..." Her gaze locked on his mesmerizing bedroom eyes, and her pulse started to race. He could be scarred from head to toe, and she would think he was the most handsome man she'd ever seen. "You caught me off guard," she managed to say. "I had no idea this was the reason you called me here tonight."

Jake grabbed hold of the metal bar over his head, and struggled to sit up straighter. "It makes sense."

None of this was making any sense. She laughed nervously, not wanting even to think about marrying this man. That had been yesterday's dream. "Maybe to you."

He raised a hand. "Just listen to me for a minute."

She folded her arms defensively.

"Now that I'm back, everyone will know I'm Joanie's father. The gossip would eventually die down if you and I married. I want to be around and help raise Joanie. You could even quit work and stay home."

Quit work. Stay home. Jake hadn't said anything about love. Ali shook her head. Of course not. Jake didn't love her. He'd never loved her. The only reason he was even considering this crazy idea was that she was the mother of his child. And what kind of marriage would that be?

Angry, she stood and strode over to the window. From her vantage point on the fourth floor, Ali concentrated on the brightly lit parking lot below, counting the cars lined up side by side. After a moment, she drew a breath and released it, then turned around and walked back to the bed.

"Don't you think the people in this town are going to gossip no matter what we do?" she asked.

Jake's jaw clenched. "Ali, I don't want my daughter to grow up with the stigma of being illegitimate." His voice held authority. "I want my daughter to have my name. She should be Joanie Hawkins. The only way to make it right is for us to get married."

"Will you stop calling her *your* daughter?" she shouted. "Joanie is *ours.*"

He glared at her. "You're the one who forgot that fact."

Jake's words pierced her heart, but she knew he was right. And she had no business hollering at him. The man was recovering from a serious accident. "I'll have your name put on Joanie's birth certificate."

"It's not enough," he argued. "I want my daughter to have a full-time father."

What Jake said was true, but she couldn't marry him. It wouldn't last. Not when he didn't love her. Not when he loved Darcie. And Ali refused to be second.

"I believe it's best if we think this over before rushing into anything. You have a long recuperation ahead of you, Jake. And there's the surgery on your leg."

Jake reached for Ali's hand and drew her closer, making her sit beside him on the bed. A warmth shot through her as her gaze met his bare chest adorned with only strips of white bandage. She glanced lower, fairly certain that he was naked under the sheet that covered his body.

"What are you afraid of, Ali?" His tone held a hint of sarcasm. "Or are you waiting to see if I'll be able to walk before you give me an answer."

She gasped, then her shock turned to anger. "You have no right to say that to me, Jake Hawkins. I was the one here, by your bedside, trying to bring you back. I never once turned away from your injuries. How dare you accuse me of thinking..." She stopped, fighting tears. No, she wasn't going to cry. "I better go." Grabbing her coat and purse, she ignored Jake's plea to stop and rushed out of the room.

"Ali, wait. Come back." Jake cursed as excruciating pain shot up his elevated leg. He grabbed his left thigh and threw his head back against the pillow, waiting for the throbbing to stop, knowing he deserved the agony for what he'd said to Ali.

About five minutes later, Margo Wells came into the room. He remembered the nurse as being Ali's good friend from school.

"How about a painkiller to help you sleep?" she offered, holding out the small paper cup.

"No, thanks." He didn't want to dull his senses.

"Okay, but sleep will do you good. If you're worried about drifting back into a coma, the pills can't—"

"I told you, I don't want any medicine," he said abruptly. "It's my pain, I'll handle it."

Margo shrugged as if she were used to handling mulish patients. "Fine. If you need anything later, just ring the nurses' station and someone will bring you the pills." The petite nurse walked to the door.

Jake called to her. "You're leaving?"

Margo glanced at her watch. "My shift's over in about an hour."

"Could you do me a favor?"

Margo's eyes narrowed.

"Could you go and see if Ali is okay? When she left here, she was a little upset." Jake couldn't help but remember the pained look in Ali's emerald eyes. He also couldn't forget how his body reacted when she'd been so close to him on the bed.

He turned his attention back to Margo. "As you can see," he said, spreading his arms, "I can't go after her."

"Jake Hawkins, you can't even go to the bathroom without help," she chided.

"Okay, you made your point."

They both smiled.

"Look, Margo. I'm sorry. It's just so frustrating lying here." Hell, he'd spent six years in the army with rigorous training and had never been injured. This helpless feeling was driving him nuts. He didn't even want to think about never regaining the full use of his leg. What the hell would he do? And what about his memory? The day of the accident was a total blank. He rubbed his thigh. What business did he have asking Ali to marry him? he thought grimly.

Margo folded her arms over her chest. "Jake, you should count your blessings that you're alive."

"Yeah, I know." He'd blown it. "So you'll stop by and see if Ali is okay?"

Margo nodded.

"And give my daughter a kiss for me?"

She rolled her eyes. "You are such a charmer, Jake Hawkins."

"Then will you put in a good word for me with both my girls?"

"I'm not Jake Hawkins's…anything," Ali told her friend as she laid Joanie down on the dressing table and worked to get her daughter's kicking feet into her pajamas.

"If you could have seen the look on his face, Ali," Margo said. "He was panicked. He still can't remember anything about the accident."

"And that's a good reason for me to accept his proposal?"

Margo's eyes widened. "Jake asked you to marry him?"

Ali refused to look at her friend. Margo knew too much about her feelings for Jake. Instead she blew a raspberry on her daughter's stomach. "It was just because of Joanie. I told him no, of course."

"Couldn't you at least say you'd think about it?"

Ali finished snapping her daughter's pajamas. "What's to think about? It's a sad state of affairs when my first marriage proposal is from a man who's been out of a coma less than forty-eight hours."

"Ali, you've never even made love to another man. Could that be because you've been in love with Jake Hawkins since you were fourteen?"

"Not anymore," she denied adamantly. "I grew up a lot this past year. I stopped believing in fairy tales. Besides, Jake only proposed because he's afraid he'll never see his daughter. I've assured him that he can see her anytime he wants." Ali carried Joanie to her crib and placed a kiss on her cheek.

Margo followed, adding a kiss to Joanie's other cheek. "So you're not even going to think about his proposal?"

"There was no proposal, Margo," she said in a whisper. "It was a spur-of-the-moment...insane idea on Jake's part. He looked shocked even as he said it." Ali watched as Joanie rolled onto her stomach, snuggled under the blanket and closed her eyes.

Flicking off the lights in the small pink nursery, Ali led Margo down the hall toward the stairs.

Her friend sighed. "But wouldn't it be a dream come true if you two were married?"

Ali stopped and glared at the woman. "Wasn't it you who cursed Jake for leaving me? And during every labor pain you threatened to call his father to ask where you could locate Jake."

"Well, he's here now," Margo assured her. "And you should take advantage of it."

"Margo, he's in the hospital. I think I'll give him a few weeks before I ask him to baby-sit, or hand him a bill for back child support."

Margo smacked Ali on the arm. "That's not what I meant. I meant that if Jake Hawkins wants to marry you, I don't think you should dismiss the idea."

Ali started to protest, but Margo raised her hand. "Just think about it. He's Joanie's father and wants to be a part of his daughter's life. He's good-looking and—" her friend wiggled her eyebrows "—I hear he's incredible in bed."

Ali's face flamed. How could she have ever told her friend that? "Like I have a wealth of experience in that department."

"You don't need any experience to know what you like."

Ali could never forget her and Jake's night together, but she needed more than memories. "But I do need love, Margo," she said sadly. "And I have a daughter to think about. If things go wrong between Jake and me, our daughter will suffer. Darcie and I lived through that with our parents. Darcie…''

They both paused at the head of the stairs. Margo finally spoke. ''Stop with the guilt, will you? Your sister was the one who left Jake. She has no claim on him.''

Ali knew that wasn't true. Darcie would always have a claim on Jake's heart.

Jake had to relent and took a painkiller to stop the throbbing in his leg. But the pill hadn't eased his headache, or the anxiety about Ali.

Why hadn't she been to visit him the past two days? And what about Joanie? He needed to see his daughter, to get to know her.

The door to his room opened, and his father came in.

Cliff Hawkins looked tired today. The lines around his eyes were more noticeable. There was a sadness in his father's expression that was completely different from the usual arrogant look that Cliff Hawkins had. Jake still didn't trust him, though. He braced himself for the barrage of questions, or worse, the argument that always ended most of their meetings.

''How are you feeling today, son?'' Cliff smiled. ''You remembering anything?''

''No.'' Jake raised the bed. ''But I'd like to know what they're going to do about my leg. If I'm going to have surgery, I'll need to be moved to a military hospital.''

''No!'' his father protested. ''You'll get better care here. I've called in a specialist from Chicago. He's flying in this afternoon.''

Jake was surprised. ''I can't afford a specialist. Besides, the army has their own surgeons.''

''I'm paying for it,'' Cliff said. ''I want to make sure you're walking around again. You have a daughter to keep up with now.''

Jake didn't know how to handle his father's concern. This man's motives seemed totally selfless. "Well, whoever does the operation, I want it over with soon." He sighed, remembering the phone call he'd made to his commanding officer that morning, informing the soldier of his medical condition. Jake wasn't even sure of the status of his leg. Until he was, he'd been given extended medical leave.

"Dr. Hostler will be here around three. He's one of the best orthopedic surgeons in the country."

"Only the best for Cliff Hawkins's son," Jake remarked sarcastically.

Cliff stiffened. "Son, I've always tried to do the best for you."

"Sure. After you're finished with Hawk Industries. Winning bids, filling contracts and making automotive parts were always your top priority. Mom and I always had to take a back seat to the plant."

"Damn it, Jake. Why do you keep dredging this up? I had to make a living. If I hadn't gone after those bids, the people in this town would have suffered. Other factories across the country were shutting down because they didn't have work. Hawk's employed a few hundred people who needed jobs."

It had always been the same argument with his father. They would never agree on what was important. But Jake knew if Cliff had put his family first, his mother might be alive today. Carol Hawkins's loneliness had driven her to the bottle...and eventually to her death. Jake vowed he would never let his own daughter go through what he had. Joanie was going to know that her father loved her. Somehow. Some way.

"Dad, do you think you can arrange it so that Ali can be here this afternoon?"

Cliff pursed his lips. "I don't see how it will hurt."

"Then you'll call her?"

His father looked at him with confusion.

"She's a little angry with me. I think it would be best if I apologize. I also need to see Joanie." He looked directly at his father. "You think the doctor can be persuaded to let her visit me again?"

A slow smile crossed Cliff's face. "Wouldn't mind seeing the little one myself. But you should contact Ali yourself." His father's dark eyes lit up. "Maybe a small bouquet of flowers to get her attention."

"I think for what I did," Jake said, "I'll need a big bouquet."

When Ali returned from her lunch break, she found a huge vase of yellow roses on her desk. Now she knew why the deputies had been grinning when she walked through the door.

With a trembling hand, she dug out the card and began to read.

Ali,
I'm sorry for being a jerk. Forgive me. Would you please come by the hospital? I miss you.

Jake.

Ali sank down into her chair, as if the strength had been sapped from her legs. She knew she had been purposely avoiding Jake the past few days, but she wanted to let him know he couldn't just have her whenever he snapped his fingers.

Ali had always been the true-blue twin, the one whom everyone could count on. Well, she wasn't going to let Jake get away with treating her as he had. Of course, he wasn't going to go away. The fact was, he was going to be a permanent influence in her and Joanie's lives. And Ali had to figure out a way to work through their problems.

"Hey, it sure smells good in here."

Ali turned to find Ray Benson in the doorway.

"That guy must be nuts over you to send roses in November."

"Maybe he's just plain nuts," Ali said unable to meet the sheriff's eyes.

Ray walked into the small glass-enclosed cubicle and took the seat across from Ali's desk. "I would think flowers would put a bigger smile on your face."

Ali loved Ray Benson, as did half the town of Webster. He had fought in Korea and came home a war hero. He had been a good friend of her grandfather, and a big help to Gran June when her husband died. Ray had also given Ali a job when she needed one. He'd even let her off work when Joanie had gotten sick, and never questioned her when she asked for extra time off to spend at the hospital with Jake.

"The roses come with strings," she confessed.

"Well, then, just set him straight. You make the rules, Ali, and if the guy doesn't like it, you send him to me." Ray winked and stood up. "But I have no doubt that you can handle Jake Hawkins without too much trouble."

Ali's mouth opened, then she closed it. She knew it was useless to deny her connection with Jake. Both he and his father were going to tell the whole town about Joanie.

"Thank you, Ray. I'll tell him."

Just then a call came in, and Ali put on her headset as the sheriff left the room. She pressed the button on the phone. "Webster County Sheriff's Office."

"Promise not to hang up on me," a familiar voice said in a husky tone. Ali immediately felt a rush at hearing Jake's voice.

"Tell me why I shouldn't."

"Because I just spent a fortune on flowers and more importantly I'm the father of your child. But mostly because I'm sorry for saying the things I said to you."

Oh, yes, he was weakening her defenses. "What did you say your name was again?" she said teasingly.

"You know exactly who this is. But if you come by the hospital, I can give you a more personal hint...that I'm sure will stimulate your memory."

Ali couldn't catch her breath; her heart was racing like crazy. She looked up at one of the deputies who was watching her, and quickly glanced away. "Look, Jake, I have to get back to work."

"Not until you promise to stop by and see me. Alone."

"Jake, I've got to go."

"Say you'll come by. I want to see you."

"Okay, okay. I'll stop by tonight. We'll talk."

"Thanks, Ali-cat. I'll be looking forward to tonight."

Ali closed her eyes at the endearment. "I've got to go, Jake. Goodbye." She hung up the phone, knowing she was in big trouble if she didn't figure out a way to keep her distance.

Jake waited, not very patiently, for visiting hours to start. At 7:20, still no Ali. Damn, he knew she wasn't coming. He picked up the remote and began flipping through the channels on the television. By the time he circled them all twice, the door to his room opened. He held his breath when Ali walked in.

He swallowed hard as she silently made her way to his bedside. She was dressed in a dark maroon sweater that highlighted her red hair and green eyes. White wool slacks enhanced her long legs.

"Okay, Jake," she began. "I'm here. What did you want to talk about?"

He smiled at her, hoping to coax an answering smile

from her. No such luck. "Well, first I want to apologize. I was rude the other day. You've had a lot to deal with, and I haven't been very patient. I've never thanked you for having my child. It would have been so easy to get rid of her—"

"Not for me," she interrupted.

He nodded in agreement. Knowing Ali as he had, she would never take the easy way out. "But still, you did give birth and kept Joanie to raise on your own. I owe you a great debt for that, along with my financial support now."

"Don't think I'm going to turn down your money."

He smiled. "I don't expect you to. I want our daughter to have the best of everything. I already think she has the best mother."

He got the pleasure of watching Ali blush. "I've given it a lot of thought, Ali. Believe me, all I wanted to do when I suggested getting married—"

"That isn't the answer," she interrupted again.

He raised a hand. "I know that now. It's too soon. But at least will you agree to let me spend time with Joanie?"

"Of course," she said. "I want you two to get to know each other. Joanie needs her father."

He grinned proudly. "I'm glad. I want to be there for her. So I've got another idea."

Ali frowned.

"I need to have surgery on my leg. Soon. They have me scheduled for this Thursday. Afterward I'll have to spend another week here, then I'll be sent home for the long recuperation."

"I'm sure your dad will like that."

"I don't want to go to Dad's. I want to stay with you and Joanie."

Ali didn't know how many more shocks she could handle. Every time she turned around, Jake was throwing something else at her. How could she be under the same roof with this man? "No, that's impossible."

"Why? I want to rent your Gran June's extra room downstairs. I happen to know that it's vacant now."

"How did you know about the room?" Since her grandfather's death, Gran had taken in a few boarders in the past few years.

"Your grandmother came by earlier."

Ali closed her eyes. She couldn't do this. She couldn't have Jake Hawkins in her house, be with him every day…every night. "It won't work."

"Why, Ali-cat?"

Her head jerked up. "Stop calling me that name."

He grabbed her by the arm. "Why? Because it brings back memories?"

Jake's fiery stare threatened to burn away any barriers. She fought to keep that from happening, and pulled away. "We have no memories, Jake. One night you reached out…and I was conveniently there."

He looked hurt. "There was more, Ali. For one thing, our child was conceived."

She felt a shiver race through her. No. She couldn't think about how it had been between them. "I don't want to bring up the past." She didn't want to be reminded that she'd only been a substitute for her sister.

Jake puffed out a long breath. "Fine, but I'm not going to let you keep my daughter from me. If I stay at the house, then I can ease into her life. This change isn't going to be easy for Joanie, either. I want her to know me as her father. Can't you understand that, Ali?"

Ali closed her eyes. Oh, God. Jake was right. Ali would have given anything to know her own father better. She couldn't deny this chance for her daughter. She turned to Jake. "Have you talked this over with Gran June?"

He nodded. "But she wouldn't agree to anything unless

you gave the okay. Please, Ali. I'll stay out of your way as much as possible. I just want time to get to know Joanie.''

He couldn't know how much that statement hurt. There had always been someone else. First Darcie. Now Joanie. She wanted to be first in somebody's life. In Jake's life. But she had to stop thinking of herself, of her deepest yearnings, and think of her baby.

She was insane for agreeing to this, but she knew from experience that Jake Hawkins was a hard man to resist. ''Okay, but there are going to be rules.''

He nodded. ''Hey, I'm an old army man. I can handle rules.''

Ali knew without a doubt that he was going to break them all, along with her heart.

Chapter Five

On Thursday morning, Ali took the day off work to be at the hospital for Jake's surgery. She told herself her concern only stemmed from the fact that the man was her daughter's father. But Ali knew, deep down, that it was more. If things didn't go well, she wanted to be there for him. And for Cliff, too.

Across the waiting area, Cliff Hawkins leaned heavily on his cane as he gazed out the window. Ali was worried about the man. He seemed so lost, so lonely. She knew he hadn't been getting enough sleep. The dark circles under his eyes proved that. And over the past week, she'd practically had to drag him out of Jake's room and down to the cafeteria for something to eat, insisting he needed to keep up his strength.

In all the time Ali had spent with Cliff talking when Jake was in a coma, the older Hawkins hadn't seemed anything like the terrible father Jake had resented most of his life.

Ali found a concerned parent who loved his son. Cliff had taken Jake's accident hard, as expected, but the man acted personally responsible for what happened.

Jake and Cliff's disagreements had been public knowledge for years. There weren't many secrets in Webster, especially for the prominent Hawkins family.

It was ironic that Jake and his father seemed to have everything—except happiness. Ever since Carol Hawkins had died when Jake was thirteen, all he and his father had managed to do was argue.

Ali knew it had been hard for Jake to grow up without a mother. When they met in high school, he had seemed confident and popular, but as their friendship grew closer over the years, she'd discovered it was a cover.

Jake had tried to get his father's attention. He'd been a 4.0 student and the star quarterback who led the Webster football team to a conference title. Cliff might have gone to all the games, but he hadn't seemed that interested in the sport, boasting only about how his son would join him in the family business.

Jake had other plans. When he went off to college, he enlisted in the ROTC program. Then he'd joined the army for the next six years. Both Darcie and Cliff wanted Jake to get a business degree and come back to Webster so he could take over the plant. That had started the terrible argument between Jake and Darcie just before their wedding day, when Darcie had run off.

Sadness gripped Ali's chest. If Darcie hadn't been able to persuade Jake to stay in Webster, what made her think *she* could? Jake loved Joanie, but Ali refused to use her daughter to hold a man who would never love her.

Thirty minutes later, Dr. Hostler approached the waiting area. Dressed in his green scrubs, the forty-year-old doctor stripped the cap off his head, revealing the thick blond hair beneath.

Cliff went to him and Ali followed. "Doctor, how did it go?"

The doctor smiled. "Good, all things considered. It was rough going, but I knew that before I went in. Setting the leg was relatively easy. The tricky part was repairing the damage around the ankle area." He frowned. "We had to put a pin in the talus bone, then repair considerable ligament and muscle damage. If Jake heals properly, he'll regain close to normal use in his leg."

"Close doesn't cut it. My son is a captain in the army, Doctor. He can't be a cripple."

Ali was surprised at Cliff's outburst, but Dr. Hostler didn't even blink. "I understand how you feel, Mr. Hawkins, but much of Jake's recovery depends on him. I've seen patients go both ways. Your son is strong, healthy—and very determined. I know it's rough, but this is a wait-and-see proposition. He still has a lot of physical therapy to undergo."

"What about his military career?"

Hostler raised an eyebrow. "Before surgery, I warned Jake not to expect miracles. It's too soon to tell."

The doctor looked at Ali and smiled. "I promised Jake that you would be in recovery when he wakes up." Hostler checked his watch. "If you'll excuse me, I have to call my service. I'll stop by the desk and tell the nurse about Jake's request." With that, he turned and walked off.

Ali's heart raced with excitement, then she saw the sadness on Cliff's face. "You go in first."

"No, Ali," Cliff began. "Jake wants you there. I'll visit him later. Besides, I need to get back to the office."

Ali hugged the man, mainly because he looked as if he needed one. She wanted to hit Jake over the head for this stunt. He had to have known his father would be waiting. "Why don't you come to the house for dinner?" she asked. "You can spend some time with Joanie. But brace yourself—your granddaughter's table manners leave a lot to be desired."

The older man's eyes lit up. "I'd love to. You're sure it's not too much trouble?"

"No, of course not. I know for a fact that Gran June is cooking chicken and noodles. She always makes plenty. Say about five-thirty?"

"Thank you, Ali." His smile faded. "Will you tell Jake I'll be back tonight?"

"I'm going to tell him more than that."

"No," Cliff said sternly. "Jake and I have to work this problem out ourselves." He finally smiled and reached for her hand. "Now, you go in and see my son. He needs you."

Ali nodded and moved down the hall. When she got to intensive care, a nurse led her inside to see Jake. Looking down at his still body, her heart began to pound erratically. The memory of seeing Jake in a coma haunted her.

The nurse adjusted the IV. "He should be coming out of the anesthesia soon. You can talk to him."

Ali stood next to the bed and leaned close. "Jake, wake up. It's me, Ali."

Within seconds, his eyelids began to flutter. They opened, then closed again. "Kiss."

"What?"

"Need…a kiss."

Ali felt the heat rise to her face. He wanted her to kiss him.

"P-please."

She glanced up at the blond nurse, who was smiling. "He wouldn't have to ask me twice," she murmured, then left the room.

Once alone, Ali didn't hesitate. She leaned forward and placed her mouth against his. A warm tingle swiftly moved through her body as his lips worked their special magic.

Remembering that the man just had surgery, Ali started to pull away. He slid a hand to the back of her head just holding her close, with a light touch, but for Ali it was enough to prolong the kiss. She gave in to the sensations. His mouth opened over hers, tasting and caressing her until she felt light-headed. Finally he released her.

Ali pulled back and opened her eyes to find Jake's dark-eyed gaze on her.

"I've wanted to do that…for a long time," he whispered.

She cleared her throat to find her voice. "You're awfully energetic."

His fingers stroked her cheek. "You're so soft, Ali-cat."

Ali took his hand in hers. His touch was too unsettling. "And you're full of it, Hawk."

He grinned and Ali's breath caught in her chest.

"Missed you," he whispered.

It was the medication, Ali told herself. "I've been here all the time."

"No, before that. After that night we were together. Sorry… I hurt you."

She stiffened. "Jake, don't apologize anymore."

"No. Not sorry we made love. Sorry I left you afterward. Please forgive me." He blinked. "I'll make it up to you…Joanie. Promise." Again he was losing the fight as his eyes began to close. He fought a few seconds longer before giving in to the drugs.

Ali watched his peaceful face as tears welled in her eyes. Had Jake meant what he said, or was it just the anesthesia?

That evening in the Pierce kitchen, Cliff laid his napkin on the table. "June, that was the best chicken and noodles I've ever had," he announced.

"Thanks, Cliff. It's been a while since I've gotten an outside opinion on my cooking skills." June smiled at him.

Joanie let out a cry. She wanted down from her high chair. Ali quickly got up and began to clean off her face. "Okay, Joanie, hold on a minute."

Cliff pointed to the child. "By the looks of my grand-daughter, I'd say that she's crazy about your cooking, too."

"This child eats anything," Ali said as she cleaned Joanie's hands. "We just have to work on her table manners."

Everyone laughed. Cliff had seemed to enjoy the meal with Joanie, mess and all. He'd accepted his granddaughter and never questioned Ali after that day at the hospital.

Tonight, when he'd appeared at the front door, he carried several toys for Joanie. He also let Ali know that Joanie had been placed in his will, and that a trust fund had been set up for her college education.

Ali was grateful to Cliff for securing her daughter's future, but it was all so overwhelming. There was more coming, too. Cliff had said to expect packages from an exclusive Minneapolis children's store in a few days. She'd let Cliff have his fun. But she didn't want her daughter thinking she could have anything by simply asking Grandpa.

Ali took her daughter from the high chair. "Looks like it's bath time."

Joanie squealed with delight.

"Water is another of Joanie's passions." Ali started out of the kitchen when the phone rang. She reached for it. "Hello."

"Hello, sis." Her twin's voice came over the line clearly.

Ali froze. "Darcie."

"I was hoping I would catch everyone at dinner. How are you?"

"Fine. We're all fine." Ali shifted her daughter to her other hip. Then she glanced at Gran June for help.

"Sorry I haven't called lately," Darcie said, then sighed dramatically. "It's just that I've been so busy. I can't believe it, Ali, my boss assigned me to one of our biggest accounts. I'm working on a new ad campaign for Choice Jeans. Can you believe it?. *Choice Jeans.* Remember when we would die to be able to buy a pair?''

''That's wonderful, Darcie.'' Ali forced her enthusiasm as Joanie reached for the phone, making chatter.

''It that little Joanie I hear?''

''Yes, it is.''

''Oh, I can't wait to see her—hold her. Let her get to know Aunt Darcie. The pictures you sent are precious with her dark eyes and curly hair. She must look like her daddy.''

Ali swallowed her panic and quickly changed the subject. ''Are you coming home?''

''I wish,'' Darcie said. ''But this campaign is a killer. It's also my big chance, and I can't blow it. I know you don't understand, Ali, but I have to put in a lot of hours to move up the corporate ladder. I'm just beginning my career, and it takes hard work.''

Suddenly irritated, Ali didn't want to hear any more about her sister's martyrdom. ''Darcie, I'm happy for you. And since I'm just a mother who needs to give her baby a bath, I'll let you talk to Gran June.'' Ali handed the phone to her grandmother, then walked out.

Once upstairs, Ali stripped her daughter's clothes off and put her into the tub. This was usually the time of day she loved most. Time she got to spend with Joanie, a relaxing time where they got to play. But tonight, Darcie's call brought back all the old memories. And the guilt of what she'd done to her sister. But there was hurt, too. Darcie hadn't come home once to see her or her niece.

Now Ali didn't want her here. Everything was so messed up. With Jake home now, it was only going to get worse.

''Would you mind if I came in?''

Ali swung around to find Cliff. "Sure. Joanie likes company. Just be careful—she splashes."

Cliff used his cane to maneuver across the room and took a seat next to the old claw-footed tub. Joanie grinned up at her grandfather, then smacked her hands against the water, splashing water all over her mother. Ali wiped her eyes as the baby and Cliff both began to laugh.

"Don't encourage her," Ali told Cliff as she began to wash her daughter. Joanie wanted to play longer, but Ali wasn't in the mood tonight. Grabbing a towel, she dried off the child, laid her down on the rug, put on a diaper, then helped her into warm pajamas. Joanie sat on the floor contentedly playing with one of her toys.

"You make it look so easy," Cliff said.

"Sometimes it's a real wrestling match."

"Ali, I came up here because I saw how upset you were about Darcie's phone call."

Ali sighed. "It's just that I never told Darcie about the baby. I mean, she knows I had a child, of course. She just doesn't know that Jake is Joanie's father. I made up a story about the baby's father being a guy from college. When we were younger, we were so close. We talked about everything. Now...it's a different story."

Ali could still remember the nights when their mother had left her and Darcie alone in the apartment. Two frightened five-year-old girls curled up in bed, trying to act brave. They'd comfort each other and pretend they weren't scared.

"I panic at the thought of Darcie coming home," Ali said softly.

"Your sister chose her life. She's the one who left Jake at the church."

"But you don't understand, Cliff. I remember how much Jake loved Darcie—he loved her for years." Ali shook her head. "I shouldn't have gone after him that night."

Deep in her heart, Ali knew she would never regret that night with Jake because of her daughter. But she also knew Darcie would never forgive her. Even though Darcie had thrown Jake away, hadn't wanted him, she was territorial. Darcie would never in a million years want Ali to have him.

Ali picked up Joanie. "I better get this one to bed."

Cliff stood, too. "Yes, and we need to get to the hospital."

"I don't think it's a good idea for me to go." She walked into the hall and headed for the nursery.

"Ali, you have to."

She turned on the dresser light in the baby's room and picked up the bottle of milk her grandmother had left for Joanie. Settling in the rocking chair, Ali cuddled her daughter on her lap as Joanie put the bottle in her mouth.

"Maybe it's not such a good idea for Jake to stay here," she said as guilt engulfed her. "But I won't stop him from seeing Joanie whenever he wants."

Cliff walked over and stood in front of her. "You listen to me, Ali Pierce. This little one needs both her parents— you *and* her father. Believe me, I know. If I could change anything, I would try to be the father Jake needed. I should have tried harder, listened to my son more and gotten help when his mother's drinking problem began." He glanced away, pain etching his face. "But we can't change the past. We have to move on." He turned back to her. "You can't let Darcie's phone call deprive Joanie of her father."

It was Ali's turn to look away. "You don't understand. When Darcie discovers that Jake and I…" She felt tears threatening. "She's going to hate me."

"What right does she have to condemn you? She's the one who chose not to marry Jake. How can she pass judgment on what happened after she left? You and Jake chose to be together that night. And you created this lovely child. Joanie has to be your first concern.''

''She is,'' Ali assured him.

''And Jake is mine. My son needs to see his daughter. I've arranged for Joanie to come to the hospital tomorrow.''

Ali opened her mouth to argue. She didn't like the fact that Cliff was taking over, especially where Joanie was concerned. ''I don't think that's a good idea.''

''Look, Ali, Jake is going to be in the hospital for at least another week, and he needs to see his daughter. It's a small request.''

Ali thought back to this morning in recovery and Jake's kiss. He'd stirred feelings in her that she didn't need or want. He was just being attentive because she was his child's mother, she told herself. But what would happen if Darcie came home?

''Don't make problems for yourself, Ali,'' Cliff warned. ''Right now Jake needs your help. He's not only discovered he's a father, but the injuries to his leg may cost him his army career.''

Ali glanced down at her daughter contentedly drinking her bottle, and wished her own life were as simple. ''All right. Tell Jake that Joanie and I will be there tomorrow.''

The next afternoon, Ali stood beside the hospital bed as Jake and his daughter got to know each another. Dressed in bright red corduroys and a white ruffled shirt, Joanie seemed to be comfortable with her daddy. She wasn't scared of Jake, but the nine-month-old often glanced over her shoulder to make sure her mother was close by.

''Our daughter isn't only beautiful, she's smart.'' Jake smiled at his child, drawing cheerful chatter from Joanie. He handed her a colorful block, and Joanie expertly showed her father her dexterity by placing the block on top of another one sitting on the bed tray. She grinned up at her daddy when she finished the task and clapped her tiny hands together.

Jake looked at Ali, his dark eyes identical to his daughter's. "How can those little fingers do that?" Ali shrugged and he turned back to Joanie. "Yes, you're such a smart little girl." He took the child's hands and pulled her up to stand next to him. "Pretty soon you'll be walking. Look at how strong she is, Ali." Joanie started bouncing up and down.

Ali grabbed her. "And she likes to bounce on beds, too."

Jake's eyes sparkled as he grinned. "I wonder where she learned that."

Ali blushed. Jake was remembering her first visit to the Hawkins's lake cottage. A group of kids was messing around, and Jake challenged Ali to see if she could bounce high enough off the bed to touch the bedroom ceiling. She'd done it. "I have no idea what you're talking about," she said primly, but it was useless to try to hide her smile.

"Wait until you get a little older, Joanie, and I'll tell you about some of your mother's wild days. She skinny-dipped—"

"I did not," Ali interrupted. "Unlike some others, I kept my clothes on."

"But you were a party to it. In fact, wasn't it your suggestion to steal the guys' clothes?"

Ali's blush intensified. "I have no idea what you're talking about, Jake Hawkins."

"Ali Pierce, I lay in this bed and listened to your confession just last week."

She gasped. "You heard what I said?"

Jake could only stare at Ali. She was embarrassed. She was twenty-five, and her innocence still amazed him, as did her beauty. Such a contrast to Darcie with her flirty confidence. "Some of it. Things faded in and out. But I remember you said that it was your idea to take the guys' clothes.

Luckily there were some extra clothes in the cottage, or that could have turned out to be an embarrassing night." He shook his head. "Who would have thought that of shy Ali Pierce?"

Joanie shook her head, too, and laughed.

Ali lowered her eyes as she pushed her soft curls behind her ears, exposing her long neck. "I wasn't that shy. It's just that Darcie liked to talk."

"And you stayed in her shadow." He thought he saw her wince, but she covered it with a noncommittal shrug. The twin sisters had been so different, Jake thought. He'd never paid attention then, because he could never see anyone but Darcie. It wasn't until the night Ali came to him that he realized how sweet and giving she was...and how little comfort he'd ever received from Darcie.

"How is your leg?"

He looked at his elevated leg, now adorned by a cast to the knee. "I took a painkiller last night, but so far today, it's not too bad. I just hate to think about staying here another week."

"The time will fly by."

In your dreams. "You're still going to let me stay at your house, aren't you?"

She lowered her eyes from his steady gaze. "I'm sure your dad will be disappointed that you're not coming home."

Jake tensed. "Cliff and I have trouble getting along when we're together five minutes. Living under the same roof while I recover could be fatal. Besides, I already told him that I'll be staying with you...indefinitely."

"You aren't staying *with* me," Ali denied. "You're renting a room from my grandmother."

"Of course," he agreed. "We wouldn't want to set a bad example for our daughter. Not before we're married anyway."

"Jake." Ali released an exasperated sigh. "Don't get any ideas."

He smiled. "Too late, Ali-cat. I've already had some pretty vivid ideas about you during the past eighteen months. And I don't see that changing in the near future." He stuck his finger out to his daughter, and she latched on to it. "I think she's used to me already. Aren't you, Joanie? By the time we're together awhile, I bet you'll be able to say Daddy."

Ali knew that Jake's living at the house was going to disrupt her life—and her sanity. Now everyone would not only know that Jake was Joanie's father, but they'd also think that something was still going on between them.

Joanie began to fuss. Ali went to the stroller, pulled a baby bottle from the diaper bag and handed it to her daughter. "She's tired."

"Bring her here and lay her down next to me." Jake patted the space beside him.

"Maybe we should go home so she can sleep in her bed."

"Please, Ali. I want Joanie to know that I can comfort her, too. I want her to get used to coming to me."

Ali hesitated, then put Joanie down on the bed next to Jake. The child's eyes widened for a second, then Jake talked to her and she settled down to drink.

Ali felt her chest tighten as she watched the touching scene between father and daughter. Then Joanie's eyes closed, and her bottle slipped from her mouth. Ali took it away. "I usually don't let her go to sleep with a bottle. It isn't good for her teeth."

"You're a good mother, Ali."

"I try, but sometimes it just seems too much. That's why I'm glad I have Gran June to help me."

"And now you have me."

If only that were true, Ali thought. But she'd never really

have Jake Hawkins. His wanderlust kept him from settling in one town, especially when that town held bad memories. But for Ali, Webster, Minnesota, had been her salvation. The only home she'd ever known—and the perfect place she'd promised to raise her daughter.

Chapter Six

In early November, Jake was released from the hospital with strict instructions to spend all his time in bed or in the wheelchair with his leg elevated.

"I told you I could do it," Jake argued as his father's driver, Harry, helped him out of the car in the Pierces' driveway.

"Sorry, sir, but you need assistance," the large man said.

Harry Reese was about forty, and he was built more like a bouncer than a caretaker and driver. Without any more argument, Jake allowed Harry to lift him into the waiting wheelchair, but vowed that when he was healed, he wasn't going to let another person touch him. Except maybe Ali.

Jake watched as Ali raised his cast-covered leg into the chair's brace to keep it elevated. Her hands were soft and caring as she fussed over him.

Kneeling, Ali looked up at him, her green eyes intense. Her long auburn hair lay against the soft curve of her jaw.

"You have to stop being so stubborn. If you fall, you could end up back in the hospital."

The thought of returning to Webster Memorial Hospital caused Jake to relent. "Okay, I'll behave."

Harry turned the wheelchair around and headed for the porch. The ramp that had been used years ago, when Ali's grandmother had had a stroke, was back in place. Silently Jake allowed Harry to push him to the top, but he was determined that he wasn't going to remain in this wheelchair for long.

They made it to the porch, where a smiling June Pierce opened the door. She was dressed in a print dress, an apron tied around her slim waist. "Well, I see you made it." She backed up so Jake could come into the large entry.

Jake smiled at her. "I'd do about anything to get one of your meals."

"You didn't have to try so hard." She leaned down and hugged him. "Good to see you on the mend."

"Thanks, Gran June. I'm feeling pretty good."

He glanced around, and a feeling of warmth engulfed him, triggering memories of the years he'd spent here. Such love and caring radiated from this old house, and he'd never forget the familiar aroma of bread baking and lemon polish.

He placed his hands on the wheels and maneuvered the chair into the huge living room, where there was a fire lit in the stone hearth. The mahogany mantel still displayed pictures of generations of Pierces, including photos of Ali and Darcie. A floral sofa was placed behind an antique Queen Anne coffee table. Lace doilies and china figurines decorated the end tables. An overstuffed chair and ottoman were positioned in front of the bay windows. Late-autumn sunlight filtered through the sheer curtains, reflecting off the grand piano that had been in the Pierce family for generations.

"I want you to feel at home here, Jake," Gran June said. "If there is anything you need…"

Jake took her hand. "I have everything I need," he told her. "And as a bonus, a few of your great meals."

Harry entered the room with Jake's army duffel bag. "Where should I put these, Mr. Hawkins?"

"Follow me," Gran said, and led the man down the hall.

Jake moved farther into the room next to the sofa. He would never admit it, but he was exhausted.

"I think you should go to your room and take a nap," Ali suggested from behind him. "This wasn't an easy trip."

Jake turned to look at Ali. She was wearing a pair of dark blue leggings and a matching sweater. Soft curls danced around her face, making him itch to touch the tendrils.

"I'm just so tired of being helpless."

Ali drew nearer and sat down next to his chair. "Jake, you nearly died. It's going to take a while to recover. Besides your leg injuries, your ribs were cracked." Her gaze moved to his face, and she touched his jaw with gentle fingers. "There are still traces of bruising. Give your body time to heal."

He swallowed at her close examination, and realized that certain parts of his anatomy still worked perfectly. He drew in a deep breath. Her soft scent reminded him of springtime.

He backed away from her gentle caress. "I know you're right, but so many things have changed. I feel like I've lost part of my life, but I've gained something wonderful, too. I have a daughter I want to get to know." He looked at Ali. "Where is Joanie?"

"She's napping, like her father should be doing."

Jake started to argue when he noticed Ali cross her arms over her chest. All at once, he wanted to grin. He was living with the two most important people in his life—Ali and his daughter. What was he complaining about?

"I'll go to my room in a little while. I just want to savor being out of the hospital."

Ali nodded, a smile on her face. "I guess a lot of things have changed since you returned to Webster."

He tipped his head back and stared at the ceiling. "You can say that. My leg for one." He could feel every sore rib, and his leg throbbed like hell under the cast. He didn't mind the pain nearly as much as not knowing what the future held for him. What if he couldn't go back to the army? His father had already offered to help him financially. But Jake refused. He had his mother's trust fund. That would take care of him...and a family. He looked at Ali. "I need to go to the veterans hospital in Minneapolis to be checked out."

"When do you have to return to the army?"

He stared down at his injured leg. "I seriously doubt I ever can."

"I'm sorry, Jake. I know how much you loved your career."

Surprised by her sincerity, he turned to her. "Thanks, Ali. You seem to be the only person who realizes what the army meant to me."

"That's not true. I know your father disagreed with your choice, but he's proud of your accomplishments. And Darcie—"

"Darcie made her statement loud and clear." He shook his head. "You know, she did us both a favor by leaving before the wedding. I doubt our marriage would have survived military life." Suddenly he didn't want to talk about Darcie or his career. He was tired. "I think I'll go lie down."

Ali got up. "Good idea. I'll help you."

Jake didn't argue as she pushed his chair down the hall,

the wheels rolling easily on the hardwood floors. Ali went ahead and opened the bedroom door while Jake rolled the chair over the threshold and into the light blue room. There was a queen-size bed against the far wall, covered by a decorative quilt. A wing chair was positioned next to the slate stone fireplace. Built-in bookcases went from floor to ceiling, and were filled with reading material.

Ali watched Jake's reaction. Gran June had fussed over the room, making everything perfect for their new tenant. Years ago, this room had been a study. Then, after Grandpa Pierce had died, Gran supplemented her income by changing it into a room to rent. There already had been an outside entrance at the end of the hall, and the big walk-in closet had been turned into a bathroom.

A few changes had to be made to accommodate Jake. The bathroom doorway had to be enlarged for wheelchair access. Without Jake's knowledge, Cliff had new door-jambs put in. The carpenters did such a wonderful job that it was hard to tell there had been an adjustment.

Ali opened the bathroom door and flicked on the light. "Here's the bathroom. It's just a shower stall...." Her voice faded off.

He patted the arms on his wheelchair. "I'm going to have some trouble taking this thing in there."

"It'll fit through the door. I'm not sure how you can manage a shower, though."

"Maybe you can volunteer to help."

Their eyes locked for a second before she glanced away. "I think your dad is sending a nurse."

"You tell him I don't need help. I'm getting tired of strangers prodding my body. I'll wash myself, thank you." He grinned. "Unless you want to help."

Ali tried to act unaffected by his comment. "I thought you were tired of being prodded."

"By strangers," he clarified. "You definitely aren't a stranger."

"And I think you're too cocky for your own good." Ali gripped the handles on the chair and pushed him to the bed. "You better rest. When Joanie wakes up, she's going to want to play. You'll need your strength."

She locked the chair in place, and Jake pulled himself up. A sudden warmth shot through her as she put her arms around his narrow waist and helped him to sit down on the mattress. She could feel the muscles in his back tense, the warmth permeating his clothing. Ali looked up to discover his face was close, so close that she could feel his ragged breath against her cheek. She released him, then escaped to the end of the bed and carefully elevated his cast-covered leg.

Taking a step back, she examined her patient and noticed that Jake was grimacing in pain. "You're hurting, aren't you?"

Jake laid his head back against the pillow. "Yeah, the leg is throbbing a little. My football coach used to say that pain builds character."

"Well, you're not on the team anymore. Where are your pills?"

He remained silent.

"Jake."

"In my shaving kit."

Ali nodded and walked to the green duffel bag on the floor. She pulled out the shaving kit on top, then reached inside and retrieved the pills. Ali poured a glass of water from the pitcher on the bedside table and handed Jake a pill.

He took the capsule and washed it down with the water. "Thanks."

She didn't move. "I wish there was something more I could do."

He touched his thigh. "The pill will take the edge off soon, and maybe I can sleep."

Ali fought with herself. She didn't want to leave him yet. Maybe she should wait until he went to sleep. She moved to the rocker and sat down.

Jake gave her a sideways glance. "Don't you have to go back to work?"

She shrugged. "I'll get there later."

"C'mon, Ali. You've taken off enough work because of me. I don't need a baby-sitter."

"Then quit acting like a child and let the pills go to work."

Jake glared at her, then turned away.

Ali saw more than pain in his eyes. She rose from the chair and claimed a seat on the bed. "What's wrong, Jake? Is it your leg? Do I need to call the doctor?"

He shifted position and finally looked at her. "No. It's just hard for me to sleep. Sometimes I dream...."

Something stirred inside Ali, and she took his hand. "Are you having nightmares about the accident?"

He shook his head. "I still can't remember anything about that day. I dream about being in a coma again."

She squeezed his hand. "Oh, Jake. I'm sorry." She brushed his hair from his forehead, like she'd done for Joanie so many times. It seemed to relax him, and he closed his eyes. After a few minutes, she caught his even breathing and knew the pills were working. What a terrible thing for Jake to go through.

She was surprised that he didn't remember the day of the accident. Her thoughts turned to Cliff, recalling his comments that he was to blame for what happened that day. Ali prayed that that wasn't true. Jake's remembering could be a nightmare.

About five, Jake woke up, managed to get back into his wheelchair and made a trip to the bathroom by himself.

Afterward he wheeled the chair into the kitchen and found June cooking dinner.

"Well, my word, Jake, seems you're managing just fine."

"With all my military training, I'm pretty resourceful."

"Just don't be too foolish with your independence. I know after my stroke, I wanted to show everyone that I wasn't an invalid. My stubbornness nearly put me back into the hospital."

"I'm not breaking any rules," he protested. "See. I'm in the chair, my leg is elevated." He glanced around and discovered that Joanie was in her playpen. "I just wanted to see my girl." He wheeled his chair toward the child as she stood up and held on to the raised side. "Hi, Joanie. How's my girl?" He glanced at June. "You think she knows me?"

"Of course she knows you. See that smile? She doesn't hand those out to just anyone."

"I mean, do you think she knows I'm her father?"

"Give her time, Jake."

Joanie held her hands out and began to fuss.

"What does she want?"

"Don't let her con you, Dad. She wants her freedom. But while I'm fixing dinner, it's safer if she's right where I can keep an eye on her."

"I can watch her."

Gran June began to laugh. "You can't keep up with her to watch her."

"How can she cause trouble? She can't even walk."

"I guess you haven't been around too many children. Joanie crawls and she's fast. She also pulls herself up on the furniture and breaks things. Worse, she can hurt herself. So while we can't keep a close eye on her, she has to be in the playpen."

"It just seems cruel to keep a child cooped up."

"Jake, this is the first time today she's been in there. I spent over an hour upstairs playing with her in her room. But Joanie needs to learn to entertain herself, too. Usually she does very well while I fix dinner." June glanced at the clock. "Besides, Joanie knows that when her mother comes home from work, she'll have playtime."

"So Ali gets to play with Joanie every day?"

June nodded, then went to the oven and checked inside on dinner. "Before you ended up in the hospital, she was home every night and on weekends. Ali's wonderful with Joanie. And if you want to find out any more, Jake, I suggest you sit back and observe the mother of your child."

Jake was embarrassed. "I know Ali is a good mother, but I'm worried that she doesn't get to spend enough time with Joanie."

"And just how am I to do that?"

Both Jake and Gran June turned to see that Ali had arrived home. Joanie let out a squeal of delight. Ali gave Jake a stern look as she hung up her coat, then went to her daughter and picked her up.

"How's my girl?" She kissed her daughter's cheeks until she giggled. Then Joanie patted her mother's cheeks in return. It was obviously part of their game. Jake felt a little left out.

"Joanie, now give Daddy a kiss," Ali suggested.

Ali held Joanie in her arms, allowing the baby to lean down and place a sloppy kiss on Jake's face.

"Thank you, Joanie." He took the child from Ali and placed her on his lap, careful not to disturb his injured leg. The child sat there, looking a little confused, then she smiled and clapped her hands.

Ali gave Joanie a toy, which quickly went into her mouth. Just as swiftly Jake reached up and took Ali's hand.

"I didn't mean that you weren't a good mother. I just want you to be able to spend time with her. She's just a baby."

"Don't you think that I want that, too? But the reality is I have to work for a living. And if I didn't have Gran June, I'd probably have to put our daughter into day care. Joanie's one of the lucky ones."

"Let me help you."

"Jake, your money will help, but I need to work to get health insurance for both me and Joanie. I'm a single mother." She picked up her daughter from Jake's lap. "C'mon, sweetie. I need to get out of my work clothes and I think you could use a diaper change." She headed out of the room without a backward glance.

Gran June came up beside Jake. "She's not the same shy girl you remember, Jake. Ali's had to grow up fast these past few years. Don't underestimate her."

Jake shook his head. Never. His only concern was how he was ever going to get her to need him in her life.

After a quiet supper, Ali stopped by Jake's room to make sure he was settled for the night.

"I thought it was nice of your dad to send over this television and VCR. There's even some movies."

"I don't watch much television."

She held up some tapes. "These are movies. There's *Top Gun, Ghost, Sleepless in Seattle, Beauty and the Beast, Apollo 13, Forest Gump.*"

Jake didn't want to spend the night alone. Ever since Ali had overheard his conversation with June, she'd been ignoring him. If he could take the words back, he would. The last thing he wanted was for Ali to feel he was critical of her as a mother. Somehow he had to get their relationship back on track.

"I'll watch one if you'll stay," he suggested. "I'll even let you pick."

She shook her head. "I have to get up early."

"Tomorrow is Saturday, and you don't work."

She raised an eyebrow. "But Joanie still gets up early."

"I'll be up. You bring our daughter downstairs, and I'll feed her breakfast and dress her."

Ali laughed. "Oh, I should do just that to show you what hard work she is."

"I can handle it. Just because I'm in a wheelchair doesn't mean I'm incapable. My hands work just fine. Since I've lifted weights all my adult life, there is nothing wrong with my upper-body strength."

"Fine," she agreed. "You have yourself a deal. But when I bring her down tomorrow, you better be awake."

They decided on the movie *Sleepless in Seattle*. Ali hurried into the kitchen for popcorn and soda. By the time she returned, Jake had repositioned himself on the left side of the bed, with his injured leg on the far side.

"Come on." He patted the empty spot next to him. "There's plenty of room." He had the remote in his hand and started the movie. "Will we need tissues?"

Ali put down the tray and smacked his arm. "Just shut up and watch the movie, Hawk." She kicked off her sneakers and climbed on the bed. He couldn't help but notice she stayed on her side.

The music began, setting a romantic mood. Ali handed the popcorn to Jake. He gave her a sideways glance. "You sure you're not going to cry?"

"Not unless you eat all the popcorn," she teased as she took a handful. "It is a good movie, Jake. Very romantic."

"Oh, a chick flick."

"You said I could pick the movie."

Jake raised his hand in surrender. "Okay." He'd agree to anything to get Ali to stay close. "Meg Ryan is pretty easy to look at."

"And Tom Hanks is adorable. See. Something for the both of us."

Ali smiled and he had to stop himself from pulling her into his arms.

Ninety minutes later, the last song swelled, signaling the end of the movie. Jake found that he liked the story. The kid was cute.

He turned to say something to Ali, only to discover her eyes were closed. He smiled. She'd fallen asleep. He started to shake her, then stopped. The last time he'd seen her asleep was at the cottage. It had been after they'd made love. It had been Ali's first time....

Jake closed his eyes and recalled how giving she'd been. Her touches and simple caresses had brought him to pleasure like nothing he'd ever experienced before. She'd given to him freely that night, erasing all the painful memories, the pain of rejection. If only he could have returned the favor.

Jake managed to roll to his side and laid his head on the pillow next to hers.

Ali was a pretty woman. She had pale skin with only a light dusting of freckles across the bridge of her nose. Her lips were well shaped, the lower full and pouty.

He pulled back, wondering why he couldn't see any comparison to her twin, Darcie. He knew that physically they looked alike, but he'd never thought they were identical. He'd never really noticed Ali until the night they'd made love. But her tenderness and caring had drawn him to her.

His gaze lowered to her sweater. It was heavy enough to hide the generous swell of her breasts, but he knew they were fuller than he'd remembered. Was it from breast-feeding their daughter?

An ache tightened his chest. He wished he could have shared that time with the mother of his child. His gaze continued the journey down to her long legs, and a sudden jolt caused more havoc. This examination was a bad idea.

"Ali, wake up," he whispered. He touched her arm, knowing he had to resist temptation.

She responded with a soft moan and rolled to her side, then curled her warm, shapely body against his. Her arm came across his chest as she rested her head on his shoulder.

Jake froze. "Oh, boy." What was he supposed to do now?

He wanted nothing more than to go to sleep with Ali in his arms. But he needed to establish some trust here. The night in the cottage, he had blamed the beer he'd drunk for clouding his judgment. But the minute he'd kissed Ali, he became full awake. She had stirred things inside him that he'd never felt for Darcie. Then he took everything she offered so freely.

What had he given her?

Heartache.

For eighteen months, she'd thought that he'd deserted her. She'd had to raise their child by herself. Put up with the gossip in town. Well, he was back, and he'd prove that he was here for her now, if she needed him. Taking advantage of her while she was sleeping wouldn't gain her trust.

"Ali," he said more firmly. "Wake up."

Ali murmured something, but finally opened her eyes. Jake smiled at her confused look. "The movie is over, and you missed a great ending."

"Oh, gosh." She sat up and rubbed her eyes. "I'm sorry. I fell asleep."

"You don't need to apologize. I never should have insisted you stay up. I'm selfish. You came and visited me at the hospital for weeks, and my first night home I make you sit with me."

Ali smiled. "I wanted to, Jake. Everyone hates to be alone sometimes. I'm glad you're out of the hospital." She got off the bed. "I better head upstairs. Do you need anything else before I go?"

He shook his head, afraid of what he might say.

"Good night, Jake."

She walked out the door. Jake listened as she climbed the stairs, then walked into the room above his. He closed his eyes, willing himself to relax, but his body wouldn't cooperate.

He wondered—and hoped just a little—if Ali was having trouble getting back to sleep, too.

At seven o'clock the next morning, a tired Ali carried her freshly diapered daughter downstairs. Joanie's usual playful mood wasn't reciprocated by her mother. Thanks to Jake, Ali had lain awake for hours last night, and just before dawn she'd made herself several promises. The first and foremost was to stay far away from Jake Hawkins's bedroom. Others included not letting him touch her or kiss her. She couldn't think straight when he did.

Besides, the only thing he could offer her was heartache. He would always belong to Darcie.

She walked into the kitchen and stopped. Jake was seated at the table, dressed in a bathrobe draped open in a large V, exposing too much of his bare chest. She swallowed as Joanie squealed happily, nearly jumping out of her mother's arms.

Jake smiled at his daughter. "Good morning, Joanie." Then his penetrating stare moved over Ali, taking in her flannel gown and old chenille robe. "Good morning, Ali-cat. How did you sleep?" he asked in a husky voice.

"Just fine," she lied as she tried to tame her wild hair. "What are you doing up?"

He grinned again. "I'm military, remember? I'm used to

getting up at dawn,'' he said, then frowned. ''That's not always true. Sometimes I'm up all night on a surveillance, so I've learned to make a decent cup of coffee.'' He pushed his wheelchair back from the table and went to the coffee-pot. ''Want some?''

''Sure.'' She pulled the high chair beside the table and placed her daughter in it. ''Where's Gran June?''

''She had to take some things over to the church for the seniors club's rummage sale.''

''Oh, I forgot. I was supposed to help her.''

''June said she's going back in the afternoon. You can help then.''

Ali watched as Jake wheeled his chair toward her. They exchanged glances, and Ali thought back to last night...the movie...being with Jake...in his bed. Again a tingle shot through her. Quickly she broke eye contact, went to the stove and turned on the teakettle. ''Oh, I wanted to tell you that Gran June has Thanksgiving dinner here,'' Ali said abruptly. ''She usually invites family and friends. This year she wants to invite your dad,'' she added as she pulled down the oatmeal and poured some into a bowl.

''I know. June already asked me. I told her that it was her house. She can do what she wants.'' He looked at Joanie and his somber expression changed to a smile. ''You think I could feed her this morning?'' he asked.

''If she'll let you. She's pretty independent.''

''She let me last night,'' Jake said as he took Joanie's hand and kissed it. The child cooed at her daddy, and Jake cooed right back.

Suddenly Ali felt as if she was intruding. Joanie only needed her in the past, but now she wanted her father. Turning away, Ali finished mixing the cereal with milk. She tested the temperature, then gave the plastic bowl to Jake. ''Be careful. She's been known to sling food across the room.''

Jake nodded and took the bowl. He spooned up a small amount and offered it to Joanie. The baby took the spoonful eagerly. The next bite went down, as well, then she tried to grab the spoon. When she didn't get it, she let out a loud scream.

"My, my. Is that any way for a young lady to act?" Jake said, but relented and handed his daughter her spoon. Joanie ignored her parents and began to eat—and make a mess.

"She's stubborn."

"I wonder where she gets that?" Ali said, then she took a long sip of coffee to hide her smile.

"Are you saying I'm stubborn?"

Jake's smile nearly knocked her off her chair. All Ali could do was nod.

He turned to Joanie. "Well, sweetie, it's only fair you get something from me since you got your beauty from your mother."

Ali felt the heat rise to her face. Darcie was the beauty of the family. Ali's looks leaned more toward cute. She went to the counter and picked up the milk carton. After pouring some into a cup, she snapped on the safety lid and put it in front of Jake. She hoped he couldn't see her hand shake.

Ali stood back and observed the two for a while, then asked, "Think you can cope while I take a quick shower?"

"Sure, we'll be okay." He grinned at the messy-looking child in the high chair. "Won't we, Joanie?"

Fine, Ali thought. Jake wanted to get to know his daughter. Ali might as well let him see Joanie's true side. Wait until he gets to change a diaper, she thought. He'd probably set land speed records wheeling his chair back to his dad's place.

Ali went to her bedroom at the head of the stairs. The yellow walls had faded over the years, but with Joanie, Ali hadn't had any extra time to repaint. The double bed still had the same white ruffled bedspread that she'd had when she started high school. Darcie's room was identical, except she'd chosen everything in blue.

Most of Ali's school things, like yearbooks and banners, had been put away, but she knew she could open a certain drawer and locate a picture of Jake Hawkins. To prove her point, she went to the mahogany dresser and slid open the bottom drawer. Sorting through her sweaters, she found the small wood-carved jewelry box that Jake had given her as a Christmas gift. From the time Jake had met Darcie, he'd spent nearly every holiday in the Pierce home, and he'd always come bearing gifts for the family. The year she and Darcie were seniors, Darcie had received a pearl necklace, and Ali had gotten the jewelry box.

Ali told herself that she was no longer the silly girl with a crush, that she'd only kept the photos for Joanie. But when she opened the box and found a picture of Jake and her years younger, her heart soared. She looked at the next one, a time when they were all together at the lake cottage. A boyish-looking Jake was pushing her on the tire swing down at the water's edge. A smile spread across Ali's face. Life had been so carefree back then. Their problems were no more than who was going to ask you to the prom, or flunking Algebra II.

She sank to the bed. Now she was a twenty-five-year-old woman. Problem was, she'd also realized that Jake was definitely a man.

Her fingers touched the photo. Every time he'd gotten close to her, her body told her she still wanted him. Her heart told her she still cared. But her head told her not to get involved, she'd only be hurt again. And she knew she couldn't handle that a second time.

Twenty minutes later, Ali returned to the kitchen to find that her grandmother had taken charge of Joanie.

"Where's your daddy? Did you tire him out?" she asked, stooping over the baby's playpen.

Gran June stood at the stove frying up bacon. "Jake had everything under control when I got here. This little one was sitting on her daddy's lap, and they were playing pat-a-cake. It was so cute."

"Where is he now?"

"In his room, getting cleaned up. Joanie shared a little of her oatmeal with him," Gran June said. "I told him you'd help him wash it out of his hair."

Ali's heart thudded against her chest. "Gran, I can't do that—"

"Relax. He won't be taking a shower. He'll be doing sponge baths for a while. But he'll still have trouble maneuvering. So I told him you'd help wash his hair."

"Thanks a lot."

Gran June handed her a plastic pitcher. "My pleasure. Breakfast will be ready in fifteen minutes." She motioned with her hands. "Now scoot."

Ali grumbled as she made her way down the hall. Jake's door was open, but the sight of him sitting in the wheelchair with only khaki boxers on startled her. She wanted to turn around and run. Instead, she averted her eyes. "Gran said you needed me?"

"Yeah." He raked his hand through his hair. "I hate to ask, but can you help me wash this oatmeal out?"

"Your dad offered to send over a nurse."

Jake gave her a stubborn look. "Look, if this is too much trouble, you can pass."

"No, of course it's not," she said, a little breathless. "Lead on."

He pushed his chair into the compact bathroom that barely had space for a toilet and shower stall, and managed to get turned around so he could back up to the pedestal sink. Ali's heart pounded as she watched his large, muscular arms flex when he maneuvered the chair into position. She had to resist the urge to reach out and touch him. Instead, she waited until he was settled, then turned on the water, adjusted the temperature and filled the pitcher.

"You can lean back now."

Jake did as she asked, and she poured some water over his thick hair. Her hand was trembling as she squeezed out a dab of shampoo from the tube. The familiar scent teased her nostrils, boldly reminding her of their one night together. The night she'd spent in Jake's arms, sharing their needs and wants... and passion. Ali drew in a breath and tried to relax as she massaged the soap into his scalp. His hair had grown since he'd come home, and feeling the long silky strands of his hair between her fingers only worked to sensitize other parts of her body, as well.

"Oh, that feels good," Jake groaned. "How are you on rubbing backs?"

"Haven't had much practice," Ali said before thinking about the implications. There hadn't been a man in her life since Jake.

Jake opened his eyes, and his dark-eyed stare bore into hers. "I'm glad you haven't had practice." His voice was husky as he raised his hand and touched her hair. "When I'm able, I'll return the favor. I'd love to get my hands in all this softness."

Ali sucked in a breath. "Jake..." Warmth shot through her at the thought of Jake's hands on her.

"What, Ali?" he whispered. "What is it you want? Tell me."

"I can't." She met his gaze.

"Okay, don't tell me, Ali. I can see it in your eyes." He slid his hand through her hair and drew her head down. "You want what I want."

Ali wanted to dispute it, but no words came. Then his mouth covered hers, and she was lost. What started out as soft caresses quickly turned into a hungry kiss as his mouth began to move over hers fervently. Passions flared as he cupped her head, burying his fingers into her hair. When his tongue parted her lips, she surrendered once again and released a moan, eagerly returning the kiss. She touched his chest, feeling his bare strength against her fingertips. Every inch of her ached with longing, a longing that only Jake could extinguish. Ali swept her hand down to his waist, and he sucked in a sharp breath.

Suddenly her grandmother's voice at the bedroom door broke them apart. "Breakfast is ready."

Ali jumped back, and somehow managed to speak. "Okay, we're just about finished."

Ali couldn't look at Jake. Her cheeks grew hot as she busied herself rinsing the shampoo out of his hair, then she got a towel and handed it to him. When she started to leave, Jake grabbed her by the arm.

"You can't keep running away from what's happening between us."

"You purposely set this up, didn't you?"

He smiled. "Did I force you to kiss me?"

Ali refused to look away. Damn the man for seeing through her.

Jake's expression grew serious. "Ali, I just want to be a part of your life."

"You've moved into my house and you spend more time with Joanie than I do. Why can't that be enough for you?"

"Because I want us to be a family."

Ali wished it were that easy. But there were too many things stopping them. "Right now, that isn't possible, Jake. You need to concentrate on your recovery. I think you should get to know your daughter. Maybe…after you change a few diapers, being a parent won't look so appealing."

"And what about after that, Ali? Will there be more tests?"

She closed her eyes in frustration. "We'll see."

His hold on her arm tightened. "All right. If I go by the rules, will you promise to stop running away from me?"

She wanted to run at that moment. This man could destroy her if she let him get too close. She wasn't sure she was willing to risk it.

"I'll stop running if you'll stop chasing." She turned and hurried out of the room.

Chapter Seven

Three weeks had passed since Jake had arrived at the Pierce home. Three *long* weeks during which he'd kept his promise, and his distance, from Ali. He hadn't come near her since that morning in the bathroom. And in all that time, he had learned patience. Being forced to sit in a wheelchair will do that to you.

Thanks to one Johanna June Hawkins, he'd also discovered a lot about being a father. He'd learned to change a diaper, as Ali suggested. He'd also become a pretty good storyteller and found a secret of how to deal with Joanie's fussy times. She loved getting rides in her daddy's chair.

Well, today there was going to be another change, he thought as he pulled a polo shirt out of the drawer and slipped it over his head. Then he managed to put on a pair of black sweatpants to accommodate his cast. It was Joanie's first Thanksgiving, and she was about to see her father stand up. Jake had decided he wasn't going to come to the dinner table in his wheelchair. Although reluctant, Dr. Hostler had given Jake permission to use crutches, but only around the house.

Jake wanted to shout the pleasure of his small freedom. He'd been lying on his back for so long, he thought he'd never stand again. Well, he was going to do more than stand; he was going to walk.

He stood next to the bed, grabbed the crutches Harry had delivered, and placed them under his arms. Testing his weight, he took one small step, then another. Luckily he'd been doing upper-body exercises and lifting weights, knowing he'd need all his strength to maneuver around the room with his bulky cast. His ankle felt better, too. He hadn't needed any painkillers for a while.

Over the past weeks, Jake had become more and more independent, handling on his own simple tasks like showering and shampooing his hair. He hated asking for help, especially from Ali. He wanted her to see him as a man, not an invalid.

He grinned. Maybe today things would start to change between them.

He couldn't think too far into the future. Next week, he'd be getting a walking cast, but he still had to face months of physical therapy. He also had to go to a military hospital to have his case evaluated. He pretty much knew the outcome already. His army career was over. He would have to take a medical discharge. But he was still determined to be a whole man again. For his daughter…and for Ali.

He'd been given a second chance at life, and he was going to make the most of it. Ali was going to see a different man today.

He grinned as he checked his appearance in the mirror. He opened his bedroom door and made his way down the hallway. He peeked into the dining room. The long cherrywood table had been decorated with the Pierce family's best linen and china. Feminine voices emanated from the kitchen, along with the wonderful smells of spices and fresh bread.

Making his way to the door, he poked his head into the kitchen without being seen, and discovered June bent over the oven, basting a large turkey. Ali was seated at the table peeling potatoes while his daughter busied herself quietly in her playpen.

Jake smiled. This was a family. The family he wanted. Deciding not to disturb the women, he stepped back and closed the swinging door.

He made his way into the living room and saw the paper turkey on the piano. A familiar ache welled in his chest as he remembered the holidays when he'd been a kid. His dad had always been too busy to stay home. Since they'd had no other family—no grandparents, aunts or uncles—to fill the house, most times it was just him and his mother...and her tears. Then she would start drinking and get angry and, finally, to Jake's relief, Carol Hawkins would go upstairs and pass out on her bed.

He rubbed his eyes, as if to erase the memories. Memories of a mother who tried to find happiness in a bottle. Why couldn't her child be enough to keep her sober?

"Jake..."

He turned when he heard Ali's voice. She was standing in the arched doorway. She looked like an angel, dressed in a long green-and-pink print dress. An old-fashioned lace collar adorned her graceful neck. Her hair lay in waves about her shoulders, and in her arms she carried their daughter, who was wearing an identical outfit—only in a miniature size.

Ali walked across the room. "Jake, what are you doing standing up?"

"Happy Thanksgiving to you, too," he said a little sarcastically. So much for impressing her.

Her expression softened. "I'm sorry. Happy Thanksgiving. But really, Jake, should you be out of your chair?"

"Yes, I should." Jake leaned forward and kissed his daughter's cheek. "How's my girl?" After he coaxed a smile from Joanie, he looked back at Ali. "If I don't overdo. By the way, you look beautiful."

Ali didn't know how to handle Jake's compliments— period. "Thank you. We kind of go overboard for the holidays around here, but it's fun, especially for Joanie."

"I remember the years I visited here." He smiled, but it didn't mask the sadness in his eyes. "Everything was wonderful." He turned away. "So different from—"

Ali reached out a hand and touched Jake's arm. "You were thinking about your mother, weren't you?"

He leaned his weight against the piano and looked at his daughter. "Yeah, she would have loved this little one."

Ali had never met Carol Hawkins, but she knew how much Jake had loved and missed her. Ali set Joanie down on the piano, but kept her hands on her. "Holidays bring out not only good memories, but sad ones, too. I remember one time when Mom left Darcie and me alone at Christmas at some motel room in west Texas." Ali toyed with Joanie's hair bow. "We were only five."

Tears welled in her eyes, remembering how she and Darcie had huddled together on the bed, scared and crying, wanting their mother to come back. She shook away the old memory and felt Jake's arm around her.

"What happened?"

She forced a smile. "I think the management called the police and they got a hold of Gran June. We came to live with her after that. Gran June and Grandpa had Christmas for us the next day, with a letter from Santa saying that he was sorry he was late, but he had a little trouble finding us." A tear fell to her cheek. Jake quickly brushed it away.

"I'm so sorry, Ali." Bracing his weight on his crutches,

he leaned forward and feathered a kiss on her cheek. It wasn't enough, and he moved to brush his mouth against hers.

Ali sucked in a breath, then raised her eyes to meet his dark gaze. He lowered his head again. Joanie had other ideas, and chose that moment to yell and grab for her mother.

"So you want attention, too?" Jake asked. "Have you ever heard of a thing called 'bad timing'?"

Jake made a smacking sound against his daughter's neck. The baby laughed and clutched her daddy's head, messing up his hair.

Ali laughed, too, and tried to smooth Jake's hair. "There. You're as good as new."

Jake stared at her, and her heart began to pound.

"I've missed you, Ali."

"I've been here," she said, nearly choking on her words. She had purposely stayed out of his way. Too bad it didn't stop her from thinking about him.

He touched her hand. "I didn't come here to live so we could avoid each other, Ali. I want to prove to you I'm not going to run out again. I'm here to stay—for Joanie…and for you."

Ali couldn't speak. She wanted to trust Jake, but so many things stood between them. His injuries, his army career, Darcie… Their lives were in upheaval. She couldn't decide now.

The doorbell rang, and Ali found her escape. She picked up Joanie and hurried to answer the door. On the porch stood Sheriff Benson and his wife, LaVerne, who was holding a covered dish.

"Happy Thanksgiving," Ali said as she ushered the couple through the door. Kisses were exchanged, then Ray took Joanie with him and headed for the living room as Ali escorted LaVerne into the kitchen.

* * *

Feeling a little shaky, Jake sat down on the sofa and slid his crutches under the coffee table. He'd just propped his leg on the ottoman when the sheriff walked into the room carrying Joanie.

"Good to see you moving around, Jake," the sheriff said as he sat down with Joanie.

"Nice to be out of my chair, Sheriff."

"Why don't you call me Ray?"

Jake nodded. "Seems a little strange. I still remember when I was in high school and you picked me up for speeding."

Ray smiled. "I remember. You had that fancy new car your dad bought you. It was right after you'd won the conference title." Ray frowned. "I believe you passed for 183 yards and were named the most valuable player of the game."

Jake blinked in surprise. "How did you remember that?"

"I was at the game—and, unfortunately for you, I was at the crossroad later when I clocked you going over ninety miles an hour."

Jake cringed. "I guess I did a lot of foolish things when I was a teenager."

Ray shook his head. "Not really. It could have been a lot worse. You could have been drinking that night, but you weren't."

"I don't drink anymore," Jake said stiffly. Not since the night he'd spent with Ali. The night they'd created a child.

Ray grew serious. "Well, I wish I could say that about the teenagers here in Webster High School. They think it's so cool."

Jake sighed. "We all think we're invincible at that age."

Ray studied him for a second. "You know, the Hawk is still talked about at the high school, especially with this being football season. Maybe you could come by and give a talk on alcohol safety."

"What could I say?"

"You're a father now, Jake. Just think about a drunk teenager out there on the road, endangering Joanie's life."

A cold chill went through Jake. "Tell me when you want me."

"I'll call you next week. We could use you for career day, too. What was your speciality in the army?"

"Intelligence. I was supposed to go overseas after my leave." Jake rubbed his leg. "Then the accident happened."

Ray nodded. "You know, when I was in the army, a lot of my buddies didn't make it back."

Jake studied the sheriff. "When were you in?"

"The sixties. I flew a helicopter in Vietnam."

"Rough assignment."

"Not as rough as some. At least I made it home to my family. I told myself I wasn't going to leave Webster again. I ran for sheriff, and—" he grinned "—the rest, as they say, is history."

Joanie got restless and crawled across the sofa to her daddy. Jake captured her and placed her on his lap. Ray was right. Being a father made everything different. He straightened the child's dress and touched her tiny white shoes. Joanie was his family now, and she needed him. Just as he needed to be around to take care of her. Somehow he had to convince Ali of that.

Joanie grabbed his finger and put it in her mouth and started to bite. "No, sweetie," Jake said. "Don't bite.

Joanie shook her head vigorously. "N-nooo."

"Hey, did you hear that? She said no!"

"Get used to it, son. She'll be saying that to you for about the next twenty years."

Jake kissed his daughter's head. "No, you won't do that to your daddy, right? Not my sweet little girl. You'll be the best daughter ever."

As if on cue, Joanie shook her head again. "No."

Both men laughed.

The doorbell rang, and Ray got up to answer it. A few minutes later, Cliff came into the living room. Although his limp was barely noticeable, he still used his cane.

Joanie immediately began to chatter and wave her arms at her grandfather.

Cliff walked over to her. "There's my beautiful granddaughter." He handed the child a sack from the local toy store. Inside was a fluffy stuffed kitten.

He finally looked at Jake. "Hi, son." Cliff glanced at the crutches under the table. "I see you've graduated."

Jake tensed. His father had visited him several times to check on his progress. He was playing the good-father and family-man roles to the max, and it rubbed Jake the wrong way. "I'll be using crutches from now on. You don't have to worry about me anymore. I'm fine."

Cliff smiled. "Good."

Just then the ladies walked in, and Cliff looked relieved for the distraction.

The doorbell rang once again. Ali answered the door this time, then ushered in Margo and her boyfriend, Scott Walker.

Margo came up to Jake. "So you broke out of the chair."

Jake smiled. "Can't keep me down for long."

The petite woman brushed her brown hair away from her face. "A little tender loving care doesn't hurt, either."

Jake felt himself blush as he glanced at Ali.

"Just be warned, Jake Hawkins," Margo said softly. "I helped Ali pick up the pieces the last time you broke her heart. I won't stand by and let you hurt her again."

Before Jake could defend himself, June entered the room to announce that dinner was ready.

Ali took Joanie as Jake got his crutches and stood. For the first time in a very long time, she had to look up at him. He found he liked it. Although Ali was five-six, she barely reached his shoulders. She blushed, then smiled as if disconcerted. Her response gave him a sudden rush, making him feel ten feet tall.

At the dinner table, they were seated together with Joanie's high chair almost between them. Ray and LaVerne, Margo Wells and Scott Walker sat across the table. Cliff was at one end, and June took her place at the head of the table along with a huge turkey.

Gran June stood up to make an announcement. "I think before we start this wonderful meal, we should thank the Lord for all the blessings we've received this past year." She linked her hands with the people on either side of her, and everyone followed suit. They all bowed their heads.

"Lord, we'd like to thank you today for family and friends. For the love in this room, especially for blessing us with Johanna June this year. And for seeing fit to heal Jake and bring him back to his family. Please keep Darcie safe in the big city. In your name we pray, Amen."

Jake squeezed Ali's hand, reluctant to let go after the prayer. Their eyes met, and Jake promised himself that somehow he was going to make her realize that they needed to be together.

Dinner was a noisy affair, but it was the most fun Jake had had in years. He'd never celebrated holidays like this as a kid. At his house, first came the alcohol, then the fights, and finally his father would storm off to the plant, leaving a child alone sharing dinner with the housekeeper.

Joanie's quiet chatter brought him back to the present. He smiled and she returned it with a toothy grin. He was a damn lucky man.

After the meal ended, the ladies were dishing out the pies when a pager went off. Four people reached for their belts to discover that it was Cliff's.

"May I use your phone, June?" Cliff asked.

Gran June ushered him into the kitchen. Jake felt his anger build. Damn his father. Nothing had changed.

Jake remained silent when Cliff returned and began saying his goodbyes. His father kissed Joanie on the cheek and hugged Ali.

Then the older Hawkins looked at Jake. "Son, I'm sorry, but I have to cut this short."

Jake got up and managed to follow his father to the door on his crutches. "Still the same old thing, huh, Dad? Work comes first, above all else."

"That's not true, son," Cliff denied. "It's just that so much of business now is worldwide, and Thanksgiving is an American holiday."

"So tell them you're unavailable on American holidays. Give them a damn list."

"Son, this is important, or I wouldn't be leaving for this international call."

Jake gripped his crutches tightly. "It's like always, Dad. Family never came first with you. Well, it's different with me. My daughter is having her first Thanksgiving, and I intend to share every minute of it. I'm not going to miss my kid's childhood like you did." He turned and walked back to the dining room, ignoring his father's pained expression.

At nine o'clock that night, the good china had been washed and put away, and Joanie was sound asleep in her crib. Ali was tired also, but too restless to go to bed. She came downstairs to lock up and found Jake sitting on the floor in front of the hearth. He was leaning against the ottoman, and a fire was going, throwing off a golden glow in the otherwise dark room.

"Jake, what are you doing sitting down there?"

He didn't turn around. "Just enjoying the end of a perfect day," he said.

Ali smiled to herself as she walked into the room to stand next to him. "That's pretty high praise even for one of Gran June's meals. I'll have to tell her in the morning. After she said her goodbyes to Ray and LaVerne, she went up to bed."

Jake finally looked at her, his eyes dark...and way too seductive. "I wasn't talking about the meal, Ali. It was you and Joanie who made the day perfect."

She had liked spending the day with Jake, too. He fit in so well. "It was nice, wasn't it?"

Jake patted the carpeted floor beside him. "Come and sit with me," he coaxed. "With all the people around today, we haven't had much of a chance to talk."

A warning went off in her head. Ali knew she'd be wise if she turned around and left—immediately. "I don't think that's such a good idea."

Jake took hold of her hand and, without much resistance from her, pulled Ali down beside him. "I only ask that you spend a little time with me."

Ali folded her legs next to her and stared into the fire. "We seem to get into trouble when we're alone together."

He took her hand, and his fingers brushed across her knuckles, sending warm tingles up her arm. She drew a breath and caught a whiff of his cologne.

"Trouble? A few kisses. Why should that matter?" he asked. "Unless there *is* something between us."

Ali wanted to deny his words, but knew she couldn't. Her feelings for Jake were as strong as ever, but that didn't mean she was going to just fall into his arms. "We have a daughter together, Jake." She pulled her hand away. "I think that could cloud your judgment on your true feelings."

He sat up straighter, then reached over and touched her chin, making her look at him. "You do more than cloud my judgment. I could shock you with what I'm thinking.

Things I want to do to you—with you. Things I fantasize you doing to me.''

Ali felt the air leave her lungs.

He leaned forward. His hand cupped her cheek. ''Ah, Ali-cat. You don't know how much I want to kiss you.'' He lowered his head and placed his mouth on the side of her jaw. He pulled back and stared into her eyes. When Ali didn't protest, he found her mouth, and nibbled on her lower lip until she gasped.

''Tell me to stop, Ali, and I will. But I think you want this as much as I do. You like what is happening between us. Don't tell me you haven't thought about me kissing you again.'' He took more teasing bites, then finally covered her mouth in a hungry kiss.

Ali melted into his arms as his mouth slanted over hers, devouring her like a man starved. His tongue demanded access, and she willingly opened to welcome him. In turn, she used her tongue to taste him, wanting to drive Jake a little crazy, too.

He groaned and laid her back onto the floor. ''Have mercy, woman. I'm a wounded man.''

Like hell he was. ''Just kiss me,'' she demanded.

He cupped her face in his hands and took her mouth in a searing kiss, followed by another and another. She couldn't say how long the kisses went on—forever wouldn't be nearly long enough for him to continue. They started out slow and easy, then became demanding as he plunged his tongue into her mouth, and she returned his fervor.

Breathless, he pulled back and looked into her eyes once again. Ali could feel his heart pounding in his chest.

He lowered his mouth to hers once more, and this time his hand moved to her breast. Ali moaned as he proceeded to tease her with slow, easy, butterfly kisses, then switched to deep, open-mouth kisses along her neck that proceeded to drive her to the edge. He didn't stop there. He reached under her sweater and quickly opened the front clasp of her bra, allowing his hand to cover her breast.

"Oh, Jake," she breathed as she arched against him, asking for more, demanding more. "Don't stop."

"I don't plan to." He pushed up her sweater and bared her breasts. "Damn, you're so beautiful." He reached out, caressed her gently, reverently, then bent his head and took her nipple into his mouth.

Jake couldn't believe Ali's reaction. With every touch, she went crazy with desire, and when she raised her hips and moved against his arousal, he almost exploded. He kissed her again, knowing he could never get enough of her. But if he didn't stop now, he wouldn't be able to.

He broke off the kiss, but Ali had other ideas and continued to use her hands and mouth to drive him mad.

"Ali, we have to stop."

"No." She pressed herself against him, creating an ache inside him that was unbearable.

"Ali, please. We can't."

Finally she stopped and blinked her green eyes in confusion.

He pulled her sweater back into place, unable to look at her hurt. "We were getting carried away."

Her hands covered her face. "Oh, God. I can't believe I did this. I threw myself at you."

Jake took hold of her hand, and placed a kiss against the palm. "I believe we both caught fire, Ali. I only stopped so you wouldn't...wouldn't regret what was about to happen. It's important that you trust me."

Her hand reached out and touched his jaw. "Oh, Jake. I do trust you."

"Don't look at me like that, or all my good intentions will fly out the window."

Ali gave him an innocent smile. "Look how?"

Jake groaned. "You're a wicked woman," he accused, and rolled onto his back, pulling Ali with him. He knew he should let her go, but he desperately needed her close to him.

She raised her head and stared down at him, her elbow resting on his chest. "You forget, Hawk. You're the one who persuaded me to sit with you."

"Like you resisted."

"I thought you said I could trust you."

He opened his mouth, but he had no argument. Only the truth. "Ali, when I'm with you, my control is nonexistent. If you only knew how much I want you..."

Just then the phone rang, and Ali got up to answer it. Jake watched as she moved gracefully across the room. He still ached for her.

Ali picked up the receiver. "Hello," she said, then Jake watched as her smile disappeared before she turned away.

Ali's heart sank into her stomach as Darcie's voice came over the line. "Happy Thanksgiving, sis."

"Hello, Darcie. Gran June expected to hear from you earlier."

"I tried, but I had dinner at my boss's house, and I just couldn't walk out to use the phone. Gran understands."

That was what Darcie had always counted on—Gran's understanding.

"I bet you had a houseful as usual," Darcie said. "I missed everyone."

Ali's back was to Jake, but she heard him struggle with his crutches to stand up. "Well, it was different this year with Joanie."

"I hope you'll send me some more pictures. I'm still trying to figure out who she looks like. All that dark hair, and those eyes. She must take after her daddy."

Ali knew her sister was fishing for information, and not

so subtly. But now was not the time to tell her about Jake. "She does," was all she said.

"I guess I need to come home to see for myself. And I will find out who Joanie's father is, and when I do, I'll give him a piece of my mind. Nobody leaves my sister and gets away—"

"Let's not worry about that, Darcie. Are you coming home for Christmas?" Ali interrupted, her hands trembling.

"Things are too busy around here right now, so I can't take any time off. I really love my career, Ali. I'm glad I listened to your advice."

Ali froze. "What advice?"

"You told me to follow my heart. I did, and took off for New York. I can't imagine being married and living on an army base."

Ali ached inside. Dear Lord. That had been innocent, loving advice between sisters. "I let you make your own decision, Darcie. You seemed so agitated after you and Jake had the fight."

Jake was standing behind her. He leaned forward and began to nibble on her neck. She gasped and moved away.

"Is something wrong?" Darcie asked.

"No, but I've got to go. I have to get up early tomorrow...."

"Sorry I called so late. Ali?"

"Yes."

"I heard that Jake was in an accident. Have you heard if he's okay?"

Ali closed her eyes and fought to draw a breath. "Yes, he's okay. It was touch and go for awhile, but he's doing fine now."

"Good. After everything that happened between us, I just couldn't bring myself to call the hospital. I'll probably always love Jake," Darcie said wistfully. "Maybe at another time in our lives things would have worked out...."

Ali was going to be sick. "Look, Darcie. I really have to go."

"I know, it's late, but I miss our talks. I'm also sorry I wasn't there for you, too, when you needed me."

"It's okay. Look, I'll call you the next time."

"Give everyone a kiss for me."

"Bye, Darcie."

"Bye, Ali."

Ali put the receiver back into the cradle, but didn't look at Jake.

"Are you okay?" he asked.

Ali nodded.

"Why didn't you tell Darcie I was here?"

Ali swung around, her anger flaring. "Maybe because I didn't want to hurt her. Darcie's going to find out soon enough that I slept with her fiancé the day of her wedding."

With the help of his crutches, Jake came to her. "Give it a rest, Ali. Darcie walked out on me before you and I did anything. What happened between us had nothing to do with her."

"How can you say that, Jake? When she discovers you're Joanie's father, she's going to feel betrayed."

"How can she feel betrayed when she walked out on me? Darcie has no claim on me. And I want us to be married. If we're a family, there will be no questions or speculation about who I want."

But you don't love me, Ali wanted to scream. Instead, she looked Jake in the eye. "The questions might stop, but how am I supposed to stop my guilt?"

Chapter Eight

On the first of December, Jake went back to the hospital for his scheduled checkup. The orthopedist, Dr. Rankin, removed Jake's old cast, and after another series of X rays, he replaced it with a fiberglass cast.

"Ankle looks good, Jake," the doctor said. "You're healing nicely."

"Will I be able to walk normally?" Jake asked.

Dr. Rankin sat down on the edge of his desk and folded his arms. "As Dr. Hostler explained to you, you're going to need physical therapy. How much strength your leg and ankle will regain, we can't say right now. A lot depends on you."

Jake stared down at the new cast, which fit his leg and foot like a high boot. "I'll do whatever it takes."

"Now I want you to use the crutches as much as possible. Try to keep the weight off your foot. And don't overdo it the first week. If you're good, I'll let you use a cane after a few weeks."

Jake's gaze shot up to the doctor. "Do you mean it?"

Dr. Rankin nodded. "We'll see how you're getting along."

"What about physical therapy? When can I start?"

"We'll talk in a few weeks." The doctor got up and escorted Jake out the door.

Heading toward the elevator, Jake found his father waiting for him. Why wasn't he surprised? Cliff had been showing up just about everywhere Jake was these days.

"How's it going, son?"

"At least I can walk with this cast. In a few weeks, I get to start using a cane."

"Well, I have one that isn't being used." Cliff held out both free hands. "The hip is completely healed. My doctor says to avoid falling down dark stairwells and I should be fine."

"Congratulations," Jake said enviously.

"How 'bout I take you to lunch to celebrate?"

Jake hesitated, and his father quickly rushed on to say, "We could grab a quick bite right here in the cafeteria."

"Okay," Jake agreed. "There's something I need to talk to you about anyway."

When they arrived in the cafeteria, Jake sat at a table in the corner, while Cliff went up to get their sandwiches and coffee. When he returned with the food, they concentrated on eating…in silence.

It was Cliff who started the conversation. "Okay, what is it you wanted to ask me?"

Jake didn't want to ask his father anything, but he had no choice. "I need a job."

Cliff didn't respond. He just waited for Jake to continue.

"I'm going into the veterans hospital in Minneapolis next week to have them check my leg. I have no doubt that the army will give me a medical discharge."

"Won't they at least wait until your cast is off?"

"Technically, yes. And I could check into a military fa-
cility for months of rehab. But the outcome would be the
same. I doubt I could pass a physical-agility test. My job
depends on my strength." Jake took a drink of his coffee.
"Before I came home on leave, I'd been assigned to go
overseas for two years. I can't discuss the job, but it's one
I can't do on a pair of crutches."

Cliff reached out and touched his son's arm. "But you
won't be on crutches forever."

Jake was surprised by his father's concern. "I've already
talked to my commanding officer. Because of my accident,
they had to replace me." Jake shrugged as if he didn't care,
but he'd worked hard to build his career. "I could possibly
stay in the service, but I'd be riding a desk for the rest of
my time. That's not for me. When my reenlistment comes
up in six months, I'm not signing." He met his father's
gaze. "Besides, I want out. I want to stay here with
Joanie."

"And Ali?"

Jake nodded. Even though Ali had been avoiding him
the past week, he wasn't giving up on her. He just had to
have something to offer her. And the only option he had
was going to work for his father.

God. How he hated to ask his old man for a job. "I was
wondering if there was anything for me…at the plant."

Cliff sat back with a sigh. "You have no idea how long
I have I waited to hear you say that." He smiled. "I've
wanted to bring you in as a partner since—"

"Whoa." Jake held up his hand. "I don't want anything
to do with a partnership. If I came to work for you, it would
be in the plant. I'll start at the bottom and work my way
up. I've been able to save a bit of money to tide me over
for a while. A career in army intelligence doesn't go far in
Webster."

"You're wrong, Jake. You specialized in electronic

equipment. That could be valuable—to Hawk Industries and to me.''

Jake wasn't ready to hear this. The last thing he wanted was a career at the plant.

''Before the accident, Jake, we didn't have much of a chance to talk. I'm converting part of the plant to design and build electronic components for car stereos. The electronics market is wide-open. I've made a few connections over the years.''

Jake made a snorting sound. ''You can't live without it, can you?''

''Without what?'' Cliff asked.

''The plant. There are other things in life besides work.''

''Jake, I know you think I'm a workaholic, but the plant has been losing business for the past few years. I've been looking to revitalize things.''

''Why, for more money? Don't you have enough?''

Anger flashed in Cliff's eyes. ''You really think money is what this is all about? How about the hundred jobs this project will create for this town? What about the other hundred people who have worked at Hawk Industries for years, depending on a paycheck every week? Should I just close the door and say, 'Sorry, but I've made enough money I'm shutting down'?''

Jake had to look away.

''I have a responsibility, Jake. That's the reason I had to leave early on Thanksgiving. I'd been trying to arrange a deal with this Japanese company for months. It finally went through. I'm closing down the plant during the week between Christmas and New Year's to remodel.'' His father looked hopeful. ''I'd love for you to help me with this project.''

Jake had to admit that he was interested, but deep in his heart he hated Hawk Industries. The plant represented the destruction of his family, the reason for his mother's death.

No way would he make the same mistakes his father had and let the plant consume his life.

"Look, Dad, I'm glad for you. And I'm sorry I jumped down your throat, but all I want is a regular job, nine to five, so I can be home with my daughter."

Later that afternoon, Jake parked his new car in front of the sheriff's office. The insurance company had paid off the claim on the accident, and Jake had just come from the Chevy dealership in town. He was now the proud owner of a new four-wheel-drive Tahoe. He wasn't taking any chances. He wanted something safe and sturdy to transport his precious cargo—his daughter.

Instead of going back to the house, he'd found himself heading downtown. He wanted to show Ali his new car—and also the fact that he could walk now. He climbed down from the vehicle, then reached back inside and pulled out his crutches. Avoiding the snow from the recent storm piled at the curb, he made it to the concrete-block building.

Pushing through the double doors, he glanced around the large room furnished with gray metal desks and file cabinets. There were three deputies on duty, and the secretary, Sara Merlin, was seated behind the main desk.

She glanced up, then grinned in recognition. "Well, as I live and breathe, if it isn't Jake Hawkins." The woman in her midsixties came around the desk to greet him. "How are you doing?"

"Just fine, Mrs. Merlin. I got a walking cast today and thought I should get a little exercise."

Ray Benson came out of his office. "Now I know what all the commotion is about." He shook Jake's hand. "Good to see you out and around, son."

"It's good to be out." Jake leaned on his crutches and looked around. "Is Ali here?"

Ray nodded and pointed to the glass cubicle at the end

of the hall. "She's due for a break." He turned back to the secretary. "Sara, will you take the incoming calls for a while?"

"Sure," she agreed, and returned to the desk.

Jake made his way down the corridor, a little apprehensive about the kind of welcome he'd get from Ali. He hadn't pushed the issue of marriage after their discussion on Thanksgiving. Ali had managed to remain scarce most evenings. This morning, he hadn't gotten up early enough to catch her before she left for work.

He was determined not to let her pull away from him again. Somehow he had to convince her that Darcie was in his past, and that he and Ali belonged together now and forever.

He paused at the doorway and saw Ali busy at the computer. She didn't notice him right away, which gave him time to enjoy watching her. She was wearing a white blouse and a dark straight skirt. When she stood up and reached for a file on the shelf, it caused the material of her skirt to pull taut over her shapely hips. A sudden surge of heat raced through him. Damn. He needed to burn off some excess energy.

"Hello, Ali," he said.

She swung around, the movement causing her long hair to fall across her face. She quickly pushed it away. "Jake. What are you doing here?"

The past week, there had been only silence between them, or polite conversation at mealtimes. He missed her. He missed the woman who'd come apart in his arms, who responded to his kisses with the same hunger.

"I drove here to see you." He smiled as he walked inside the small cubicle. They needed to talk. "And to show off my new cast. I can walk on both legs now."

"That's wonderful," she said as her green eyes grew large. "But should you be out?"

"I had a doctor's appointment this morning." Jake glanced over his shoulder through the glass partition. To his surprise, the entire office staff seemed to be interested in what was going on. "And I thought I'd stop by to see where you worked."

"Jake, I'm a little busy now. Maybe another time."

Her words were a crushing blow to his ego. Jake wanted her to drop everything and be happy to see him. "Okay. Why don't you tell me when there will be a good time? I've tried all week for us to spend time together. You've found every excuse to avoid me. We can't go on like this. We need to talk—about Darcie."

Her gaze danced around, never making contact with his eyes. "We'll talk when we get home."

"Will that leave you enough time to think up excuses not to spend time with me?"

She sighed. "Jake, that's not fair. I'm at work now. I can't just stop everything to talk to you."

That hurt, but damn it, she wasn't going to know it. "Fine. I just came by to show you my new car, but if you're too busy... I'll leave. See you at dinner."

She stopped his departure. "Thanks for coming by."

He nodded and walked out. Once outside the building, he heard his name being called. He turned to find Ray approaching him.

"You ran off pretty fast."

He glanced over Ray's shoulder to the office building. "It wasn't a good time."

Ray nodded, but didn't comment. "I was hoping you'd come by so we could arrange a time that's convenient for you to talk to the high-school students. If you've got a minute, I'll buy you a cup of coffee."

"Sure," Jake said.

Ray squinted up at the winter sun. "Can you handle a short walk to the diner?"

Jake nodded and they started off toward the town circle, and Charleen's Diner. They sat in a booth, and Ray held up two fingers. Quickly Charleen brought over two mugs of coffee.

Ray leaned his elbows on the table. "Do you think you can make it to the high school on Friday? They're having a career day. I'll be there, but maybe the great Hawk might have some effect on them."

"I'll do what I can."

"I'll pick you up about 1:00 p.m."

"Sounds good."

Ray leaned back. "I bet it's nice to be up and around."

Jake smiled. "I can't tell you how nice."

"Have you remembered anything more about the day of the accident?"

Jake shook his head. "Not a thing. Can't remember any part of that day."

"It's probably the trauma of the accident. It'll come back to you, son."

Jake realized that he might never know what happened that day. It made him crazy. What in the hell had caused him to go out and drive in a blizzard?

"Since we couldn't find any evidence of any other car involved," Ray continued, "we're stating the cause of the accident as weather-related. The insurance company agreed and closed the case."

"I know. They've already settled the claim. I bought a new car today."

Ray let out a low whistle. "I saw it parked out front. Pretty impressive."

Jake hadn't gotten the opportunity to show Ali. "I'll be driving around some pretty special people."

Ray smiled, then it slowly disappeared. "Look, Jake. I'm going to overstep my bounds here and ask you to give Ali a little time."

Jake tensed at the sheriff's suggestion, but he waited to hear the other man out.

"Since returning to Webster with the baby, she's been pretty private about her personal life. She never told anyone about Joanie's father. Then you return home, and it doesn't take long for people to figure things out, especially since Ali's been glued to your bedside and Cliff has been playing the proud grandfather. I know she was a little cold with you today, but she's feeling overwhelmed with all the attention people are paying to her. Ali's been stopped at the grocery store by people asking about you."

"I care about Ali, Ray. The second I found out about Joanie, I wanted to make things right. I asked Ali to marry me. I know a quick wedding won't stop the talk, but it will be a buffer for Ali so she'll no longer have to stand alone. I want to take care of her and Joanie. I should have been here all along."

The sheriff blew out a long breath. "It's not always easy, son, I know. But be a little patient with Ali. Give her time. I'm sure she'll come around."

"I want us to be a family. I want my daughter to know she can depend on her father." Something Jake had never known, remembering how alone he'd felt growing up. He didn't want that for his child. "Soon she'll be wondering why her parents aren't married. Damn this town. No wonder I tried to escape."

"This isn't the town's fault, Jake. You're the one who took off without a backward glance. Ali was the one who was left to face everyone alone."

Jake's heart lodged in his throat. Everything the sheriff said was true. He had been the one who took off. Well, no more. "I am going to stay now. I've even taken a job at the plant."

Ray held up his hands and grinned. "Slow down, son. I'm not the one you have to convince."

The man was right. Ali was the one he needed to win over.

That night, despite his cast, Jake spent nearly an hour pacing the floor, but it wasn't because he was waiting for Ali. He was comforting his daughter. With his new cast, he was able to maneuver the stairs to reached the nursery. Joanie had been crying since she woke from her nap. June and he had both tried rocking the child, but nothing seemed to calm the baby.

When Ali arrived home, she took charge of Joanie, but that didn't help much, either. She finally called the doctor and was told to bring Joanie into the clinic. Jake insisted on driving while Ali comforted the baby.

At the office, the doctor diagnosed an ear infection, and before they'd left the office, Joanie had been given antibiotics along with some Tylenol. And by the time they reached the house, the baby was asleep.

Ali carried her daughter upstairs with Jake following close behind. They both stayed in the nursery to watch Joanie until she settled down for the night.

"Ali, I need to talk to you," Jake said.

"I can't now. Joanie needs me."

"Joanie's asleep," he countered. "Besides, she has a good set of lungs and can make herself heard." He took Ali's hand and led her across the hall into her bedroom.

"Jake, I don't want to leave Joanie."

"You can go back in a few minutes, but right now we need to talk."

Ali pulled her hand from Jake's and folded her arms across her chest defensively. "We have nothing to talk about."

"We have several things, but right now I'd like to know why you treated me like a stranger when I came to see you today."

Ali didn't want to hash this out now. She was tired and hungry, and she knew her daughter probably wouldn't let anyone get any sleep tonight. "I was just surprised. And busy."

"You're not a very good liar," he accused. "Ray told me you were due for a break."

"Okay. Is it so bad not wanting to broadcast my private business?"

"You mean, you don't want anyone to know that I'm Joanie's father?" There was a pained expression on his face.

"I never got a chance to decide. Your dad has told the world about his granddaughter."

"Are you begrudging my father his bragging rights?"

Now she felt like a heel. "Of course not." She brushed her hair away from her face and let out a tired breath. "You don't understand, Jake. You always belonged to Darcie. You never gave me a second look while she was around. Then Darcie leaves town and suddenly you want me. Then you leave town and I have a baby, and never once did you call me over eighteen long months." She fought hard not to cry. "Nothing like being second best. Darcie will come back sometime. What will happen then?"

Jake dropped his crutches, and Ali gasped as he reached for her. Without warning, he pulled her against his body and his mouth covered hers in a devouring kiss. A warm tingle started from the base of her spine and worked its way up, making her forget everything except this man and what he was doing to her.

He broke off the kiss. "How many times and how many ways do I have to convince you that you are the only one I want? You're the mother of my child, not Darcie."

He took her mouth again. Then he pulled away once more, breathing raggedly. He gripped her arms tighter. "I can do this all night, Ali. You belong to me. I'm not about to let you go. How can I convince you?''

Ali, too, was having trouble breathing, praying he meant what he said. Her hands moved up his chest and circled his neck. ''I think what you were doing is a good start.'' She drew his head down to hers, and their mouths met in a searing kiss. ''Convince me, Jake. Take the doubts away.''

The next day at work, Ali was distracted. All she had managed to do all morning was think about Jake. She felt herself blush when she remembered last night, and how they couldn't keep their hands off each other. A few kisses led to still others, until Ali couldn't think clearly. It had been Jake who'd stopped things from going too far. Then he took her downstairs and made them both a sandwich for a late dinner. They continued to talk, promising each other to try to work things out. A few more kisses, then Jake sent her off to bed. It hadn't done any good. Ali lay awake for hours, fighting the urge to make the trip down to Jake's room.

Even this morning, she'd wanted to stay home with Joanie, who seemed much better, but Jake insisted that he could handle things. After giving her a long passionate kiss, he'd sent her out the door to work. She hadn't come down to earth since. She needed advice and called her best friend and asked her to lunch.

''Tell me what to do,'' Ali begged Margo, who was seated across the table at the restaurant.

Margo looked shocked. ''You want my advice?''

''Of course. Why do you think I asked you to lunch?''

Margo smiled. ''To be your maid of honor?''

Ali gasped and glanced around the busy café to see if anyone had heard. ''I never said anything about getting married.''

''Why don't you just put the man out of his misery?''

she suggested. "You've been in love with the guy forever."

"That doesn't mean marrying Jake is the right answer.
If I make the wrong choice here, it could hurt Joanie."

"If I thought this was a bad idea, I'd never suggest you
do it. Besides, I didn't say get married right away. But at
least give the man a chance."

A chance to break her heart, Ali thought. The fact remained that Jake hadn't seen Darcie yet, hadn't tested to
see if the old feelings still remained. "I'm not sure...."

"What can a few dates hurt?"

"I don't know. I've never been out on a date with Jake."

Margo laughed. "Yeah, you have done things a little
backward."

Ali crossed her arms over her chest. She'd had the man's
baby, but never gone out on a date with him. "Not anymore," Ali insisted. "Starting tonight, I'm going to be
courted by Jake Hawkins. When Darcie comes back, I need
to be sure and so does he."

On Saturday night, after their date, Jake walked Ali up
the steps to the house. They'd just spent hours together, in
a dark theater, watching a romantic movie.

"Don't tell me I lost my chance with you to Tom
Cruise?"

Ali released an exaggerated sigh. "Could be."

"Damn, I knew I should've dragged you out of there
when the guy started running around without a shirt," Jake
teased as he used his crutch to make it up the ramp.

"And miss all that good popcorn," she said, and moved
closer. "Besides, you don't look so bad without your shirt,
either. And the best part was, I got to hold your hand."

Jake made it to the front door and turned toward Ali.
"That was the best part for me, too."

"But we could have stayed home and rented a movie."

Jake shook his head. "No. We've never been out on a date. Not to say this evening was that great." He looked down at his injured foot. "Damn, what I really wanted to do was take you dancing—but as you can see, I'm not exactly light on my feet."

Ali's mouth opened in surprise. "The only place to dance around here is Rudy's Roadhouse. Not the best reputation."

Jake leaned a hip against the railing and looked out at the snow-covered lawn. It had snowed last night, just enough to leave a blanket of white everywhere. He drew in a deep breath of clean, cold air. "It's smoky, and a little sleazy, but at least I'd get to hold you in my arms."

Ali's gaze locked with his in challenge. "Who says you have to have music to hold me?"

Jake's heart did a couple of skips, then began to pound as he reached for her and pulled her between his legs. "That's right. I can hum."

He began to hum a deep baritone sound and placed a kiss on her forehead. Then he carefully cradled her against him, causing his body to react immediately. But he wouldn't go any further. It was enough to enjoy the feel of her in his arms.

Ali's arms moved to circle his waist over his heavy jacket. "Jake, I want to thank you for tonight. I had a nice time."

"That sounded awfully polite. Are you giving me the brush-off?"

She pulled back and looked at him. "No. I'm just saying I had fun."

"Good, because I want to make sure I still get my goodnight kiss."

Ali smiled and something tightened in his gut. Without giving her a chance to back away, he cupped her face and kissed her gently. "I've been thinking about doing that all night. Ever since Thanksgiving, I've been thinking about doing more than just kissing you, Ali.''

She tensed.

"But I'm not going to push you into anything that you're not ready for. I want us to spend time together. I want you to care about me…to trust me.'' His mouth closed over hers, and Ali released a soft moan. She leaned into him as his tongue delved into her mouth, tasting her sweetness, letting her know how much he wanted her. He broke off the kiss and moved to her ear and breathed, "You make me crazy, Ali.''

A shiver ran down his spine as he used his arms to pull her tight against him and just held her for a moment. Then finally he released her, but he didn't let her go far.

"I better get you inside.''

"I'm not cold. I like to be outside in this weather.'' She went to the railing. "Can you believe Christmas will be here soon?''

"Yeah, our daughter's first.'' Jake smiled, remembering how they'd shared Joanie's first Thanksgiving just days ago. "I'm really looking forward to being with her.'' His hand touched her cheek. "And you.''

Ali went all tingly inside. She wanted that, too. She wanted them to be a family. "I can't wait until Joanie sees all the decorations and Christmas lights. I wonder how she'll react to Santa Claus?''

Jake smiled. "Why don't we find out together?'' He drew Ali back into his arms.

"Jake—'' Her words were cut off by his mouth covering hers.

The kiss began slow and easy as Ali's arms circled his neck. Then he added some heat, and Ali purred with pleasure as his tongue pushed into her mouth, driving her passion higher. Finally Jake released her. Their eyes locked, and silently they made their way into the house. Once inside, Jake leaned against the closed door and drew Ali to him again. He took her mouth in another kiss, then another.

"Oh, Ali. I want you," he whispered. "I want you so much."

She felt the proof of his words and moved closer, hungry for him, too. Time stopped when Jake was kissing her. She couldn't think clearly when he touched her—Joanie was evidence of that. But Ali knew where things were headed, and somehow she managed to pull away.

"Jake, we have to stop."

Jake was breathing hard and refused to release her. "I hate it when you say my name and the word *stop* in the same sentence."

"You know it's the wise thing to do."

"I'm in pain, woman," he growled.

"Is it your leg?" she asked.

He grinned. "You're not even close."

Ali felt herself blush and buried her face against his chest. She inhaled his wonderful scent and almost changed her mind. "I think it's best if we officially end our first date."

"Not until you promise to go out with me again," he said, holding her tight against him.

Enjoying their closeness, Ali took her time in answering. "I'd love to. But I think we need a chaperone."

Jake pulled back. "A chaperone. Who?"

"I was thinking we'd take Joanie out to see the Christmas lights."

Jake wiggled his eyebrow. "Wow, a date with my two favorite women. What else could a man ask for?"

Chapter Nine

For as long as Ali could remember, the tree-lighting ceremony had been the official start of the Christmas season in Webster.

At the downtown circle, a decorated fifty-foot fir stood high above the crowd that gathered, waiting patiently for Mayor Anderson to plug in the lights.

The weather had cooperated, too. Although there was only a small amount of snow on the ground from the last storm, it was enough to set a perfect backdrop for the Christmas festivities. In fact, the mild temperature enabled Jake and Ali to camp out for a good spot behind the ropes. Joanie was bundled up warm and snug in her stroller, drinking her bottle, as the First Community Church choir sang Christmas carols.

Ali pulled her wool scarf around her neck as she watched the white cloud of her breath. "They'd better hurry, or Joanie will fall asleep."

Jake shifted his weight against his new cane. Today was his first attempt at walking without crutches. "I doubt she'll sleep much with all this commotion."

Ali glanced over her shoulder at him. "Is the standing too much for you? I should have brought a folding chair."

"I'm fine," he assured her. "What about you? Are you warm enough?" He came up behind her and pulled her close to him.

Ali leaned her head back against his shoulder and smiled. "I'm very warm, thank you."

"Well, I wouldn't want you to catch cold," he teased.

"I don't think there is much chance of that. Your body throws off plenty of heat." That wasn't a lie, either, Ali thought, remembering their past few days together. Jake had stolen every chance he could to touch her…to kiss her. He'd stirred up enough heat between them to ignite flames. But was that enough?

Jake bent down and whispered, "You do unbelievable things to me, Ali Pierce."

His breath tickled her ear, and Ali shivered. With Jake's arms around her, she looked down at her contented daughter. Could life get any better than this?

Ali smiled as she watched people milling around, exchanging greetings with friends and neighbors. One of the reasons she loved living in this town was the friendly people. Even when she couldn't make it on her own, and had to return to Gran June's with a baby—and without a husband—they'd welcomed her home, though she'd feared they would not. There were a few people who hadn't, she thought, as she glanced around the circle and found Mrs. Tillson and Mrs. Ellis whispering, then looking in her direction. Ali knew those two ladies were notorious for being the town gossips.

Ali's pulse began to pound as her protective instincts took over. She moved out of Jake's embrace. "If they don't start soon, we're going to have to leave. I don't want Joanie to catch a cold."

Jake looked concerned. "Ali, what's wrong?"

"I just don't want my child out too long in this weather."

Jake frowned at Ali's sudden mood change. He reached for her hand and made her look at him. "Tell me why you suddenly want to leave?"

She blinked at the tears pooling in her eyes. "It's silly."

"Nothing that makes you unhappy is silly, so tell me."

Ali pulled away. "People are talking about us."

Jake stiffened as his gaze combed the crowded town circle. "Who's talking?"

"It's just that Mrs. Tillson and Mrs. Ellis are over there. I know they are saying things about us."

Jake slowly began to relax. "Honey, those two old ladies have been finding something to gossip about since we were kids. No one listens to them." He drew her close, desperately needing to hold her. "Our friends—the people who care about us—have greeted us warmly. Do you really care," he nodded to the women "what those two say?"

Ali shook her head. "I guess not. I just don't want Joanie to ever be hurt."

Just then the two elderly ladies made their way across the circle, greeting people along the way, then finally they reached her.

"Hello, Darcie," Mrs. Ellis said, smiling. "Are you home for the holidays?"

"I'm Ali, Mrs. Ellis."

The woman's gloved hands covered her mouth momentarily. "Oh, my. I am sorry, dear. I just took for granted that since you were with Jake..." Then both women seemed to notice Joanie sitting in her stroller. "So this is your little girl."

Ali nodded, feeling her heart sink into her stomach.

Mrs. Ellis looked at Mrs. Tillson. "Isn't she just adorable, sister?"

"Just as sweet as can be," Mrs. Tillson said.

The choir stopped and Ali noticed the mayor starting for the podium.

"Where is your grandmother?" Mrs. Tillson asked, looking around.

"She has a cold and decided to stay home."

"Well, would you tell her we said hello and wish her a speedy recovery?"

Ali nodded; the rest of her was numb. Who did she think she was, trying to take Darcie's place in Jake's heart? Was she dreaming? All she could do was just watch the two ladies walk away.

Something tugged at Jake's heart when he saw Ali's pain. "I should have said something."

"No, Jake. The only one I care about is Joanie."

Angry with himself for not putting those two old biddies in their place, he said, "I swear I won't let anyone hurt you or my daughter. I care so much about both of you."

Ali's eyes lowered.

"Ali Pierce, I may have to take drastic steps here and prove it to you in front of the whole town. Then the gossips will have plenty to talk about."

She looked up, her eyes wide. "I believe you," she whispered.

Jake refused to let her go, and took the opportunity to press a quick kiss on her mouth. He pulled back in time to see her face redden.

She gasped. "Jake, you promised…"

"Sometimes, Ali-cat, you test a man's sanity. Count yourself lucky. If I did what I really wanted to, we'd get arrested."

Before Ali could react, the mayor reached the podium

and the crowd became silent. Jake lifted Joanie from the stroller and held her up so she could see the tree.

"My fellow townspeople," the mayor began. "It's my pleasure to officially open the holiday season." As the high-school band played a drumroll, he picked up the extension cord and plugged in the lights.

There was a renewed hush over the group, then a loud burst of cheers and applause as the tree came to life glittering with colorful lights. Even Joanie seemed mesmerized. She pointed and began chattering away.

Jake was in awe, too, and a sudden rush of emotion swept through him. Holding his daughter in his arms, with Ali at his side—what more could he want? This was going to be the best Christmas ever. The first Christmas with his family.

Jake arrived at Hawk Industries on Monday morning. He paused as he stepped inside the huge double doors of the plant, feeling the assault of his painful past. It nearly staggered him.

For twenty years, Jake had been haunted by the memories of being an eight-year-old pawn in his parents' game.

For years, Carol Hawkins had never seemed happy unless she was drinking. Jake's stomach turned over. He could still remember the rancid smell of bourbon on her breath. He recalled the night his mother came into his room and woke him with her sobs. As usual, his father wasn't home, so Jake tried to help her into bed, but she fought him, insisting she had to see her husband. She had to tell him that she was sorry, and that she loved him. She needed Jake to go with her to the plant. Jake didn't want to go anywhere, especially to listen to another one of his parents' fights. He'd hoped she would just lie down and pass out, which was often how things went. But his mother ordered him to get dressed. Jake did as he was told and was ready when the taxi pulled up in front of the house.

At the plant, the security guard stopped them, but even though she was drunk, Carol Hawkins managed to persuade the man, insisting she wanted to surprise Mr. Hawkins for his birthday. Little did Jake know that night would change his life forever.

That was the last time Jake had been inside the plant until today. Jake glanced up to the second floor of the large warehouse to where his father's office was and shuddered. But he wasn't here today to see Cliff Hawkins. Jake had an appointment with the plant supervisor, Dave Keller. Reluctantly Jake ascended the metal stairs, then walked along the catwalk just above the main machine floor, wondering all the way if this was a good idea.

When he reached the supervisor's office, it was empty so Jake waited outside. Taking a breath, he gripped the catwalk railing, and looked down at the activity on the floor below. Once again, the haunting memories clouded his vision.

All he saw was an eight-year-old kid coming off the elevator into the deserted hall. Everything was dark, and a little scary. He sensed something wrong, and tried to talk his mother into leaving. She ignored him and like a woman possessed, grabbed his hand and pulled him along until they reached the reception area.

That was when they heard the voices coming from his father's office. His mother pushed Jake behind the open door, into the shadows, and hushed him. The office door opened, and two people walked into the room, laughing. Through the crack in the doorjamb came a sliver of light. Jake recognized his father with his tie gone and his shirt unbuttoned. The blond woman was Cindy, his dad's secretary. They were holding hands and whispering, then his father pushed Cindy against the desk and kissed her. His hands moved over her, sliding over her leg and under her skirt.

His mother gasped, and Jake's heart was pounding so loud, he thought they'd be discovered in their hiding place. Finally his dad and Cindy went back into the office and closed the door.

With a trembling hand, Carol dragged her son out of there. Instead of waiting for the elevator, they ran for the stairs, then stole out the same doors that Jake had walked through today.

In the cold darkness of the cab, his mother remained silent. When they reached the house, Jake ran to his room. His anger refused to be contained, and he punched at his pillow in fury. Now he knew why his father never came home, why his mother was so lonely. Why she drank. Finally the tears came until he fell asleep, exhausted.

Later that night, Jake heard a crashing sound. He jumped out of bed and ran downstairs to the living room. He found his mother throwing things. Pieces of crystal that had been gifts from his father were being thrown against the fireplace. Finally she fell to the floor sobbing.

Trembling, Jake went to his mother. Bravely he reached out and touched her. When she didn't respond, he got scared. He called her name and said he loved her, that he would take care of her. She shrugged his hand away, and Jake remembered Carol Hawkins didn't like to be touched. Not even by her son.

She pulled her drunken body up. "Jake." She grabbed his arm. "You love me, don't you?"

"Yes, Mom. I love you." He did.

"Then you've got to swear to me…swear you'll never tell anyone about tonight."

Jake nodded as he fought his tears.

"I mean it. I never want your father to know we were there."

"I won't tell anybody, Mom. I promise." He couldn't help himself and flung himself at her, wrapping his arms around her. He felt her go weak and knew she was close to passing out. He guided her into the master bedroom, then helped her into bed. He stayed with her until she stopped mumbling her apologies and fell asleep, then he returned to the living room to clean up the mess. The broken glass was just the remains of a little boy's shattered family.

At the sound of his name, Jake shook away the memories and came back to the present. When he turned around, he found Dave Keller.

The gray-haired man in his fifties smiled. "Glad to see you made it." He offered his hand.

Jake reached out and shook the man's hand. "I need a job."

"Well, let's go see what we can do."

Grabbing his cane, Jake followed Dave inside his office. "I hope my coming by isn't an inconvenience to you," he said.

"No problem. Have a seat." Dave shut the door, muffling the loud machine noise from the floor below. "It's nice to see you're recovering so quickly."

Jake sat in a chair, then placed his cane against the wall. "The surgeries are over, but the cast will be around for a while, and I'll need physical therapy."

Dave sat down on the edge of the desk. "So you want to come to work here."

Jake nodded as his insides churned. It was the last thing he wanted, but his choices were limited. "Only if there is something available. I won't take a job away from anyone."

"Nor would I offer you another person's job. I have something else in mind. As you probably already know, we're going to branch out in a new direction after the first of the year. We were awarded a contract from a Japanese company to build electronic circuit boards. We've already brought in several experienced people to train the employees."

"Is Hawk Industries going out of the automotive-parts business?" Jake asked.

Dave shook his head. "No. We're expanding our assembly to accommodate the times. Assembling electronic circuitry requires a lot of growth, but it should be good for all of us."

"Dad's always been interested in making money," Jake murmured. How much did the man need, anyway?

Dave frowned. "We're not going to be making much money the first quarter. But this new contract means we'll be hiring more people, and more importantly, not laying off any of the current ones."

That didn't sound like the Cliff Hawkins he knew. Could it be that his father had changed? Layoffs were a common occurrence at the plant. Jake shook away the thought and looked back at Dave. "What is it you want me to do?"

Dave folded his arms over his chest. "I want you to be supervisor for the new assembly crew."

Jake felt as if he'd been hit in the gut. "You're kidding. I don't know anything about supervising an assembly crew."

Dave shrugged. "You were a captain in the army. You had men under your command, and you had to give orders." He stood and went behind his desk. "Jake, we can train you in what you need to know about the circuitry. In fact, we'll all be going through training. What we need is your leadership capabilities and your electronics expertise." Dave quoted a salary for the position.

Jake had trouble holding his temper. The money was more than generous. Obviously his father was trying to buy him. He reached for his cane, then politely said, "I'll think about it." Jake wanted to go up and tell his dad exactly what he could do with his job offer.

Dave stopped him. "Look, Jake. I can see you're angry, but don't blame your father."

"Don't try and tell me he didn't instruct you to get me to take this particular job."

The supervisor shook his head. "Cliff suggested you for the position, but it was my decision to approach you. It wasn't until I went through your application that I decided you'd be right for the job.

"Just think about it, Jake," Dave went on. "There isn't much opportunity out there in this area. If you're going to stay in Webster and build a new career for yourself, don't let your problems with your father make you turn down a great offer."

Jake tensed. It wasn't a secret that he and his father hadn't gotten along. There had been several fights over the years, but for the most part, they'd tried to keep their business private.

Apparently they hadn't been too successful.

Suddenly the walls seemed to be closing in on him. He had to get out of there. "I'll think about it, and let you know."

Jake walked out the door. He stared down at the assembly line below, thinking about the position he'd just been offered. All his life, he'd tried to avoid this place. Now he was supposed to walk in and be a supervisor at his father's plant? He had no doubts he could do the job Dave offered him, but could he work for his dad? He'd hoped he could get a position in which he wouldn't come in contact with Cliff, but that wasn't what was being offered. Still, it was the only game in town, and although he'd saved diligently over the six years he'd spent in the army, he needed the money he'd put aside for a home for Ali and Joanie. And though he hated to admit it, he was intrigued about the new electronics division. Who knew if this job could lead to something more?

Something made him look up to the windowed office across from him. Cliff Hawkins stood at the glass panel, overlooking the machine floor. Jake's chest tightened and his hands gripped the railing.

His father waved, but Jake ignored him. All he could think about was that night all those years ago, and an eight-year-old kid who'd started hating his father.

The following week, Jake talked Ali into going Christmas shopping at the mall in St. Cloud. June offered to baby-sit Joanie, and since Ali had the next day off from work to recover, she agreed.

They'd already made headway with their shopping list when they stopped to have dinner at a quiet restaurant at the mall.

"You should have warned me how exhausting shopping is," Jake said.

Ali glanced down at the many bags on the floor beside him. "If you had left something in the toy stores, you wouldn't be lugging around so many packages."

"This is our daughter's first Christmas. I want it to be special," he admitted.

Ali smiled at the excitement on Jake's face. A face she had come to love more each day. Was she headed for heartache, knowing he could never return her love? "Why do I have a feeling I'm going to hear this every year? Jake, Joanie isn't going to remember all these toys. One gift would have been plenty."

He frowned. "But most of them are educational. Joanie is so advanced for her age, she'll get bored playing with just one."

Ali shook her head. She knew Jake had been reading books on child care, but she never dreamed he'd become an expert. "Between you and your father, that child gets a present every week. She's going to start expecting it. I don't want her spoiled." Ali took a sip of coffee. "We can put some of the toys away and bring them out later, maybe at her birthday."

"Good idea," Jake agreed, and glanced at his watch. "Now come on. We've got some more shopping to do." He gathered up his packages and grabbed his cane.

"Jake, you already bought tons of stuff. What more could you need?"

"There's your gift. I haven't bought you anything yet."

"I don't need a gift, Jake." Just your love, she cried silently.

"But I want to get you one." He walked briskly, even with a cane, and Ali had trouble keeping up. Finally Jake stopped at a jewelry-store window.

Ali came up beside him. "Oh, look, Jake. Those cuff links would be a perfect gift for your dad." She pointed at the gold links in the window.

When Jake didn't answer, she looked over to discover his attention was on something totally different. Diamond engagement rings.

Ali's heart was drumming like crazy.

Jake grabbed her hand and pulled her inside the store. Immediately a sales clerk came to welcome them. "May I help you?"

Ali jumped in nervously and said, "Yes, we'd like to see the gold cuff links—"

"No," Jake interrupted. "I'd like to look at the diamond ring that's in the window," he said, and pointed to the display.

The clerk smiled and showed them to a seat, then went to the window and removed the display. "This is one of my own designs. It's a two-carat diamond in a Tiffany setting.'' The man removed the ring from the black velvet holder and handed it to Jake.

Jake examined it closely, then showed it to Ali.

''What do you think?''

The large sparkling stone took her breath away. ''It's beautiful, Jake. But I don't think...''

''Is it too big to be practical?''

Ali met his dark-eyed gaze, and searched for something that told her he loved her. That Jake wasn't only wanting to marry her because of Joanie. She didn't see it.

''Would you rather just get matching bands?''

Ali's attention darted to the salesman, then back to Jake. ''It's a perfect ring, Jake.'' It just wouldn't mean what it's supposed to, she almost cried. ''The problem is, it's too soon,'' she whispered, then got up and walked outside, fighting the urge to run.

When she was clear of the store, she leaned against the wall and closed her eyes. How could Jake do that to her? How could he force her into a corner and embarrass her?

''Ali?''

She opened her eyes to discover Jake's concerned look. It was a little late for that.

''I want to go home,'' she said.

He nodded and they headed for the parking lot. Once there he placed all their packages in the back of the car, then walked Ali around to her side.

Instead of opening Ali's door, Jake turned her around to face him. Before she could protest, he raised his hands to her hair and cupped her head, tilting her face toward him. Then he lowered his mouth until he was almost touching her. Their breaths mingled. ''I guess I need to convince you that we need to be together—that we were meant to be together. I want to marry you, Ali.''

The second his lips touched hers, skyrockets went off in Ali's head. She wanted desperately to believe she belonged to this man. For so many years, she had loved Jake Hawkins. He was buried deep in her heart.

In the darkness of the parking lot, Jake tasted and nibbled at her lips until she moaned, then begged him for more. Ali's grip tightened, wanting his body against her, wanting him to stop the endless ache inside her.

Jake pushed her backward, pressing her against the car as his mouth moved to her neck, creating unbelievable sensation in her.

"Jake..." Ali gasped as he reached the sensitive spot just below her ear.

He clutched her hips and moved her against him, unable to hide his desire.

"I want you, Ali. Not just for one night. I want you forever," he breathed, then his mouth closed over hers once again. Sparks shot off as he thrust his tongue into her mouth, imitating what he wanted to do to her.

Ali's hands wrapped around his neck, pulling him closer against her to deepen the kiss. Then the sound of voices caused them to break apart. Jake held a trembling Ali until the group of shoppers passed by.

"Let's get out of here." Jake opened the car door and helped her inside. He went around to the other side and climbed in. Before he started the car, he reached over and gave her a long hard kiss.

"We're not finished with this, Ali," he warned, then he turned the key and started out of the lot.

It was about ten o'clock when Jake pulled into the driveway of the Pierce house. He knew for a fact that Joanie was already in bed, as was Gran June. There wouldn't be anyone to interrupt them. He got out of the car, then limped around to the other side and opened Ali's door.

When she climbed out, he immediately drew her against him, and together they walked to the house. He only released her when he unlocked the door. He pushed open the weathered oak door, allowing Ali to step across the threshold ahead of him. Once they were inside the warm house, Jake reached for her and pulled her against him again.

There was nothing gentle as his mouth took hers in a searing kiss. A kiss, he prayed, that would affect her the same way it affected him. His tongue swept into her mouth, hungry for a taste of her sweetness. His hands moved over her body, reveling in her softness, at every luscious curve.

He broke off the kiss. "Ali, I want you."

"Oh, Jake," she whispered. "I want—"

Jake's mouth covered hers again. His body grew hotter and harder as his tongue dueled with hers. He stripped off her coat, letting it drop to the floor. He held her captive with a kiss as his hands roamed under her sweater. Finding her bra, he quickly released the front clasp, and her breasts sprang free into his palms.

Ali's hands gripped his shoulder.

Jake released her. Their eyes met in the soft light. He searched her face. "I want to make love to you. Now. Tell me you want the same."

He saw only passion in Ali's eyes. "Oh, Jake. Yes. I want you, too."

His cane forgotten, Jake reached for her hand and they walked down the hall. The bedroom was shadowed by the moonlight coming through the window. Jake stood Ali next to the bed, keeping her close, then he covered her mouth in another kiss.

When he drew back, he removed her sweater, then her bra. "You're so beautiful," he breathed.

"Thank you. I've added a little...weight since Joanie was born."

His gaze raised to meet hers. "You were perfect before."

"I was flat chested," she said, and laughed nervously.

His fingers reached out and toyed with her nipples. Immediately they hardened into tight buds. "You may have been small, but you were so responsive." He bent his head and took her into his mouth.

"Oh, Jake," she cried out, and her knees gave way.

He gripped her tighter, and eased her down on the bed. He stood back and stripped off his jacket and shirt, all the time watching the way Ali's auburn hair spread across the pillow.

He joined her. "Ali, I haven't been able to stop thinking about you since the last time we made love. I should have called you. I wanted to, but I thought you hated me." He couldn't resist her mouth and kissed her.

"I couldn't hate you, Jake." Tears formed in her eyes. "I couldn't even stop thinking about you...our night together. Every time I looked at Joanie..."

"Shh. I'm not going to leave, Ali. Not ever. I want to marry you so we can be a family."

"Oh, Jake."

The rest of their clothes were soon discarded, and Jake proceeded to caress every part of Ali's body until she was whimpering with need. Jake reached into the bedside drawer and pulled out a foil packet. He turned on the small dim light, quickly rolled on the condom, then turned back to her.

He placed openmouthed kisses on her sensitized skin, adoring her until she was begging him to make love to her. Her hips rose and rubbed rhythmically against him. His name was a whisper on her lips, and he felt her shiver when his hand moved between her legs.

"Please, Jake. Make love to me."

He wanted this night for Ali—wanted to be totally self-less, concentrating only on her needs. His finger slipped inside to discover her wetness. Then he found her sensitive spot and used his thumb to circle around it, urging her toward the edge. He kept telling himself to hold back, to let Ali find completion first. It was enough to watch her beautiful face, to see her arch her head back, receiving the pleasure he was giving her. Suddenly she exploded in his arms, trembling and crying out his name.

Unable to wait any longer, Jake moved over her. He spread her legs and entered her swiftly. The invasion caused her to spasm once again. He tried to keep himself in check, his muscles fighting from the strain as he began to move inside her. He closed his eyes. Heaven. Pure heaven.

Jake couldn't hold back, nor would Ali let him as she wrapped her legs around him. He began to plunge in deeper...deeper with each of her encouraging whispers. Then all too quickly the tremor began, and he became helpless as he began to fall into the oblivion of pleasure. Crying out her name, he collapsed on her.

Later he moved off her and pulled Ali against him. He couldn't speak. The emotions he was feeling were overwhelming. Ali had stirred something inside him. She had touched a place that he'd never let anyone get to before. He had no protection from this woman who had found a way into his heart.

Ali curled up next to Jake and smiled as she savored the effects of their lovemaking. Now she understood what *afterglow* meant. She moved her hand over Jake's chest.

"You were incredible," she breathed. "Even wounded." She realized his cast hadn't hindered him at all.

He laced his fingers through hers. "You were pretty fantastic yourself," he said as he turned toward her and placed a sweet kiss on her lips. "I wanted this time to be good for you."

Holding her emotions in check, Ali raised her head and met his dark-eyed gaze. "You were wonderful. Just as wonderful as it was the first time."

Jake's fingers brushed her hair away from her face. "I

was selfish that night. All I worried about were my needs. God, Ali, I didn't even take care that you were a virgin. I didn't care about anything.''

Ali also remembered some things about that night, too. Like the fact that she had been the one who'd gone after Jake, and when she found him, she'd been the one who'd done the seducing. After all the years Ali had longed for Jake, she'd found her chance that night at the cottage, and took it. Took what didn't belong to her. What might never belong to her.

She should have waited until he saw Darcie again, waited to see if Jake was truly over her. Ali swallowed back the pain that lodged in her chest, knowing she'd just made her second mistake. ''Jake, you were wonderful to me that night as you were tonight,'' she said, starting to panic. God, she had to get out of here. ''I've got to go.''

''Not yet.'' Jake pulled her against him, tempting her with his body.

''I have to.'' She fought back the tears.

Reluctantly Jake released her. ''I guess I don't need Gran June throwing me out of the house,'' he teased.

As modestly as possible, Ali gathered her clothes and hurried into the bathroom. Don't cry, she told herself as she jerked on each piece of her clothing.

When she returned, she found Jake asleep. Relieved not to have to face him again tonight, Ali picked up her shoes, then went upstairs. Stopping to check on Joanie, Ali found her daughter curled up and sound asleep. Even in the dim light, the child looked like Jake. Ali pulled the blanket up around her precious daughter.

''Oh, Joanie, what am I going to do?''

Ali loved Jake. That was fact. But how could she let him break down the barriers, and get into her heart again? She knew she was leaving herself open to hurt again, for the day when Darcie returned and demanded Jake back.

Chapter Ten

Two days later, Jake took a flight to North Carolina, rented a car and drove to Fort Bragg Army Base. At the hospital, he was put through numerous tests and examined to see if he was fit for military service. He was classified borderline. With less than a month left on his enlistment, it didn't matter. Jake was getting out.

After a lengthy visit with his commanding officer, Jake went to his small apartment off base and cleaned out his personal belongings. He hadn't accumulated much over the past couple of years. The three rented rooms had never felt like home, just a place to visit between assignments.

He made arrangements with a moving company to pack up and ship everything home, then he closed out his bank account and said his goodbyes to the friends from the base. He would miss North Carolina, but everything he wanted was back in Webster, and hopefully waiting for him.

His thoughts turned to Ali. He'd been so used to seeing

her every day that just forty-eight hours apart felt like an eternity. He ached to hold her, kiss her…make love to her. His blood stirred as the memory of her gasps of delight and passionate cries echoed through his head. In his thoughts, she begged him for release—begged him to take her over the edge.

The commuter plane touched down at the St. Cloud airport runway, jerking Jake back to the present. He glanced out the window as the plane taxied to the terminal. The sky was clear and blue, the open fields covered in snow.

When the plane stopped, Jake retrieved his carry-on bag and headed off. He hoped that Ali would meet him. But the chances were slim. He had thought that making love would bring them closer; instead, it had created a distance. The morning after, Ali had seemed to regret their love-making.

After two days and nights away to think, Jake realized he'd bulldozed his way into Ali's and Joanie's lives. Maybe it was time to let Ali have some space to think about their future together. Call it male pride, but he wanted Ali to come to him.

Using his cane, Jake made his way into the terminal, and looked around at the people milling about. Some meeting planes, others waiting to board. Kids were glued to the windows, watching in awe at the planes taking off and landing.

Jake continued to scour the area until he found what he'd been seeking. *Ali.* His heart pounded against his ribs as his hungry gaze combed over her. She wore a pale green sweater and matching slacks. Her auburn curls were clipped back from her face, making her emerald eyes seem large and incredibly beautiful.

Then Ali noticed him, and a slow sexy smile touched her lips, causing Jake's body to smolder. Oh, what she did to him. He swiftly glanced down to see his daughter seated in the stroller. His family. Dear God, he'd missed them.

Nearly pushing people out of the way, he crossed the room. "You came."

Ali blushed, almost as if she were embarrassed to admit it. "I had the day off. I thought Joanie would like to see the airplanes."

He didn't care what excuse Ali used to justify coming; she was here. He dropped his bag and took her in his arms. "Just tell me you missed me," he coaxed.

She chewed on her lower lip. "I missed you, Jake," she whispered.

That was all Jake needed to hear. His mouth closed over hers in a kiss that showed how he felt about her coming to meet him. When her arms came up around his neck, he deepened the kiss and pushed his tongue inside her mouth, hungry for her taste…her sweetness. Finally he broke away and grinned like a schoolboy. "I'm so glad you're here."

Ali smiled. "I'm glad I came, too. How was your trip?"

"Fine. You're now looking at a civilian. It will be official in about thirty days. I'll receive my honorable discharge then."

Her sparkling eyes suddenly turned serious. "I'm sorry, Jake. I know how much you loved the army."

"It's okay, Ali." He studied the woman before him, knowing it would bother him a lot more to lose her. "This is where I want to be."

"Webster can get pretty boring."

"Boring sounds wonderful, but I doubt Joanie will let that happen." Jake picked up his daughter and kissed her, too. "Did you miss Daddy?"

Joanie smiled and patted his face. Then she stuck her fingers into her mouth, acting shy. Jake laughed and hugged her again, then put his arm around Ali.

"Damn, I'm happy to see you both. Let's go home."

Jake strapped Joanie back into her stroller, then retrieved his cane. He picked up his bag, and together they headed for the car.

In the parking lot, Jake discovered Ali had driven his Chevy Tahoe.

"How do you like the way the car handles?" he asked as he tossed his bag in the back.

"It's wonderful to drive. You've spoiled me," Ali admitted. "I hate to go back to my old compact."

"Then don't. You can drive this."

She looked shocked. "Jake, I'm not taking your car."

"Then you can borrow it."

"No," she said, and lifted Joanie into the child's safety seat. "My car is fine."

Jake's temper flared as he climbed behind the wheel. After Ali finished securing Joanie, she got in the front seat, but he didn't start the car.

When Ali began to buckle her safety belt, he stopped her. "Can you at least tell me why you won't drive our daughter around in a vehicle that is better in the snow than your little compact?"

"Because it's your car, not mine. I'd feel funny."

"Ali, Joanie is my daughter, too. I want her to be safe."

"I know." Ali sighed, and refused to look at him. "It's just... I don't want people to think you're keeping me."

"Ali, we can solve these problems if you just marry me."

"A car isn't a reason to get married, Jake."

He fought to remain calm as she turned away.

Ali refused to talk to Jake on the drive home. She'd taken time off work to pick him up at the airport, but she hadn't expected him to start badgering her about marriage the second he got off the plane.

Of course, she'd encouraged him two nights ago, when

she had gone to bed with the man. They couldn't go back to taking things slow, nor did she want to.

Ali glanced across the car just as Jake turned to look at her. He tossed her a sexy grin that nearly melted her right there in her leather seat. Damn. He wasn't playing fair. But one thing she'd realized while Jake had been gone: she missed him. Missed him desperately.

"Ali, I called Dave while I was in North Carolina. I took the supervisor's job at the plant," Jake said. "I'll be starting work the first of the year. So if you're worried about my being able to support you and Joanie…"

"Jake, I'm not worried about the money. I just never thought you wanted to work for your father."

He shrugged. "Things change." He reached into the breast pocket of his corduroy jacket and pulled out his checkbook and handed it to her. "I also have enough money saved to take care of both of you for a while, or enough for a decent down payment on a house. I haven't spent much the past few years."

Ali held the leather checkbook in her hands. She didn't need to go through Jake's finances. She knew he could take care of her and Joanie. But at what cost to him? Would Jake be happy staying in Webster, working for his father, the man who'd driven him away in the first place?

"Jake, I'm sure that you have enough money for whatever you plan to do." Ali sighed in frustration. How could she keep resisting this man? "You realize that, counting back to the accident, you've only been home…"

"About seven weeks," he answered.

Ali frowned. "So you understand it's too soon for us to make a decision about the future, especially one that will affect our lives, as well as Joanie's."

"Ali, I've known you since you were fourteen. I was at your house nearly every day during your high-school years." He took his attention off the road. "Two people should be able to get to know each other in that amount of time."

"Darn it, Jake. You knew Darcie, not me. She's the one you spent time with." She's the one you loved. Ali looked out the window, not trusting herself to speak just then.

Jake turned down Mulberry Street where bare trees lined the parkway, their trunks practically covered with shoveled snow. The long Minnesota winter had arrived.

Jake had been in a warmer southern climate the past few years.

Ali loved the cold weather, but how could he really want to return to the blizzards and Arctic winds?

"I've spent time with you, too, Ali." Jake stressed each word. "I know you're shy. You hate your freckles. You think you're too skinny." He gave her the once-over, causing Ali to blush. "I think your body is perfect. You also like to read a good mystery on rainy days. You hate crowds, and anything that draws attention to yourself." He grinned.

Ali felt naked. She had no idea Jake had paid that much attention to her.

Jake glanced across the car. "I don't need any more time to know we belong together. You're an excellent mother. Joanie is proof of that."

"Jake, I'm not going to marry you because we have a child."

He pulled the car into the driveway, shut off the engine, then unfastened his seat belt. "I never said I wanted to marry you just because of Joanie. I want to marry you because of *you,* Ali. Because I care about you, and want us to be a family. We both know about rotten marriages— our parents showed us the worst. And I think you and I would be a lot better at it than they were." He reached over and pulled her across the seat until she was nearly in his lap. "Besides, there's a hell of an attraction between us, Ali-cat." His head lowered until they were only a breath apart. "Have I ever told you that you have the sexiest mouth? I've been fantasizing about kissing you all the way home." To prove his words, he took her mouth in a blatantly possessive way that made her forget any argument.

Ali lost all willpower as Jake tore away her defenses. But at this point, she didn't care. She wanted Jake as much as he wanted her. Somehow she had to keep a level head. With the last of her strength, she pushed him away. "Jake, this isn't getting us anywhere."

Ignoring her, Jake began nibbling on her neck, then her ear. "I can be more convincing, if you'd like. But I'd prefer seducing you somewhere besides the car. We could draw a crowd, or Joanie could wake up and learn the facts of life a little earlier than planned."

She couldn't help but smile as she glanced in the back seat and found that Joanie had fallen sound asleep. "Jake, will you stop this teasing and talk to me?"

Finally letting her go, he looked at her with passion-filled eyes. Ali knew one thing for sure—this man wanted her. But wanting her didn't match the love Ali felt for him, and she had to decide if desire was enough.

"Jake, Christmas is only ten days away. Why don't we just continue to spend time together?"

"Why do I get the feeling that a few kisses is all I'm going to share with you for a while?"

Ali met his eyes. "Because sex can't be the only thing that is between us."

He tossed her a mischievous grin. "Correction. Make that great sex."

Ali groaned. "Jake. Please. We shouldn't have let that happen. We have to think about our daughter and try to set an example for her. What happens when she comes to us and says she wants to have sex?"

He turned around in his seat and looked at the sleeping

child. "She'll never get the opportunity, because I'm not going to let my little girl date."

"Jake, that isn't realistic. Someday she's going to have questions. We already have enough questions we have to answer."

He raked his hand through his hair. "Okay. We'll spend time together as a family. But can I at least take you out on a few dates?"

Ali smiled. "I'd like that."

"Finally we've agreed on something." He pressed a quick kiss on her mouth before getting out of the car. Ali sat motionless, wondering if this was going to work. Could they really be a couple? Could she replace her sister in Jake's heart? Could she survive if Jake never grew to love her?

As promised, Jake spent the week before Christmas with Ali, and didn't pressure her about marriage. With Ali's job and the preparations for the holidays, Jake found it nearly impossible to schedule any official dates. Both he and Ali agreed that time with their daughter was the important thing. Joanie's bedtime was something Ali and Jake both looked forward to together. Now that Jake was more mobile, he'd taken over as Joanie's primary caretaker during the day, giving Ali and Gran June time for themselves.

On the sixteenth, Joanie turned ten months old, and the family celebrated the milestone by decorating the Christmas tree and baking a birthday cake. Cliff stopped by the house with a gift, but Jake soon discovered the real reason for his father's visit. Plant business. With cold politeness, Jake told his father that his evenings were reserved for his family. He would report to work after the first of the year as he'd promised. Until then, he was concentrating on Joanie and Ali.

Early Christmas Eve, Ali rushed out to finish her shopping. She'd bought everyone's gift, but she still she had to pick up Jake's. Ali wasn't ready for the holiday, her first with her daughter—and with Jake. She'd planned a big family Christmas, something Jake had never had before. Ali looked up into the gray sky, hoping the dark clouds would produce snow soon. A white Christmas would be perfect.

By the time she pulled into the driveway, her wish became reality. Big white flakes were floating down from the sky. Excited, she rushed into the house.

"It's snowing," she called out.

Jake came out of the kitchen carrying Joanie, both of them wearing evidence of Gran June's double-chocolate fudge on their faces.

"Hey, sweetie. It looks like it's going to be a perfect night for Santa," Jake told his daughter.

Joanie reached for her mother, and Ali took her. "It isn't going to be perfect if she eats any more chocolate," Ali said. "She'll be up with a stomachache. Jake, too much sugar isn't good for her."

"It looks worse than it is. She's only had a little taste." He grinned. "I ate most of the fudge." He patted his rock-hard stomach. "Which I've got to stop. I bet I've put on ten pounds since June's been feeding me."

Jake had an incredible body. And since he'd been released from the hospital, she knew he'd been working out. He definitely hadn't lost any muscle tone. "You needed the weight after the accident."

A confused look flashed over Jake's face. "You know, I haven't thought much about the accident lately."

"That's because Joanie's been keeping you too busy," Ali teased.

Jake touched his daughter's cheek, then leaned forward and placed a soft kiss on Ali's mouth. "I guess I do have other things on my mind."

"If it's me, I'm glad."

"It's definitely you." Jake moved closer and whispered, "In fact, later I'd like to tell you how much you've been on my mind."

"Jake, we've got too much to do tonight...."

"I mean *later*, Ali. When Joanie is tucked into bed, dreaming about Santa. Later, when all the presents are wrapped and under the tree. I want time for us. Private time to share our own celebration."

Ali's heart raced. "Tell me when, and I'll be there."

A little after midnight, all the presents had been wrapped and placed under the tree. Joanie was tucked in her crib and finally asleep. Ali came down the stairs and stopped just outside the living room. The twinkling lights on the big Christmas tree shone like stars in a night sky. Ali inhaled deeply and caught the scent of pine in the air. She looked at the hearth and found Jake sitting on the floor, basking in the warm glow of the fire.

Nervously she brushed her hair back and straightened the belt on her new emerald green jumpsuit. Taking a breath, she walked into the room.

Jake stood up and took her trembling hands into his. "Merry Christmas, Ali."

"Merry Christmas, Jake."

For a long time, neither spoke, as Ali's gaze locked with Jake's sable eyes.

He slipped his hands in the pockets of his jeans. "I was afraid you weren't coming."

"Joanie woke up. Probably too much excitement."

"Well, you're here now. That's all that matters," he said, then tilted her head toward him. He gathered her into his arms, and his mouth covered hers. The kiss was like the man—hot and steamy. Soon they were on the floor by the hearth, Ali nearly consumed by Jake's passion.

Jake pulled back. "I've wanted to kiss you like that all day."

Smiling, Ali reached up and combed her fingers through his hair. "I wish you had." She pulled his head back down and closed her lips over his. Her tongue slipped timidly into his mouth, and soon her teasing strokes had him groaning in frustration. When it ended, they were both breathing hard.

"Lord, Ali. I love what you do to me, but we need to slow down a minute. I want to give you one of your presents."

Before Ali could say anything, Jake sat up, pulling her with him. Then he reached behind the chair and brought out a small black velvet box. Ali's breath caught as she looked up at Jake.

"Ali, I'm crazy about you. And I know in my heart you care for me, too. I don't know all the fancy words to tell you how I feel. How I want to share my life with you—be there with you to help raise our child, to watch Joanie grow up. I promise, I will be a devoted husband to you, Ali. Will you marry me?"

Ali couldn't breathe. This had to be a dream. But if it was, she never wanted to wake up.

There was only one thing that kept Jake's proposal from being perfect. The words she'd longed to hear Jake say never came. The words of love. She knew he cared for her, but without love could they make a life together? Build a real marriage? Having spent the past few weeks with him, and loving this man the way she did, Ali decided she'd take whatever Jake was offering her. Living without him hurt too badly. She prayed her love would be enough to see them through.

"Yes, Jake. I'll marry you," she answered at last.

Jake blinked as his pulse raced even faster. Ali had said

yes. He began to smile. "You mean it? You'll really marry me?" He couldn't believe it.

Her green eyes pooled with tears, and she nodded.

"Oh, Ali." He pulled her into his arms and kissed her. Then he kissed her again and again until soon they both forgot anything else existed. Jake finally drew back. He reached for the velvet box and opened it. He showed the diamond ring to Ali.

"Oh, Jake…it's beautiful." Her gaze raised to meet his. "It's the ring we saw at the jewelry store."

He nodded. "I called the store the next day." He took the ring out of the box, and realized his hands were shaking, but he still managed to slide it on Ali's finger.

"It fits," she said, holding the sparkling diamond up to the light.

"I hope you don't mind, but I borrowed one of your rings from your jewelry box to get your size."

"You were pretty sure I'd say yes."

"No, Ali. But I've been praying for the past two weeks that I could prove to you that we can make this marriage work. I swear, Ali. We'll have a good life together."

"I know," she said, convinced herself.

Jake gathered Ali in his arms and lowered her against the carpet. He lay beside her, studied her beautiful face, then, unable to resist, he slowly began to place kisses from her forehead to her jaw, to her neck. Then his attention went to her jumpsuit. With each breath she took, her breasts pressed against the soft fabric, making her hardened nipples stand out. His arousal swelled behind the fly of his jeans. He looked up at her eyes to see her own desire flare.

"I want you, Ali. I want to make love to you."

"I want that, too."

Jake stood, then reached down for her hand and pulled her to her feet. Silently they walked to his room. Tonight

Ali had agreed to be his wife, and he wanted to show her just what she meant to him.

In the bedroom, he switched on the light beside the bed, then he pulled her into his arms and kissed her. Her mouth was hot and sweet and wonderfully familiar. He moved his arms around her back and drew her nearer, nestling her between his thighs. Ali moaned and pressed closer as her hands lifted to trace the shape of his face. Then she pulled his head down to meet hers, opening her mouth to urge him in. When he plunged his tongue inside, she moved against him, asking for more.

Jake broke off the kiss. He was losing his composure fast. He tugged down the zipper on her suit, only to discover that she was naked underneath.

"Goodness, woman, are you trying to kill me?" He stripped her, then took off his own clothes. He laid her down on the bed. "I thought I could wait…make this last all night, but…" He jerked open the drawer beside the bed and tore open a foil packet.

Ali laughed. "I want you, Jake. Hurry."

He came back to her, kissing her fervently as his hand moved to her breasts, first one, then the other. Finally he drew her nipple into his mouth. She cried out and arched off the bed. He didn't stop the sensual assault as he went to her other breast and adored it also.

"Please, Jake," Ali cried, urging him over her.

Her own hands were busy roaming over his chest, causing his muscles to jump at her erotic touch. Then her tongue sought out and found his nipple. He shuddered as she stroked him. He nearly lost it, but refused to tell her to stop the sweet torture. He'd never felt like this before. His whole body was flooded with emotions, a burning need to give everything to this woman. He wanted to shelter and protect her, to always keep her safe, but mostly he just wanted to love her.

His breath rasped in and out of his lungs until he couldn't take any more. He slid his hand down and pushed her legs apart, then rose over her. Ali opened willingly, and he thrust inside her. A throaty moan escaped her lips, and she wrapped her legs around his waist as he began to move.

Ali began to writhe, her body lifting to his as she whispered his name. A sweat broke out across Jake's shoulders as he pumped slowly, drawing out the pleasure for both of them, then thrust powerfully, deeply into her. Suddenly she tensed and came apart in his arms.

Jake's climax followed hers, and a rush of sensation took over his body, filling him with a pleasure he'd never experienced before. He groaned out her name in release, then he buried his head next to hers as the aftershocks surged through his body. Later, still gasping for air, he rolled to his side and pulled her over to lie on top of him.

"Ali," he breathed against her ear. "It's never been like this before."

Ali raised her head and brushed back her hair. "I'm glad. A woman likes to think she can keep her husband happy."

Jake hugged her again. "Oh, Ali. You more than make me happy."

It was six o'clock on Christmas morning, and Ali was slow to get up. She hadn't made it upstairs to her own bed until after 3:00 a.m.

A smile crossed her lips as she sat up and glanced at the sparkling engagement ring on her finger. A shiver of excitement raced through her. Jake Hawkins was going to marry Ali Pierce. It seemed impossible, but it was true. They were going to have a life together—her, Jake and Joanie. The family she'd always dreamed about, and with the man she'd always loved.

Ali felt almost giddy as she slipped her robe on and walked across the hall to the nursery, hearing her daughter's familiar morning chatter. She stopped in surprise to find Jake at the dressing table already changing Joanie's diaper. She leaned against the doorjamb and checked out the view of her man.

Jake was dressed in a dark T-shirt that outlined broad shoulders and muscular arms. Memories of the previous night flashed through Ali's head, how her fingers had traced over the slick skin of his chest, then her tongue....

Her breath quickened, and her gaze moved to enjoy the firm curve of his buttocks encased in a pair of jeans, the seam in the left leg split to accommodate his plastic cast. She smiled and a warm feeling swept through her body. Jake's bad leg hadn't hampered his movement whatsoever.

"Say Da...da..." Jake repeated to his daughter. "Da..."

Joanie continued to chatter, but nothing sounded remotely like the word *daddy*.

"Looks like you're up bright and early," Ali said as she walked inside.

He glanced over his shoulder and smiled. "Good morning, Ali-cat. Hope you slept well," he said, then finished the job of snapping his daughter's pajamas.

Ali went to the changing table and wrapped her arms around his waist. "You know how I slept, since I spent most of the night beside you," she whispered against his ear, and felt him shiver.

He picked up Joanie and turned around. "I don't recall that we did much sleeping last night." He tossed her that sexy grin she loved so much.

"I know." Ali pressed her lips against his. "I like not sleeping with you." She sighed. "You are an incredible man."

"And you are a beautiful and incredible woman."

Joanie started making impatient noises.

"Maybe we better take this one downstairs and feed her."

Jake kissed Ali's ear. "I know what I'd rather do."

This time Ali shivered. "Maybe later." She looked into his dark eyes and saw his desire. "Definitely later."

"I like how you think, lady."

Ali tugged at his arm. "C'mon. I want to see what Santa left. Right, Joanie?"

All three went downstairs and found Gran June in the kitchen making breakfast. She turned from the stove as Ali came across the room and kissed her. "Merry Christmas, Gran."

The older woman returned the kiss. "Merry Christmas, honey." She went to her grandchild and kissed her, then reached up and planted one on Jake's cheek. "Now sit down and we'll have some breakfast before we open the presents."

Jake put Joanie in the high chair, then pulled Ali next to his side. "We'll eat, but first there is something that we'd like to tell you."

Ali felt her heart race. What if Gran didn't accept the idea?

"Ali and I are getting married," Jake announced.

A slow smile crossed Gran June's mouth as Ali showed off her diamond ring. "Well, it's about time," she said, giving hugs all around. "When is the event going to take place?"

Ali gasped. "Oh, gosh. We hadn't talked about setting a date."

"Soon," Jake said. "Definitely soon."

Ali wanted to be Mrs. Jake Hawkins as soon as possible, too. "How about right after you get the cast off?"

Jake stared down at his booted foot. "You know, Ali, I'll more than likely be limping for a long time." His forehead creased in worry. "Maybe always. Will that bother you?"

Ali saw the questioning look in his eyes. "It doesn't

matter, Jake." Didn't he realize that she loved him so much that nothing as trivial as a limp could ever change that? She felt the tears well in her eyes, remembering the sight of him in a coma. "We almost lost you, Jake. A slight limp isn't going to stop this wedding."

Jake took her into his arms and kissed her. "I don't know how I got so lucky to find you."

Ali swallowed hard, wondering if he would ever come to love her someday. "I've been here all the time."

When everyone finished breakfast, they started into the living room just as the doorbell rang. Ali opened the door to find Cliff carrying an armload of gifts.

"Oh, my, a man bearing gifts. Something a woman can't resist."

"I hope you don't mind, but I wanted to stop by to see Joanie open her presents."

"Of course. Come in," Ali said as she guided Cliff into the room where Joanie had already begun tearing open packages.

When the little one spotted her grandfather, she crawled toward him. Cliff got down on the floor, and then handed her more presents to unwrap. He gave one to everyone else in the room.

Ali went to the tree and reached for the gift that she had bought for Jake. Nervously she gave it to him.

He ripped it open to find a beautiful antique frame with a recent photo of her and Joanie. "You had this done for me?"

Ali nodded. "You're really hard to buy for." She handed him another package.

"You didn't have to get me anything, Ali." He opened a new wallet complete with a different picture of them.

She blushed. "I kind of went with a theme here."

"I love it all." He leaned closer. "But the best present you've given me was agreeing to be my wife."

"Oh, Jake." She kissed him tenderly, then whispered, "I think you should tell your father that we're engaged."

Jake didn't look happy, but he relented. "Dad, Ali and I have something to tell you."

Cliff raised an eyebrow. "What's that, son?"

"We're getting married."

Ali raised her hand and showed off her new engagement ring.

Cliff smiled. "This is great." He got up, shook his son's hand and hugged Ali. "Welcome to the family."

Just then they heard the front door open. Everyone turned around.

"Who's there?" Gran June called out.

Ali gasped as she saw who rushed into the room.

"Surprise, everyone. It's me, Darcie. I'm home."

Chapter Eleven

Total silence swept the room. All except for the loud drumming of Ali's heart as she watched her twin sister make a grand entrance.

Darcie Pierce was dressed in a jade-colored business suit. Her skin was flawless underneath perfectly applied makeup. Her hair was cut in a sophisticated style that touched just below her chin.

"Well, isn't anyone going to say anything?" Darcie pouted.

Ali was jolted out of her daze and jumped up. She followed her grandmother and hurried to greet her sister.

Gran June hugged her other granddaughter. "Why didn't you tell us that you were coming home?"

"I didn't know, Gran," Darcie said. "I only found out just an hour before I caught the red-eye out of New York."

With a plastered-on smile, Ali stepped up. "Hello, Darcie."

"Hi, sis." Darcie returned the hug, but was distracted by Jake on the sofa. They eyed each other for what seemed like an eternity, then finally Darcie said, "Hello, Jake."

Jake stood. "Hi, Darcie," he answered in a cool tone.

"I'm sorry about your accident." Her gaze drifted to his leg. Darcie crossed the room and sat down on the sofa next to Jake. She reached out and touched his arm. "Ali said you were doing just fine, though."

He nodded. "My cast will be coming off in a few weeks."

Darcie's attention lingered on Jake, and Ali could see there was something still between them. Old memories flashed in Ali's head. She recalled seeing the same looks exchanged many times over the years. How could she forget Jake and Darcie had a history together?

Suddenly Joanie began making noises from her spot on the floor, causing Darcie to notice her. "Oh, my gosh. This must be little Joanie."

Ali's heart began to pound in panic. Before she could stop her, Darcie went to the child. For once, Joanie played shy and started to fuss, then crawled to her mother.

Ali hurriedly picked up her daughter, and explained, "Joanie's had a busy morning. I'll make her a bottle and get her cleaned up so she can visit with you." Ali had to struggle to keep the trembling out of her voice. "And we can visit, too. It's been a long time."

"Too long," Darcie agreed as her gaze went to Jake. Ali's heart sank. Suddenly Ali felt as if her whole world were suddenly falling apart. Darcie was back. Was she going to assert a claim on Jake?

An hour later, Ali had run out of excuses to stay upstairs and came down with Joanie. Her daughter had been bathed and dressed in her new red velvet dress, white tights and black patent leather shoes. A red bow adorned her short dark hair.

Ali had also taken extra care with picking out her own outfit, choosing her black wool slacks and hunter green sweater. She'd taken the time to French braid her hair and put on small pearl earrings.

She went into the kitchen and found Gran June and Cliff seated at the table, drinking coffee. She glanced around nervously, relieved to see they were alone. She walked to the playpen, set Joanie down in the middle of her toys, then turned and glanced out the window at the half inch of fresh snow on the ground. The sky was a clear blue, and the sun was already warming things up. A perfect Christmas day. Ali's heart sank, and she felt near tears. It wasn't perfect for her.

She looked at her grandmother. "Where's Darcie?" she asked, suspecting she didn't want to know the answer.

Gran June got up from the table and went to Ali. "Darcie and Jake had to face each other sooner or later. It's best they finish the business between them, so everyone can move on."

But were they going to move on together? Ali didn't want to spend the day wondering if Jake and Darcie could have something still between them.

"I know, Gran. But why did Darcie have to come back today?" Ali said angrily. "Things were so perfect."

"Then it shouldn't matter that Darcie's here."

Ali knew that should be true, but Darcie had been notorious for making trouble—and getting her way.

The scraping of the kitchen chair reminded Ali that Cliff was in the room.

"I think I'll be leaving. I needed to drop off some presents." He smiled. "But I'll be back for dinner." He hugged Gran June, then walked over to Ali. "Trust your love for my son. Things will work out, Ali."

She nodded, but didn't share his optimism. "Thanks, Cliff. And thanks for the presents."

"You're welcome." He said his goodbyes, then saw himself out.

Ali looked to her grandmother and started to speak when Joanie pulled herself up to a standing position by holding on to the side of the playpen. She cried for her mother.

Ali went and picked her up. "What will I say about Joanie?"

"Honey, if you and Jake are to have a future together, you have to stop running from your sister. Darcie's coming home is probably the best thing that could have happened. Your sister should have been told about Joanie a long time ago."

"Why?" Ali asked defensively. "Darcie's the one who ran off to New York. Never once did she come home in the last eighteen months. She didn't try to find out about Jake, or about his accident." Ali felt her voice tremble. "And now she decides to show up, thinking..." She looked at her grandmother. "She must be coming back to Jake. But why now?"

Gran June reached out and stroked Ali's cheek. "Oh, honey. You don't know that. Besides, if you and Jake truly love each other, your sister coming back isn't going to change anything, no matter what *she* had in mind."

A tear ran down Ali's face. "That's just the problem, Gran. Jake doesn't love me. He's marrying me because of Joanie." Ali turned abruptly and walked out. She couldn't bear to be the recipient of Gran's pity.

In the living room, Ali put Joanie down to play with her new toys, then sat on the sofa and stared at the huge decorated tree. The smell of pine filled the air, and the lights still sparkled as they had last night when Jake had held her in his arms and asked her to marry him. Later, when he'd made sweet love to her, he'd promised they'd have a wonderful life. Together.

Why did it suddenly feel as if it had all been a dream? And why did she feel so damn guilty, as though Boyfriend Stealer were imprinted across her forehead in scarlet letters? Ali stared down at her diamond ring. The dream had been shattered when Darcie had walked through the door.

She hugged herself protectively as she watched her daughter play contentedly with her colorful blocks, and gave in to her misery. "Oh, Jake. Darcie is going to hate us both." Another tear fell on her cheek, and she swiped it away. Her grandmother was right. She should have told Darcie—and Jake—about Joanie a long time ago.

Suddenly the front door opened, and Jake's and Darcie's voices echoed through the hall. Swallowing her panic, Ali stood as the two walked into the room. They were both smiling, and their faces were flushed from the cold.

Her sister pulled off her gloves, stuck them in her pockets, then slipped off her coat. Jake took it from her and hung it on the hook in the hall.

"Oh, Ali. Jake's been filling me in on what's been going on the past few months." Darcie's eyebrow raised. "He said you came to the hospital every day."

Ali shot Jake a look as he stood leaning on his cane. She knew immediately that he hadn't told Darcie about Joanie.

It didn't matter, though, since their daughter handled the matter herself. The ten-month-old crawled over to Jake and pulled herself up by grabbing his pant leg, then raised her tiny hand, crying to be picked up.

"Da...da...da," her soft voice cried.

Both Ali and Darcie jerked their attention toward Jake as he reached down and swung Joanie up into his arm.

Jake's eyes lit up with joy. "Did you hear that, Ali? She said, 'Dada.'"

Darcie smiled. "Isn't that cute. Joanie thinks you're her father."

Dead silence reigned.

Suddenly Darcie tensed, her gaze darting back and forth between Jake and her niece. She was seeing the resemblance, too.

"Darcie," Jake said softly. "Joanie calls me Dad because I'm her father."

Ali watched as her sister's face suddenly went pale. Her twin's throat worked nervously, but no words came out.

Finally Darcie managed to choke out, "But that…can't be. You and Ali…" She swung around to Ali, and her green eyes flared in anger. "You. You went to bed with my man?"

Jake moved to Ali's side. "No, Darcie. Ali did nothing wrong. You and I were no longer together. Remember, you walked out on our wedding."

Darcie turned back to Jake. "But I wrote you a letter and explained."

"If you did, I never got it." Jake shook his head. "But, Darcie, I deserved more than a letter. You owed me the courtesy of speaking to me in person."

"So because I didn't come and apologize," Darcie said, "you went to my sister and used her as my replacement?"

Ali felt as if a knife pierced her chest. It was all she could do not to cry.

Jake raised a hand. "I didn't use Ali as anyone's replacement. You left me, Darcie, then I discovered Ali. But nothing happened between us while you and I were together."

Darcie folded her arms over her chest. "Just exactly when did you two consummate your…friendship?"

"That doesn't matter," Jake insisted.

"Since Joanie is only ten months old, and we were to be married in May nearly a year and a half ago… My God, did you two go to bed together the night of the damn wedding?''

Ali blushed, but refused to look away.

"It's none of your business when it happened," Jake said. "Ali and I have a child and we're going to be married."

Darcie paced the room. "This is too crazy to believe. You and my sister. You can't be serious." She threw up her hands and stomped out of the room, then a few seconds later she raced up the stairs.

Ali couldn't hold the tears any longer, and they poured down her cheeks. "I knew this would happen. Oh, Jake. She hates me."

"She has no reason, Ali. You did nothing to her." He tried to pull her into his arms, but Ali resisted. She couldn't let her feelings for Jake confuse her now.

She brushed the tears from her eyes. "I have to go help Gran June with dinner. Go up and talk with Darcie."

"Why? We have nothing else to talk about. Besides, do you really think she's going to listen to me now? Let's give her some time to cool off. She made the right choice going to New York. She just needs to remember it."

Ali stared at Jake. Did he really believe that? How had he felt when Darcie walked through the door? She was beautiful and sophisticated. He had to have some regrets.

"Please, Jake, go up and see if she's okay." Ali took her daughter from him.

"I'll go, but I'm not going to like it." He frowned as he drew her against his side. "I had other ideas on how we were to spend our first Christmas together."

Ali had, too. She trembled, not wanting to leave the safety of his arms.

He pulled back. "We're going to make it through this, Ali. We've come too far to let anything pull us apart."

Ali nodded, but in her heart she didn't believe it. No

matter how much she loved Jake, he was never going to be hers. She'd seen the look in Darcie's eyes. Her sister still wanted him, and what Darcie wanted, Darcie took.

She'd let nothing—and no one—stand in her way.

Ali felt the age-old pain of being second best and wished she'd never let herself dream. But Ali had dreamed. She'd dreamed about a life with Jake for her and her daughter. Had Darcie's return put all that in jeopardy?

Two hours later, Ali went up to the nursery to check on her napping daughter. She found Jake in the room and told him she wanted to talk to him. They went out into the hall.

Looking up into Jake's face, Ali was suddenly nervous. "I'd like to wait to announce our engagement until the first of the year," she said.

"You don't want anyone to know?" Jake asked.

"No, it's not that," Ali insisted. "It's just with Darcie home, maybe it would be best if we wait…awhile."

Jake folded his arms across his chest. "You're not considering giving me back the ring?"

"Oh, no," Ali breathed. "I just…feel that it would be better for…Darcie if we don't officially announce the engagement until after the holidays."

Jake was so angry, he saw red. Instead of showing his temper, he decided this woman needed a little convincing about how he felt. Glancing around to make sure no one was in the hall, he grabbed Ali's hand, yanked her into her bedroom, shut the door, then pinned her against it. When she gasped, he bent his head, rubbed his lips against hers teasingly, then finally, hearing her moan, he took her mouth in a searing kiss.

With her soft sigh of surrender, he shifted his body against hers, letting her feel what she did to him. When she moved her hands restlessly over his chest, then began to tug at his shirt, he knew the fire in her was lit. He pulled her sweater up and unfastened her bra while she worked the buttons of his shirt. Soon they were pressed together, skin to slippery skin, sharing an intimacy that he only wanted to experience with her—no one else. It made his heart dance just to touch her. His hands traced her body in a rhythm that pushed them both higher and higher.

His mouth continued to devour hers, his tongue pushing inside to find her sweetness. He released her mouth, muttering her name. Then he rained kisses down her neck until he found her breasts. His lips closed over her nipple, sucking until she cried out.

They were quickly out of control. Heat exploded between them, igniting the inferno of their passion. He reached down, unfastened her slacks and his hand slipped inside to find her heat. When he stroked her, she nearly came apart in his arms. Not long after, Ali arched her back and moaned out his name. Jake felt her release and held her tight.

She clung to him until her breathing slowed, then she raised her head. "Why did you do that?"

He smiled, hiding his own painful need. "You needed to know how much I want you."

"But what about you?"

Her wide eyes were like emeralds, her hair slightly mussed, her lips swollen from his kisses. She looked as if she'd just been thoroughly loved.

"You give me all I need, Ali."

She groaned and buried her head against his chest. He held her close for as long as he dared. Wanting Ali seemed to be a constant condition. "C'mon, I think we better put in an appearance downstairs."

Just then Joanie cried out.

Jake sighed. "I'll go and take care of the baby. That will give me a little time to…cool down."

Ali smiled.

He bit back a grin. "So, you like what you do to me?"
Her eyes grew wide and innocent.

"God, woman. You make me crazy. I'm not happy that
we're keeping our relationship a secret, but I'll go along
with it." He pushed her back against the door. His head
lowered to hers. "I'll just have to keep trying to convince
you that we belong together."

Ali tried to push him away. "Jake, we have to get Joanie.
What if someone comes looking for us?" she argued.

Jake didn't budge. Without a word, his mouth closed
over hers. The kiss was gentle, but he didn't feel in a giving
mood. He wanted to brand her. Tell the world that Ali was
his woman. Maybe then she'd believe that he truly cared
for her. He broke off the kiss.

"Don't treat me like a stranger, Ali. We're engaged. You
and me. This has nothing to do with Darcie, so quit pushing
me at her. What happened between your sister and me was
over a long time ago."

A slow smile crossed Ali's face, and Jake felt as if the
sun just came out.

"I believe you, Jake. But give us all some time. Please?"

He finally nodded. "Just remember, Ali Pierce. I can be
a very convincing man."

Later that day, the Pierce house quickly filled with people. Friends and neighbors stopped by to share Christmas.
Margo and a couple of the other nurses from the hospital
showed up. Ray and LaVerne were there with far too many
gifts for Joanie. Everyone was polite to Darcie and welcomed her home, but they still hadn't forgiven her for leaving her family to deal with a church full of wedding guests.
It didn't stop Darcie from vying for attention by telling all
about her wonderful new career in New York.

It was Joanie who stole the spotlight from Aunt Darcie,
though. Even a beautiful woman had trouble competing

with a cute ten-month-old for attention. Jake spent the day playing the doting father, and Ali could see that Darcie didn't like that, either. In all fairness to her sister, Ali knew it couldn't be easy to return home and discover that your twin had had your ex-boyfriend's baby. It all sounded so sordid, almost like a soap opera.

Ali spent the day helping her grandmother in the kitchen. About five o'clock, a huge buffet of ham and numerous salads had been set up in the dining room. Pies and cakes covered the sideboard, then everything quickly began to disappear through the course of the evening.

About nine o'clock that night, the house had quieted considerably. Joanie was in bed asleep, after putting up a pretty good fight.

The last Jake had seen of Ali, she was in the kitchen cleaning up. He didn't want to know where Darcie had gone. He'd spent the day avoiding her, especially when she tried to lead people to believe they were going to pick up where their relationship had ended nearly two years ago. Jake wanted no part of Darcie—or her scheming.

He wandered into the living room, where he found Ray. "Too much excitement for you, Sheriff?" Jake teased.

"I ate too much." The older man patted his slightly rounded stomach. "Seems to be a problem of mine around the holidays." He sighed. "Now Laverne and my doctor will be on my case." He tossed Jake a sideways glance. "I have high blood pressure."

"Can't that be controlled with medication?"

"It's better to control it with diet."

"Yeah." Jake sighed, staring at the tree, remembering how he'd held Ali in his arms last night. "Too bad we can't control more things."

"Son, you're too young to sound so troubled."

Jake came out of his trance. "Sorry. I was just thinking how much things have changed. A year ago, I was career military.'' He looked down at his cast. ''I never thought that I'd be back in Webster and thinking about getting married. I'm even going to work for my father.''

''You're not happy about that?''

Jake shrugged. He didn't have much choice. He couldn't ask Ali to follow him around the country until he found out what he wanted to do with his life. ''I have a child to support, and soon a wife. I'm sure the job will be interesting, but it's no secret that Cliff and I don't exactly get along.''

''Maybe this is your chance to get closer.''

''Yeah, it would take a miracle.''

''Who's to say you'd have to make a career of the plant. Something else could come down the road.'' The older man smiled. ''I never thought about being a sheriff after I got out of the service, but here I am nearly thirty years later.''

''You plannin' to retire?''

Ray raised his hand. ''Elections aren't for another year, but LaVerne's been making noises that we're not getting any younger.'' He sighed. ''But it's hard to give up something that you love doing.''

Jake thought back to his visit with his commanding officer just a little over a week ago. The army had been good to him during the past six years, and he'd loved it, but that career was over. He had to think of a future for him and his family, even if it meant spending his life at the plant. He'd do anything for Ali and Joanie.

''So, Jake, you ever think you might be interested in law enforcement?''

Ray's voice brought Jake back to attention. ''I don't know. Right now I'm more interested in getting my leg back in shape.''

''Wouldn't hurt to maybe mull the idea around. I watched you with those high-school kids when you gave the talk for career day. You were good with them. You had their attention.''

The only thing Jake remembered was being asked a lot of questions about his football days. ''They seemed more interested in my skill as a quarterback than anything else.''

''The point is, they communicated with you. You have their respect. Believe me, as an officer of the law, that's most of the battle. With your military background and your knowledge of Webster, you might be a good candidate.''

Jake was taken aback. Sheriff? What a crazy idea.

Besides, he'd already committed to the job at the plant, and despite the fact that he'd be working for his father, Jake had been looking forward to helping get the new division off the ground. He'd be able to work regular hours, and do the therapy needed to strengthen his leg.

Most important, he'd be able to spend time with his family.

The Pierce household was finally quiet after everyone had gone to bed for the night. Ali was especially grateful that the busy day had come to an end. Exhausted, she slipped on her flannel nightgown, then pulled the blanket back on her bed. She started to climb in, when there was a soft knock on her bedroom door.

The clock on the beside table showed that it was well after eleven. Was it Jake coming upstairs to say goodnight? Excitement raced through her as she hurried to answer the door. Her smile died quickly when she discovered Darcie waiting in the hall.

Her sister didn't wait to be invited in. She just pushed past Ali, the satin of her long black nightgown trailing behind her. Quickly, Darcie glanced around the dim bedroom.

''So you *are* alone,'' she said with a look of satisfaction. ''Why does that not surprise me? When Jake and I were together, he'd never leave me—''

"Look, Darcie," Ali interrupted her. "I'm tired and I have to be at work early in the morning." She wasn't in the mood for any of her sister's games. "What do you want?"

"I want what belongs to me."

Ali folded her arms over her chest.

Darcie looked hurt. "How could you do this to me, Ali? I'm a laughingstock in Webster now. The whole town knows that the man I was supposed to marry slept with my sister—my twin sister." She paced a while, then swung around. "And *you*. Don't you have any pride? Couldn't you get a man of your own?"

Ali winced as if her sister had slapped her. The bitterness in Darcie's voice only added to the pain. As much as Ali tried not to let her sister's words affect her, they'd hit the bull's-eye.

"I wasn't out to get your man, or any man," Ali began to explain. "What happened between Jake and me wasn't planned. It just happened. But the result is that I have a child, and Jake is her father." Ali was shaking now. "We're going to be married."

Darcie jammed her hand on her hip. "Then you really are a fool. You know that Jake will always love me."

Another direct hit.

"We were together a long time." Darcie's gaze swept over Ali. "You were just my skinny sister who he used to tease."

Ali stiffened her spine. She had to fight back. "Obviously Jake's done a little more than tease me."

Darcie's nostrils flared. "I guess you don't care that you're second in his heart."

"I'm not second."

Darcie went still. "We'll see about that. Anyway, if you think that a man like Jake Hawkins can survive in this town, you are crazy. The one thing we did have in common was wanderlust. That was the reason Jake went into the military. He never wanted to settle in one place. Jake and I talked about traveling together, but I just couldn't see myself wasting away on a military base. So at the last minute I chose New York. But the point, Ali, is that he wanted to leave this hick town as much as I did, and never look back.''

Darcie shook her head. ''And you'll never leave Webster, Ali. You're just like Gran June. You love this old house and this stupid town. You like knowing your neighbors and going to town council meetings.'' Darcie sighed. ''You'd better think long and hard, Ali. All too soon, Jake will get bored with this bucolic life here…and with you.''

Ali's heart pounded so loudly, she heard the sound in her ears. ''Okay, Darcie. You've had your say—now get out.''

With a smirk of satisfaction, Darcie tossed her hair off her shoulders and marched out of the room. Once the door closed, Ali sank to the mattress, her trembling hands clutched together, her feigned confidence gone.

Was Darcie right? Would Jake grow tired of her…or of Joanie? Her thoughts went back to her own parents, how devastated she'd been when they divorced, then later deserted her and Darcie.

''No.'' Ali stood and pushed aside Darcie's cruel words. Jake wouldn't do that to her. And he loved Joanie. He was starting a job at the plant on Monday. They were going to have a future together, a house, more children…. Ali stopped. Oh, God! Was Jake taking the job at the plant for *her?* She couldn't let him do that. She had to find out for sure. Didn't he know that he didn't have to take the job at the plant?

She reached for her robe and slipped it on, then she walked out the door. Somehow she had to try to convince Jake that the plant wasn't his only option.

Mostly she needed to let him know how much she wanted them to have a future together.

"What the hell are you doing here, Darcie?" Jake sat up in bed. The unmistakable scent of her perfume gave her away the second she came into his room. He never thought she'd be brazen enough to try to seduce him.

"C'mon, Jake. You know you've missed me." She sat down on the edge of the bed, then reached out and began to stroke his bare chest.

"Cut it out, Darcie. You're going to regret this in the morning."

"Oh, Jake. Are we going to do some regrettable things? That sounds exciting." She leaned forward, her breasts threatening to spill out the top of her satin nightgown.

He grabbed her hand and moved it away. "We're doing nothing. Ali and I are going to be married."

She laughed. "Right. Like my mousy sister can keep you satisfied." She moved closer.

"As a matter of fact, she does. Ali is an incredible woman and a wonderful mother." There was a subtle beauty about Ali that drew him, unlike the brassy made-up woman who was before him now. He'd outgrown his taste for women like Darcie. Even her perfume turned him off.

"That's it, isn't it. You wanted children and I didn't."

Jake closed his eyes and prayed for patience. "That's part of it. But there's more, Darcie."

Her hands were back on his chest. This time she pressed her body against his. "What we had was good, too. Jake, remember the time we—"

Jake pushed her away. "Stop it, Darcie. It's over between us." He got out of bed. Wearing only his boxer shorts, he limped to the closet, grabbed a robe and jerked it on. "I guess you have a short memory, but nineteen months ago, you walked out on me. You said that you didn't want to live with me, or my choice of career. Well, I finally woke up. It took me almost dying to realize that I wanted something else, too. You were right to go after what you want. I plan to, as well. I want your sister."

She looked sad as she walked across the room to him. "I guess you're right, Jake. We did want different things back then." She looked up at him and flashed those big green eyes.

Though both sisters' eyes were similar, he thought Ali's eyes were prettier.

"I always wanted you." Darcie put her hand on his chest again. "We were so good together, so hot." Somehow she rose up and pressed her lips against his. He remained motionless. Maybe curiosity was the reason he allowed her to kiss him. To see if there was still something between them. When nothing happened, he pulled back, relieved.

He started to tell Darcie to leave when something caught his attention. He looked up and saw Ali standing in the doorway. The hurt look on her face made his own heart ache.

He called as he started toward her, but she quietly disappeared.

"Ali, wait!" he shouted again. He hurried after her, but his cumbersome cast slowed him down. She was upstairs when he finally made it to her room. He knocked on her bedroom door, but she didn't answer. "Ali, please let me in. We have to talk."

Darcie strode up the stairs and past him to her room. "Knock on *my* door, Jake. I won't leave you out in the cold." She smiled, then went inside.

"Ali, please." He continued to knock. "Let me in."

Ali finally jerked open her door. "Will you stop making so much noise. You'll wake up Joanie."

"I'll shout the house down if you don't listen to me, Ali."

She raised her chin stubbornly. "There's nothing to say."

"There's plenty to say. What you saw isn't what you think. Darcie came into my room. I tried everything to get rid of her."

"Did the kiss work?" Ali asked.

"All right, so I let her kiss me. She wasn't going to leave me alone until I proved to her that she didn't mean anything to me. You're the one I care about."

He watched her blink at the tears in her eyes.

"Jake, it's really late. I have to go to work early. Can we talk about this some other time?"

"Damn it, Ali. You aren't even listening to me. Darcie came after me because she knows that I want you, not her."

Ali felt herself go soft inside. Jake wanted her... not Darcie. Her sister had been the one who'd gone to Jake's room.

"Oh, Jake," she cried as she went into his arms.

"I'm sorry, Ali. I really tried to get rid of her, but—"

Ali put her finger over his mouth. "I don't want to talk about Darcie," she said as she rose up on her toes and kissed him.

She wanted to block out all their problems. For just a short while, they could pretend that everything was perfect between them, that Jake wasn't going to work for his father to please her.

And if things didn't work out, would that drive Jake into Darcie's waiting arms?

"I'm sorry, Ali," Jake whispered as he pulled back. "I'd do anything to keep from hurting you. You know it's you I care about."

She nodded. "I know, Jake. You've made so many changes for me and Joanie."

"That's because I want us to be a family."

"But, Jake, you don't have to go to work for your father.

I know how hard that is for you. I know you hate the plant.''

He pulled her into his arms. ''Look, I told myself I was going to give it a shot. I can't make you any promises, Ali, but if it doesn't work out, we'll face our options together.''

Ali was afraid. ''Maybe we should postpone the wedding until you see if the job pans out. And you've only been out of the hospital a short time...''

Jake backed her against the wall, pressing his body against hers. ''I don't need any more time. I know exactly what I want, Ali. You.''

Chapter Twelve

Three days after Christmas, Dave called Jake and asked if he would mind coming in to the plant to familiarize himself with the operation. Jake agreed, since hanging around the house meant he had to put up with Darcie. He couldn't wait for her to return to New York, to the job she'd claimed was so hectic. He'd even help put her on a plane. Maybe then, things would get back to normal and he and Ali could get on with their lives.

What lives?

Even though he and Ali had talked things out the other night, she'd still been distant, acting as if she didn't deserve to be happy. How was he going to help her get rid of the guilt, when she believed she'd taken away her sister's man?

Jake cast all thought aside, as he pulled up to the plant, then got out of the car into the cold morning.

Dave met him at the door. "Glad you could make it." He shook Jake's hand and ushered him inside.

Together they walked through the remodeled section of the plant, the newest high-tech equipment already in place. A work crew was busy adding the finishing touches and testing machinery. As Jake walked past the assembly line, his heart thumped loudly in his chest. Although the army had been his only job since college, he found he was getting excited about this opportunity.

They stopped at a glass-enclosed room. "This will be your office."

Jake stepped inside the small room that was taken up mostly by a scratched gray metal desk and a dented file cabinet. He certainly couldn't accuse his father of showing his son special treatment.

"I know it isn't much," Dave said, almost looking embarrassed.

"It's fine," Jake assured him. "I'll be on the floor the majority of the time anyway. Right?"

Dave nodded. "You're in charge of the crew. In fact, we've already hired a first shift." He went to the cabinet and pulled out a thick file, which he handed to Jake. It was the employee listing. "We trained them the week before we shut down at Christmas."

"When do I get trained?" Jake didn't want to appear incompetent before the crew. His years in the military had taught him the importance of having the respect of those under his command.

"I'd like to have you come back tomorrow if you can make it. Ruth Carson, one of our best employees, will be showing you the ropes. Watch out, she used to be in the military also. Marines. Still thinks she's a drill sergeant."

Jake groaned and Dave laughed.

"Now, Jake, we're not expecting miracles, so take it easy. I'll be around to help until you get used to the job."

"What time do you want me here tomorrow?"

"Eight will be fine."

Jake nodded. "Dave, next week my cast comes off. I'll need to go in for physical therapy. I'll try and set it up for after hours if possible, but I'm not sure of the therapist's schedule."

"Take whatever time you need," Dave said, then grinned. "I bet it's going to feel good to be walking on two feet again."

Jake hoped the same thing. But he still didn't know if he would be able to walk without a cane. Would he have a limp? He worried about Ali's reaction. Would it make a difference to her? She'd said it wouldn't, but one thing he knew for sure: he'd do his damnedest to come to her a whole man. He waved his cane. "You don't know how badly I want to burn this thing."

"I'll bet." Dave shook his hand. "I'll see you in the morning."

"Eight o'clock," Jake verified. Both men started out when Jake felt as if someone was watching him. He glanced up toward his father's office. A woman stood at the large picture window. Darcie? He blinked and looked again. It *was* Darcie.

"What the hell…?" He charged across the machine floor, heading for the elevator. When he reached the third floor, he marched through the reception area, and without stopping to have the secretary announce him, he swung open Cliff's office door.

He found Darcie seated across the desk from Cliff Hawkins. She smiled, but his old man looked nervous.

"Now, why doesn't this surprise me?" Jake closed the door to keep their business private.

"Hello, Jake," Darcie said. "I just stopped by to see Cliff. After all, he was almost my father-in-law."

Ignoring Darcie, Jake directed his gaze at his father. "So you're the one who brought her home."

Cliff rose. "No. I admit that I called Darcie months ago

when you had your accident, but she let me know that she couldn't come back.''

Jake raised an eyebrow.

''Believe me, son, I was desperate,'' Cliff admitted. ''I needed to find some way to bring you out of the coma. But then Ali stepped in to help. And I'm crazy about the idea that you two are going to be married.''

Jake should have known that Darcie wouldn't have time for anyone but herself. It was Ali who'd been there, who had *always* been there for him.

Darcie rose from her chair. ''It's a good thing I'm back now. Someone has to stop you from making a big mistake.''

''Mistake?'' Jake asked.

''Marrying Ali.''

Jake's fist clenched at his side. ''Why is marrying Ali a mistake?''

His father stood. ''You two need to work this out alone.'' Cliff quietly exited the room.

Jake glowered at his father's back, cursing the man for leaving him alone with Darcie.

He turned back to her. ''Why is marrying Ali a mistake?''

''You shouldn't have to pay forever for one night of passion.''

Jake stood still for the longest time, finally realizing how selfish this woman was. It was hard to believe that he'd ever thought what he'd felt for her was love. But he'd been young, and there was no doubt that Darcie was beautiful and had sex appeal. What high-school boy wouldn't go for her, and overlook the quiet, reserved twin sister?

His thoughts turned to Ali. She was beautiful, too, but in a different way. Her beauty was quiet, subtle, both inside and out. Darcie's was only skin-deep.

"I have a daughter, whom I love. She and Ali are my future now. Why can't you understand that?"

Darcie moved around the room in her trim-fitting slacks and tailored blue blouse. "Because I know you, Jake Hawkins. I didn't say you couldn't be Joanie's father. You'll be a good one. But you don't have to marry Ali."

Jake folded his arms over his chest. "What if I want to?"

Darcie looked unconvinced. "And live in this town the rest of your life? I hear you're going to work for your father, Jake. If I'd known that, I wouldn't have run away from our wedding. You know how much I wanted the big house on the hill and dreamed of you going into partnership with your dad. It could still happen."

It still hurt to know that Darcie had never really wanted him, only what the Hawkins money could buy. "You and I wanted different things then, Darcie."

She came up to him and smiled. "As I remember, we wanted a lot of the same things, too."

He stepped back. "You have a tendency to remember just what you want to."

His rebuttal didn't seem to faze her. "I remember a lot of things, Jake. How you couldn't keep your hands off me. How we'd make love all night..."

His jaw tensed. He could only remember the passionate loving he'd shared with Ali. "That was a long time ago, Darcie."

"But I still care about you."

"If that was so, why didn't you come back when Dad called you about the accident?"

Her smile fell. "I tried...really. I just couldn't get away. I called the hospital, and they kept me informed on how you were doing."

Jake watched her, finally realizing that Darcie Pierce

didn't care about anyone but herself, and probably never had. "Ali found time. She was by my bed for hours."

"Well, hurrah for Saint Ali," Darcie said. "But I guess 'saint' is the wrong word for her. She probably planned this for years. Then, when she found her chance—when you were vulnerable—she seduced my man into bed."

Jake shook his head. "Maybe what Ali and I did wasn't right, Darcie. But I won't let you blame her. *I* seduced *her*."

"Only because I broke your heart."

"Damn it, Darcie. Not everything is about you." He drew a deep breath and ignored her hurt look. "Get this straight. I wasn't thinking about you when she and I made love. Ali was the one I wanted that night, and every night thereafter. I haven't thought about us being together in a long time."

Darcie tensed, her eyes piercing him. "I don't believe you. You loved me, Jake."

He shook his head. "Maybe once, but I'm not even sure of that. I *do* know that I love Ali and our daughter." He suddenly stopped at the realization of his words. He smiled. He did love Ali. He had for a long time, but his fear of rejection had kept his feelings locked inside.

Darcie opened her mouth, but closed it before uttering a word. She turned, grabbed her coat and headed for the door, then stopped. "We were together too long, Jake, for you to forget me so easily. You'll come to your senses and want me back. If you're lucky, I'll take you." She walked out.

Jake collapsed against the desk, feeling as if he'd just gone ten rounds in a boxing match. How was he going to convince Darcie it was over? More importantly he needed to convince Ali she was the woman he truly loved.

On New Year's Eve, Ali stood at her jewelry box and picked up Jake's engagement ring. It was hard to believe that he'd only given it to her a week ago. She clutched the diamond, then brought her hands to her mouth. The stone felt cool and hard against her lips, the brilliant fire shadowed by darkness.

Everything had changed since Darcie came home. Now she was taking some more time off, saying she'd been working too hard. Would her sister always be a barrier between her and Jake? A ghost from the past who would prevent them from being happy? Seeing the two of them together that night had made Ali realize that Jake would probably always have feelings for her twin. Would Jake be like Darcie said and quickly grow tired of living a quiet life in Webster with her? Would wanderlust hit and take him away from her, and Joanie?

A soft knock on the door drew Ali's attention. She put the ring away and went to answer it. Jake stood in the hall.

He smiled. "Hi, Ali."

"Jake."

"I know it's late notice, but I was wondering if you'd spend New Year's Eve with me."

"Jake, I can't go out. Who will watch Joanie?"

"We can celebrate here." He stepped closer. "I just want us to start the new year out right…together."

A shiver raced through her. "I'd like that, too."

"Good." He bent his head and placed a gentle kiss on her lips.

Ali knew she should protest, but it had been so long since Jake had touched her…kissed her.

All too soon, he pulled away and smiled. "I promise you more of that at midnight."

She blushed.

He slowly traced her cheek. "I've missed you, Ali. I've missed you like crazy."

Between his words and his touch, every nerve ending in her body throbbed with longing. "I've missed you, too. We won't be alone tonight," Ali told him. "Gran June is having a few of the neighbors over."

A sexy smile appeared across his handsome face, and desire radiated from his well-deep eyes. "That's okay. I just want to be with you. Besides, the company will have to go home sometime. Then, Ali-cat, you're mine. All mine."

Ali's heart tripped. Oh, my. He made it all sound so perfect. So very perfect.

It was after eleven-thirty, and the party was in full swing. Most of the guests were neighbors who could walk home if they had too much to drink.

Jake played bartender, talking and joking around with everyone while he purposely made the drinks weaker. And Ali noticed that he didn't have anything stronger than ginger ale himself.

Jake fit in so well with her life—soon to be *their* life—in Webster. Her thoughts, as usual, went to Darcie. Her sister was absent from the festivities. She'd gone to a friend's party, which made it easier on everyone.

After mingling with the guests, Ali went into the kitchen to find Jake talking with Cliff. Surprised, but happy, she listened as they discussed the new division. Jake seemed genuinely excited about starting his job, which lifted her spirits. But even more importantly, he was making an effort to get along with his father. Maybe there was a future for them, after all.

Finally twelve o'clock arrived, and everyone cheered, welcoming in the New Year.

"Happy New Year, Jake," Ali said.

"Happy New Year, Ali."

Jake pulled Ali into his arms and kissed her. A kiss that hopefully told her how he felt about her. Besides his daughter, she was the only woman he wanted in his life. He broke off the kiss but didn't release her, just pulled her tighter against him. Before he could say more, they were both being pulled apart by well wishers.

In the midst of all the commotion, Jake managed to slip upstairs into Joanie's room with Ali. They stood at the crib, looking down at their sleeping daughter.

Jake raised his glass of sparkling cider toward Ali's. "To the first of many New Year celebrations together." She stared at him as the soft sound of music from downstairs echoed around them. "I want us to be a family," he said. He took the glasses and placed them on the dresser, then he took Ali's hands in his. "I want to marry you."

"I want to marry you, too."

"Then wear my ring. And let's set a date for the wedding."

"But what about—?"

He placed his finger against her lips to stop her protest. "Let's just worry about us. You, me and Joanie are all that matters."

Ali gazed at him for a long time, unable to answer. There were so many questions running through her head. But at that moment, she could only think with her heart, and deep down, she knew that Jake cared about her. She gave him a trembling smile, walked out of the room and rushed to her bedroom. She pulled the ring from her jewelry box, then hurried back to Jake.

Smiling, she handed him the ring with its precious stone. "Ask me again, Jake."

He, too, grinned. "Ali Pierce, will you marry me?"

"Oh, yes, Jake," she cried. "I'll marry you."

She raised her shaking hand, and he slipped the ring back on her finger. Then he pulled her into his arms and kissed her, a kiss that promised a life filled with love.

A week later, Jake arrived at his appointment with Dr. Rankin, hopeful but realistic about his ankle. Whatever the results after they removed his cast, he knew it was going to take a lot of therapy. That was the reason he hadn't told Ali about his doctor's visit. If things weren't good, he wanted to deal with it by himself first.

Once the cast had been removed, the doctor ordered an X ray, then he examined the ankle closely, rotating it. "How does it feel?" the doctor asked.

"A little stiff," Jake said. "But it feels good."

The doctor slid his low stool back. "I want you to stand and put some weight on it."

Jake used the railing along the wall to pull himself up. Tentatively he set his foot down on the floor, then shifted his weight. No shooting pain, nor did his leg give way. "Feels good."

"Try stepping off the foot."

Jake knew this was the problem area. He rested his foot on the floor then slowly took a step. There was a lot of resistance and stiffness. More than Jake had hoped for. "No pain, but it's like my ankle and leg don't want to cooperate."

The doctor grinned. "Believe me, Jake, you're doing well—much better than I ever expected. Just the fact that your ankle can hold your weight makes me want to shout for joy."

Jake smiled, too. His heart raced as he waited for some pain. "So do I pass? My leg feels fine."

The doctor raised his hand. "This is only the first step. You're still going to need a lot of physical therapy, but yes, you passed."

"I'll do as much as needed. I just want to walk before my daughter does."

Jake couldn't wait to see Ali. After changing into a pair of jeans that hadn't been split for a cast, he drove to the sheriff's office. Still using his cane, he walked through the doors and down the hall to her cubicle.

Smiling, Ali stood when she saw him coming toward her. "Jake. What are you doing here?"

She was dressed in dark slacks and a white sweater. He caught the sparkle of the diamond on her finger, and his chest swelled with love. "I've come to see my future wife. And tell her the good news." He raised his leg. "Look, no cast."

"Oh, Jake. That's wonderful." Her eyes danced with excitement. "Why didn't you tell me you had a doctor's appointment today? I would have gone with you."

He wrapped his arms around her and held her close. He loved the feel of her body against him. Soon he began to ache with desire, remembering how long it had been since they'd made love. He placed a kiss on her forehead and stood back. "I didn't say anything about the appointment because I wanted to do this on my own."

She looked up. "You mean, you were worried that you might not be able to walk?"

He shrugged. "I wanted to make sure that I could carry my own weight...before I saw you."

"Oh, Jake. I told you it wouldn't have made any difference."

He swallowed back the lump in his throat. Was Ali's love truly that unconditional? "I started my therapy today. Ali, it's going to be a long time before I'm back to normal. In fact, I may never be. More than likely, I'm going to have a limp."

She frowned. "And you think that matters to me?"

"Well, there will be some things I can't do. Running a race is one of them."

"Will this stiff ankle of yours stop you from being a good father to Joanie?"

"Of course not," he said. "But…there may be times that this leg will slow me down. How do you feel about that?"

Ali watched as Jake stumbled over his words. She never thought she could love a man more. This had to be so humbling for him. She had to make him realize what he meant to her.

"Jake Hawkins, when I was hanging around in the hospital, you were in a lot worse condition. You didn't scare me off then, and you're certainly not scaring me off now."

He seemed relieved. "What did I do to deserve you?"

Jake started to reach for her when the phone rang. Ali sat down in her chair and picked up the headset, then pushed the button on the phone.

"Webster County Sheriff's Office," she said, then started writing down some information. Once she hung up, the phone immediately rang again.

"Sheriff's office," she said.

"Please, you got to help my husband," the caller pleaded. "He's having chest pains. I think it's a heart attack."

"Ma'am, give me your name and address."

"It's Alice Hartley at 370 Mulberry Street. It's my husband, Ben," the woman said. "Please help him."

Ali fought to keep her composure as she recognized her elderly neighbor's voice. "Mrs. Hartley, this is Ali Pierce," she said, trying to stay composed herself. "I want you to stay calm." While Ali was talking, she pressed the button for the hospital on the other phone, and dispatched an ambulance to the address.

"Mrs. Hartley, there's help on the way. Stay on the phone with me and we'll wait together." Ali talked to her neighbor for what seemed like hours, but in reality it was only minutes until the paramedics arrived. Finally Ali hung up, drew a deep breath, then released it.

"I always hate those calls. This is a neighbor, too." She

quickly dialed her home number and told her grandmother about Ben Hartley. Afterward she hung up and collapsed back into her chair, offering a quiet prayer for the Hartleys.

"That's rough," Jake said. "But help is there now."

Ali ran a trembling hand through her hair, suddenly remembering the day she'd been working as dispatcher when the call came in about Jake. The deputy had her dispatch an ambulance to the accident scene, where a truck had hit a tree head-on. A man near death had been trapped inside. That man was Jake Hawkins.

Tears flooded her eyes. Jake saw them.

"What's wrong?"

She tried to swallow. "I'm sorry. I couldn't help but think about the day of your accident."

He squatted down by the chair. "Honey, I'm sorry." He hugged her.

"When the deputy called in the accident…he said your name over the radio, then described your injuries…." She looked at him. "Oh, Jake. I thought you were going to…die."

Ali bit her lip to stop the trembling. "If you hadn't made it, I don't think I could have lived with myself. What if you never knew about Joanie? It would have been my fault."

He leaned forward and kissed her. "Ssshh. It's over now, Ali. And if anyone's to blame, it's me. After our night together, I should have stayed around to make sure you were okay." He brushed away her tears and smiled. "But I'm going to be around for a long time. Right here in this town with you and Joanie."

Jake walked across the street through the town circle. The snow had been cleared from the storm a week ago, leaving piles along the curbs. Having lived the past few years in North Carolina, Jake found he'd missed the snow a little. He also found he'd missed the friendliness of the people in Webster. They knew his name and called to him in greeting.

"Hey, aren't you going to say hello?"

Jake's head came up, and he saw Sheriff Benson. "Sorry, Ray. I guess I had my mind on other things."

Ray placed his hands on his lean hips. "I can understand why. I saw Ali's ring this morning. So you guys are officially going to get hitched?"

Jake nodded. "I hope it's soon. I want my family together."

"She's a great gal." He glanced down at Jake's leg. "And you got your cast off."

"Sure did. Just yesterday. Already had my first therapy session."

"How did it go?"

"My therapist seems to think I'll get a lot more out of this leg if I keep working it."

Ray cocked an eyebrow. "Enough that you might think about running for sheriff next November?"

Jake felt the adrenaline run through his body at Ray's suggestion. But he knew that Dave was depending on him. "I've already made a commitment to the job I have now."

"The elections aren't for a while yet. Gives you plenty of time to think about it."

"I've only had my cast off a few days. I'm not sure how much strength I'll have in my leg. I've got a lot of physical therapy before I can tackle a job like sheriff."

Ray nodded. "Don't sell yourself short, Jake. You can do this job, and do it well, or I wouldn't be endorsing you as a future candidate."

Jake didn't want to get too excited. He had a long way to go before he could think about running for sheriff. He had to discuss this with Ali, and what if he couldn't pass the physical? Of course, he had nearly a year to consider it. By then he could fulfill the commitment he'd made to Dave.

"Thank you for your confidence, Ray. I'll let you know."

They shook hands, and Jake continued toward the diner. He greeted more people, some of them he knew from high school. When he heard his name again, it was Darcie, and his pleasant feeling evaporated.

"Buy a girl a cup of coffee?"

"Look, Darcie, I'm not in the mood for any more games."

The wind whipped her hair against her cheek, and she pushed it away. "No games, Jake."

He nodded and didn't say anything as they walked to the diner. Inside, they went to a booth in the corner. Jake remembered it had been their place to sit when they were in high school.

The waitress came by the table with two mugs and a pot of coffee. She filled them up and walked away.

Darcie doctored hers with sugar, then took a sip. After putting down her mug, she said, "I wanted to talk to you...alone."

"We have nothing to say but goodbye. I think it would be best if you head back to New York. I think that's where you'll be the happiest."

She tried to smile. "Jake, do you ever wish you could turn back the clock and do some things differently?"

Jake's mind turned to his mother and her drinking problem, then to his father. "Sure. Who doesn't?"

"If I hadn't gotten scared about the wedding—"

"No, Darcie." He stopped her. "Don't go there. I'm not sure if we had gone through with the wedding, we would have stayed together."

"But we loved each other."

"Did we?" he questioned her. "Then why couldn't I give up the army, or why couldn't you come with me?"

Darcie shrugged, her eyes suspiciously bright.

"I know all this hurts, Darcie. But you know I'm right. We don't belong together, and we didn't then."

"Sometimes I just hate being alone." She looked so sad that his own heart ached.

"There's a guy out there who wants the same things you do, Darcie. He'll love you enough to do whatever it takes to make you happy, and you'll do the same for him."

Darcie's green eyes lifted to lock with his. Ali and Darcie might be twins, but they were so different. There was a softness about Ali that Darcie never had. An openness for caring and loving that Darcie would never understand.

"But I can't forget you...."

He shook his head. "Look, Darcie, I don't want to hurt you, but what we had was over a long time ago."

Darcie still looked doubtful. "You're just marrying Ali because of Joanie."

Jake shook his head again. "No, I'm not. I can't imagine life without her. I love her."

For a long time, they sat and didn't say a word, then Darcie checked her watch. "I guess I'd better go. Walk me to my car?"

They got up and Jake dropped some bills on the table, then followed Darcie out the door. They crossed the circle to where she'd parked her rental car at the curb.

He took her by the arm and turned her toward him. "Darcie, you know I only wish the best for you."

She nodded. "I just wanted to tell you I'm sorry for walking out on our wedding. It was a cowardly thing to do."

"Sometimes running seems like the only way. I know I've done it." He smiled. "I wish you good luck...in New York, Darcie. I hope you'll come home for the wedding."

Darcie glanced away. "We'll see." She forced a smile.

Jake surprised them both when he drew her into his arms and hugged her. "Try, Darcie. Ali needs you."

He released her and looked up to see Ali standing across the street, just outside the sheriff's office. By the look on her face, Jake knew that she'd seen them. He waved to her, but Ali turned away, walked to her car and drove off. Darcie saw it, too.

Ali couldn't see her way home through her tears. Why was it that every time Jake and Darcie got together, they ended up in each other's arms? Why couldn't Darcie just go away and let her and Joanie have a life, a future?

She pulled into her driveway, got out and walked into the house. Immediately she rushed upstairs into Joanie's room to find her still napping. The child looked peaceful all curled up with her hands tucked under her chin, but when Ali's hand touched her daughter's cheek, a warning signal went off. Joanie was running a fever.

"It won't do you any good running away, Ali."

Ali wiped the tears from her face as she looked up to see Darcie.

"What are you doing here?"

"The last time I looked, this was still my home."

"If you're going to warn me to stay away from Jake, I think I got the message already." Ali twisted the diamond ring on her finger. "But you're not scaring me off. You aren't what Jake needs anymore."

"Oh, and you think you are?"

Joanie began to fuss, and Ali picked her up, cradling her daughter against her breasts. "Yes, Joanie and I are exactly what Jake needs."

"Maybe you've confused love with obligation. After Jake's childhood, do you honestly think he'd walk away from his daughter? You just happen to come along with her."

Ali stared at her sister, almost afraid to take her next breath. "That's not true."

"Jake and I talked today. Right now he's crazy about marriage and babies, but you've got to ask yourself something, sis. Can a man who's had an exciting career in army intelligence be happy living in a small town like Webster? Do you think *you* can keep him happy?"

With her best confident look, she answered, "I know Jake is happy."

Darcie laughed and she walked toward the door, then paused. "There is one more thing, Ali. You're kidding yourself if you think he'll stay forever."

Ali felt the blood drain from her face as her sister left the room and disappeared around the corner. Oh, God. What was she going to do? Jake couldn't live here and she couldn't live anywhere else.

Ali sank into the rocking chair, feeling her hands shake. She couldn't leave this town…her grandmother. All those years her mother hauled her and Darcie around the country, they had never had a home. Not like here in Webster. This town was her security.

And she'd promised Joanie.

Chapter Thirteen

Jake made it back to the house, but not before Darcie. He didn't want to leave the explanation of what had happened between them up to his future sister-in-law. She could be telling Ali anything. Lies.

When he walked in the back door, he found June seated at the table peeling potatoes for dinner, but no Ali or Joanie.

"Hi," he said, but his attention was on the door to the dining room, hoping that Ali would walk in any minute and welcome him home.

June drew his attention back to her. "Did Darcie catch you?"

"Yes, we had coffee earlier."

June nodded. "Good. She was worried she wouldn't get a chance to talk with you. I know sometimes Darcie acts self-assured, but she isn't always. Finding out about you and Ali has been hard on her."

It had been hard on all of them, especially since Darcie

wasn't accepting any of it. "I know," Jake said, but he didn't want to talk about Darcie. He was more concerned about Ali. "Is Ali upstairs?"

"Yeah. Joanie hasn't been feeling good. She's been runnin' a fever again."

He stopped. His chest tightened as he remembered that his daughter had been feeling warm this morning. "Her fever hasn't gone down?"

"No. Joanie was better for a while, then when she woke up from her nap, she was hot again."

Jake needed to reassure himself the baby was all right. He took off upstairs, then hurried into the nursery and found Ali sitting in the rocker. She was holding Joanie in her arms, wrapped in a blanket. Ali looked up as he walked toward them.

He immediately saw the worry on her face, and he was alarmed. "Hi."

"Hi," she said.

Jake knew whatever he and Ali had to work out, this was not the time. Joanie needed them.

He squatted down to get a closer look at his daughter. "Hey there, sweetie. Grandma said you're not feeling well."

Joanie's rosy mouth puckered up, and she gave a weak whimper, then nestled quietly against her mother's breast. This was not like her. Whenever Joanie didn't feel good, she let the whole world know about it.

He touched her forehead and felt the heat. "What's her temperature?"

"It's 104 and rising." Ali's eyes looked bleak. "Jake, I'm scared."

"Have you given her some Tylenol?"

Ali nodded. "I called the doctor, and he said to give her a cool bath to help bring down her temperature. But neither the Tylenol or the bath worked. It's still high."

Jake kissed Ali's forehead. "I'll go and call the doctor again." Fear knotted inside him as he hurried downstairs and into the kitchen. With shaking hands, he got Ali's phone book with the doctor's number.

"What's wrong?" June asked.

"It's Joanie. Her fever's gone up to 104 degrees. I'm calling the doctor back."

June got up and walked to Jake, concern lining her face. "Think it's her ears again?"

He shook his head and punched out the numbers. It rang several times, then was answered by a doctor's service.

"It's important that I get a hold of Dr. Hall," Jake said. "It's concerning my daughter, Joanie Pierce. Please tell the doctor that the Tylenol and the cool baths didn't work. She's still running a high fever of 104. She's listless, too."

"We'll page him."

Jake gave out the phone number, then carried the portable phone upstairs to Joanie's room. June followed.

"The doctor will call back as soon as possible," Jake said when he entered the nursery.

Joanie started to fuss, but not with much vigor. "She's so listless, Jake."

"Here let me take her for a while." Jake picked up Joanie and placed her against his chest. He began to murmur the soothing words that usually put his daughter to sleep.

All three kept vigil until the doctor called back. After Ali repeated Joanie's symptoms, Dr. Hall told them to bring the baby to the emergency room.

Ali set down the phone. "The doctor wants us to go to the hospital." A look of terror crossed Ali's face.

Gran June soothed her. "It's a precaution, Ali. Kids run fevers all the time." June helped Ali gather things for the diaper bag. Darcie showed up to help as Jake was wrapping Joanie in a heavy blanket and carried her downstairs. Jake and Ali grabbed their coats, and on the way out the door promised to call with any news.

Jake had to fight to keep from speeding, knowing he wanted to get them all to the hospital in one piece. Finally, ten minutes later, he pulled the car to the emergency-room entrance. Once inside the quiet waiting area, they hurried to the desk. Luckily Margo was on duty.

"I'm so glad you're here," Ali cried to her friend.

Upon seeing the sick child in Ali's arms, Margo turned professional. "What's wrong with Joanie?" She came around the desk.

That was all it took for Ali's tears to come pouring out. "She's been running a high fever."

Margo took her goddaughter and began to remove the blankets. "How's my precious girl?" the nurse spoke softly, then glanced up at Jake and Ali. "Go fill out the forms," she said. "I'll hold the baby."

Jake escorted Ali back to the desk, where the receptionist handed them three pages of forms. Jake took Ali's insurance card and passed it on to the woman. "I had Joanie put on my medical insurance at the plant, but it won't start up until the first of the year," he explained.

Ali nodded, but he knew she was barely holding it together. He worked on the forms, his own hands shaking as he tried to write. Oh, God, don't let anything happen to Joanie, he prayed.

Margo approached them. "I'm taking Joanie to the examining room."

"Not without us," Jake insisted, tossing the papers to the receptionist. "I'll finish these later."

"But, sir—" the girl began.

"No, not now," he interrupted. "I'll pay cash if need be." He tossed his checkbook on the counter. "Or, if that's not enough, call my father, Cliff Hawkins. I think he helped build a wing or two in this place. If that isn't enough, too bad. You're not keeping us from our daughter.'' He took Ali's hand, and together they went back to the examining area.

By the time they found Joanie's cubicle, Dr. Hall had arrived and was listening to the child's heart and lungs. Handing the baby back to the nurse, the fifty-year-old doctor pulled the stethoscope from his ears, and faced Ali and Jake.

''Her temperature is up to 105. We're going to draw some blood. Maybe that will tell us more about Joanie's infection.''

''Oh, gosh,'' Ali gasped. ''It's really serious?''

The doctor raised a calming hand. ''A high fever in a child is always a concern, especially since the cool baths and Tylenol couldn't bring it down. But we have many ways to fight these things. We're not going to let anything happen to her.'' He looked at Jake. ''I take it you're Joanie's father.''

Jake swallowed hard. ''Yes, I am.''

''Good. I want you to assure Ali that everything is going to be all right.''

Just then Joanie let out a squeal as the nurse drew blood from her small body. Ali rushed to her child's side. Tears welled in Jake's eyes. He felt so damn helpless. His little girl was sick, and all he could do was stand around unable to help her.

Ali scooped up Joanie and held her in her arms until the baby's crying subsided. When Joanie calmed down, Ali carefully diapered her, then put her in the tiny hospital gown that Margo gave her.

Thirty minutes later, the blood-test results came back. Joanie had an elevated white count.

''What does that mean?'' Jake asked.

The doctor removed his glasses and sighed. ''That means

we need to do more tests to rule out meningitis. You'll need
to sign a consent for a spinal tap.''

"Oh, God.'' Ali cried. "You mean she…she could
die?''

The doctor said gently, "It's a precaution. But the test
can tell us more.''

Jake's hands curled into fists. "So you're saying all we
can do is stand around…and wait?''

"We can watch her, feed her fluids and use cool packs
to help keep her fever down so there's no chance she goes
into convulsions.''

Jake put a protective arm around Ali as they glanced
down at Joanie. The baby looked flushed and lethargic, but
mostly helpless. No! He wasn't going to let anything happen to his child.

"Ali, come on,'' he encouraged. "We need to think positive. Joanie is going to be fine.'' He glanced over his
shoulder at Margo. "We've got the best people in this hospital taking care of her, and her godmother's here to help.
We're going to pull her through. Remember when you
helped me? Well, it's my turn now to help Joanie. I won't
let anything happen to her. Please believe me.''

Ali nodded, but her lips were trembling. "Oh, Jake. I'm
just scared.''

"I know, honey. So am I,'' he confessed. "So am I.''

Margo took Joanie from Ali and placed her on the gurney
to be moved upstairs into pediatrics where the baby could
be monitored more closely. Ali followed and Jake said he'd
be there as soon as he called June.

Ali stayed glued to her daughter's bedside, and watched
as she slept. Margo had just given Joanie a cool sponge
bath to help with the fever. Joanie cried the whole time.
Finally when the ordeal was finished, Ali got to rock her
baby. But all too soon, they wanted Joanie back in the bed.

Ali stood by the side rail and held on to her daughter's hand, soothing her with quiet words until she fell asleep.

Jake took over for a while so Ali could go and freshen up with some things that Gran June and Darcie had brought over.

Gallons of coffee kept his blood surging through his tired body. He prayed as he sat next to his daughter's bed, promising God anything and everything if He would just get Joanie through this.

He looked down at her small fragile body lying still in the bed, and the sight brought a new set of tears to his eyes. He loved Joanie so much. This precious child had given him a reason to live a few months ago. He glanced down at the tiny fingers tucked into his so trustingly. He was supposed to protect her.

"Oh, God. Please, let my daughter live. I love her so much."

When he opened his eyes, he saw his father standing in the doorway. Suddenly anger pulsed through him. Jake got up from his daughter's bed and walked out into the hall.

"June called me. How is Joanie doing?" Cliff asked.

"Suddenly you're here to show concern?" Jake said. "How touching. Since when did you have time for family?"

Cliff started to speak, then stopped. The color drained from his face.

"You've never had time to play father," Jake went on. "Now you want to play grandfather. I don't think so. I don't want Joanie to think she can count on you. You're not going to disappoint her the way you—" Jake broke off and drew a deep breath. "Why don't you just go back to the plant? Just leave me and my family alone." He turned around and discovered Ali standing behind him. She had a shocked look on her face. He ignored it, and went back to Joanie's bedside.

* * *

Ali stood in the hall, embarrassed and ashamed over Jake's behavior. How could he talk to his father that way? She walked up to Cliff. "Cliff, he's just upset. We're all going crazy—"

Cliff raised a hand. "You don't have to apologize for my son. The worst part is that he has every right to hate me. I wasn't there for him when he needed a father." Cliff frowned, looking much older than his years. "But I'd hoped that after his accident, we'd be able to work through the past and start over." He sighed. "Tell Jake that if he needs anything, I'll be at home." He started to walk away, then stopped. "And, Ali, tell Jake I'm sorry. I'm really sorry." The man turned and went to the elevators.

A few minutes later, Ali returned to her daughter's room, unable to put the scene between Jake and Cliff out of her mind. How could Jake have said those awful things to his own father? Didn't he know how much the man loved him? Cliff put in hours at the hospital while Jake was so sick. Now all the man wanted to do was help his son get through this crisis, and Jake rejected him. What was it that made Jake hate his father so much?

Ali came up behind Jake. He turned and their eyes met, then Ali went into his arms. He comforted her, easing her fears. It was nice for a change to have someone to lean on. Jake always seemed to be there for her and Joanie. She hoped he always would be.

As Jake continued to hold her, Ali bargained with God to take care of her child and make her well again. Finally a peaceful calm came over her, and she knew that everything was going to be just fine.

"She's going to be all right, Jake."

He pulled back and wiped his eyes. "Of course she is. Joanie's a fighter."

"Like her daddy."

They both looked down at the child in the bed. Even

though the fever wasn't gone yet, Joanie seemed to be sleeping soundly.

Jake drew a shuddering breath. ''God, Ali.'' He squeezed his eyes shut. ''If anything happens to Joanie, I don't know...''

This was the first time that Jake had showed her his fear. ''No, Jake. We have to have faith. I believed that you would come out of your coma, and you did.'' She smiled. ''Joanie is going to make it through this, too. They've already ruled out meningitis.''

Another hour had gone by, and the sun was dawning on a new day. Jake sat in a chair beside the bed, his head braced against his hands. Suddenly Ali heard their daughter making noises and the sounds, ''Da...da...da...'' filled the room.

''Oh, my gosh.'' Ali shook Jake, then reached out and touched her child's rosy cheek. ''Oh, sweetie, how are you feeling?'' She noticed a rash along her daughter's arms and legs.

Joanie made a cooing sound, then glanced around with her big brown eyes. When she spotted Jake, she smiled. ''Da...da.''

Jake smiled back. ''That's right, Joanie. It's Dada and I love you.'' He turned to Ali. ''And I love you.''

''I love you, too,'' she whispered, her heart so full. She had everything she could ever want.

Jake pulled her into his arms and held her. Ali felt safe and secure for the first time in a long time. Then she looked up and saw Darcie standing in the doorway.

Her sister looked lost, sad. ''May I come in?'' Darcie asked.

''Sure.'' Ali smiled. ''Joanie's fever has broken. She's going to be all right.''

''I know, I heard,'' Darcie said. There was a long hesitation before she spoke again. "I wanted to say goodbye. I'm going back to New York."

Ali had waited to hear those words for a long time, but they didn't bring her the satisfaction she'd thought.

Jake stood and placed his arm around Ali, but remained silent.

Darcie lowered her gaze to the child in bed, then looked back at her sister. "I also wanted to say... I was wrong. Anyone can see how much in love you two are. I spent the night in the waiting room, watching how you drew strength from one another, how you reached out unselfishly offering comfort."

"Our child was sick," Jake explained.

"It was more than that." Darcie wiped a tear that trickled down her cheek. "And I'm sorry, Ali, that I ever tried to interfere."

Ali walked around the bed and took her sister out into the deserted hallway. "I was wrong, too, Darcie. I should have told you about Jake and me a long time ago. I just didn't know how."

Darcie nodded in understanding. "It's past history. You and Jake are together where you belong. I can see what a good mother you are with Joanie. I guess it's something we didn't learn from our own."

"It's all I ever wanted to be—a wife and mother."

"I know," Darcie agreed. "And I spend my life running away from commitment. Hell, I've dated a lot of nice guys since coming to New York, but if they get too close, I start backing away."

Ali's heart went out to her sister, wishing she could help. "Someday there's going to be a guy who cares enough that he won't let you."

"Easy for you to say—you've got a great guy."

They both laughed. "And I'm not giving him up."

Darcie hugged Ali, fighting back more tears. "I don't

blame you. You got what you deserved, Ali. And Jake ended up with the right sister.''

The doctor verified that Joanie was on the road to recovery. She had a case of roseola. By the end of the morning, her temperature was back to normal and she was released by early afternoon.

At home, Jake didn't leave Joanie's side the entire day, and Ali allowed him to take care of the baby. Finally, at about eight that night, their daughter was asleep for the night. That was when Ali told Jake she wanted to talk to him. She escorted him into her bedroom across the hall, so they could be close to Joanie in case she cried.

As the door closed, Jake pulled Ali into his arms and kissed her. The kiss told her of his desire and need, but Ali had to refrain from getting carried away. There were too many things that needed to be worked out before she could think about the physical side of their relationship.

''Jake, we have to talk.''

''This is the only talking I want to do.''

Ali allowed herself to get lost in the moment as Jake kissed her again. His hands moved over her body, quickly igniting her passion.

''It seems like an eternity since I held you, kissed you.'' He nestled her in his arms and began to move against her.

''Jake.'' Finally Ali pushed against his chest until he released her and she walked to the other side of the room.

''We need to talk about what happened in the hospital.''

Jake looked puzzled, then embarrassed. ''If you mean how I broke down, I didn't...''

''No, Jake.'' She waved her hand. ''It's normal to let go of your emotions during a crisis. I'm talking about what you said to your father.''

He looked embarrassed. ''You weren't supposed to hear that.''

Suddenly Ali was remembering what Darcie had told her yesterday: Jake hated their hometown and he hated his father. A cold chill rushed through her body. She'd seen that for herself, firsthand, last night at the hospital.

"Jake, what's going on between you and Cliff?"

He ran a hand through his hair. "The same thing that has always been going on. We've never gotten along and we never will."

"Isn't it about time you and your father tried to work it out?"

"No! That'll never happen. There's too much..."

Ali felt her panic building. "Too much what?"

Jake drew a long breath and released it. "I just can't, so don't ask me to."

"Then how can you be happy working for him, living in this town?"

He looked at her, his eyes bleak. "I'll manage."

"Jake, we can't build a life together like that."

He came to her and placed his hands on her arms. "For the first time, Ali, I'm going to have a family. I can handle anything as long as I have you and Joanie."

Ali heard the underlying desperation, and it scared her. "For how long, Jake, if you keep this resentment for your dad locked up. How can you work together?"

His gaze avoided hers. "I can handle it."

"For how long?"

"For long enough. Look, my dad and I have been this way all our lives. We're never going to have a close relationship."

"But, Jake, if you don't get rid of this baggage from your childhood, it could sabotage our marriage."

"No, Ali. That will never happen."

Tears formed in her eyes. "It could."

His dark gaze searched her face, then suddenly he smiled. "I don't have to keep working at the plant. Ray has been talking to me about running for sheriff next November. I haven't had a chance to talk to you about it.''

''Do you want to be sheriff?''

He smiled again. ''I think I might like it…a lot. What about you? How do you feel about me going into law enforcement?''

''Oh, Jake, you'd be good at whatever you do, but it doesn't erase the real problem.''

He raked a hand through his hair. ''Look, Ali. Let me handle my father.''

''Ignoring him isn't going to work anymore. The blowup at the hospital should tell you that.''

He marched around the room, visibly upset. ''Then after we're married, we'll go somewhere else where we don't have to deal with Cliff Hawkins.''

Ali's heart tightened. ''I can't, Jake.''

''Why?''

''You know that after my parents divorced, our mother dragged Darcie and me around the country. We didn't know where we were going, or if we were staying long enough to have a home. Most of the time, the places we lived were so awful.…'' Ali trembled.

''I'd never do that to you and Joanie. I'll make a good living.''

''I know you will, Jake. But I can't survive without my family around. My grandmother isn't getting any younger.''

''We can stay close by.''

Ali shook her head.

Jake gripped her shoulders. ''If you loved me, you'd go.''

She gasped, feeling as if he'd slapped her. ''I can't, Jake. I have to think about Joanie. The day she was born, I promised her that she'd always have a home, and a family. Here.''

"Are you saying that I'm incapable of giving my own daughter a home?"

She shook her head. "It's not the town, Jake. You're running from your father, and your past. You've been running for years. You've got to stop."

Jake raked his hand through his hair in agitation. "You don't know anything, Ali. You don't know what it was like—" He stopped as if he was going to say too much. "After your grandparents took you in, you and Darcie had all the love you could ever want. I wasn't so lucky." He gave her a sad smile. "I remember coming to this house and hanging around, just hoping to absorb some of that love."

Ali watched as Jake moved restlessly around the bedroom.

"But the end result was that I had to go home sometime. As a kid, I had more of a relationship with the housekeeper than I did with my own parents." He spun around to face her. "Do you know when I was eight years old, I wished I'd become an orphan just so I could go live somewhere else. Maybe have a real family."

He pulled Ali into his arms. "I need you and Joanie in my life. I love you both so much. I promise you that I'll make you a good husband. Just come away with me."

Ali was weakening to his plea. But her own fears kept her from saying yes, kept her from leaving the only place she'd felt safe. "I can't, Jake. It wouldn't solve anything. You've got to make peace with your father before we can have a future."

"How can you take that man's side? Cliff Hawkins has never been a father to me. The plant was the only family he needed."

"Jake, I'm on your side," she said. "But what's happening is tearing you apart. Every time your father is around, I can feel you tense up. I see the resentment and hate.''

"I won't play the loving-son routine with my father. We've never had a relationship, and we're not about to start now."

Ali was shaking, feeling her entire world start to unravel. She knew Jake well enough to know he wasn't going to relent. As much as she loved the man, she couldn't marry him. Pulling the ring off her finger, she handed it to him. "I can't marry you, Jake."

He looked shocked and hurt. "Why?"

"Because we want different things."

Jake rushed out the door, slamming it shut behind him. The hurt he felt caused an excruciating pain in his chest. He'd thought that Ali loved him.

For years he'd known she had feelings for him. The first day he'd walked though the Pierces' front door, he had seen that Ali was attracted to him. Back then he'd only thought of her as the skinny twin sister of the girl he loved—or maybe he should say lusted after. Darcie had been the early developer—head cheerleader and every high-school boy's sexual fantasy.

No one had looked twice at shy little Ali, except Jake. He'd seen the beauty beneath the freckles and wild hair. Ali had been the quiet one, but she knew how to listen, whether it had been his problems with Darcie or helping him decide on college. Ali had been the only person he could talk to, the one person he could depend on to give him her undivided attention. Never Darcie, not his coaches or teachers, certainly not his dad.

He jumped in the car, started the engine and backed out of the driveway. Now she'd stopped caring about him. He blinked back the moisture in his eyes and headed toward the highway. The night was freezing cold, but he barely felt it—he was numb. He'd lost Ali. His family. No matter what he did, he couldn't have her back, because there would always be a part of his past he couldn't share with her. He couldn't share with anyone.

His thoughts turned to his father as he pressed on the accelerator. Suddenly the car fishtailed, but Jake regained control of the slide and soon made it onto the two-lane road. He shifted into four-wheel drive and picked up speed again.

Ali wanted him to talk with his father. Jake laughed. Right. How many years had he tried to get Cliff Hawkins's attention? How many years had he struggled to earn his approval? Nothing had worked. Why would he even want to try again?

"Wasn't taking a job in the damn plant humbling enough for you, old man?" Jake shouted in the quiet interior of the car. "Wasn't my coming back here and letting you act like you hadn't done a damn thing enough for you, Cliff?"

The car hit a patch of ice. Jake's grip on the wheel tightened as he fought to stay on the road. Once he hit dry pavement again, Jake pushed the gas pedal to the floor and the Tahoe shot off.

"Damn you, Cliff. You're still wrecking my life."

Suddenly, up ahead in the distance, Jake caught sight of a large dark shape. A deer. He swerved to avoid the animal. His car went off onto the shoulder, meeting with the combination of snow and ice. The vehicle went into a spin, and Jake clutched the wheel. Using all his willpower, he pulled the car under control. Finally the car stopped, facing the wrong direction and half off the road.

Jake gulped much-needed air into his lungs and laid his head on the steering wheel, trying to block out thoughts of what could have happened just seconds ago.

All at once, a picture flashed into his mind of him driving another vehicle. That time he hadn't stopped. The blowing snow was blinding him so he couldn't even see the highway. Suddenly his truck hit a patch of ice and went airborne and hit a tree. A strangled cry tore from his throat and pain seared through his chest as he remembered being the man trapped in the twisted metal. Tears formed in his eyes. He remembered the day of the accident. Oh, God. Oh, God.

Just then there was a knock on his window.

Jake jumped and glanced out to see a sheriff's deputy flashing a light at him.

"Mr. Hawkins, are you okay?"

Jake managed a nod and pushed the button to lower the window.

"Sir, I saw you nearly hit the deer, then when you went off the road, I thought you were a goner…again." The young deputy smiled. "You need me to call someone?"

"No. I'm just a little shaken up."

The deputy eyed him closely. "Think you can get back on the highway?"

"Yeah, I can make it back."

"Okay, I'll wait until you're back on the road." The deputy turned and walked through the snow to his Blazer.

Jake took several breaths and carefully put his car into gear. He pushed down on the gas and eased the vehicle off the icy shoulder and onto the cleared pavement again. Once headed in the right direction, Jake waved at the deputy and moved down the road. This time at a slower speed—and this time with a destination.

He was going to see his father. To confront him with the past. Now he knew why he'd been out driving in a blizzard.

Chapter Fourteen

At ten o'clock, the house was silent and Ali made her way downstairs to the kitchen. She boiled some water for tea, but when she sat down to drink it, her hands shook so badly she couldn't hold the mug. Long hard sobs rocked her body, and Ali buried her face in her hands.

A moment later, Gran June came into the kitchen, tying the belt to her robe. "Oh, what's wrong, honey? Is it Joanie?"

Ali shook her head, fighting for control. "Jake's gone, Gran. I told him I couldn't marry him."

Gran June pulled some tissues from her robe pocket and handed them to Ali, then sat down at the table. Ali knew from experience that her grandmother was waiting for an explanation. Ali wasn't sure she had one.

"Jake wants me and Joanie to move away."

"Isn't that what usually happens when you get married, Ali? You go live with your husband."

"I know." Ali wiped her eyes. "But Jake wants me to move away from Webster. Gran, I can't leave."

"Why not? Don't you love Jake?"

"Of course, but I don't want to leave you. And Webster is my home. I feel safe here. When Joanie was born, I promised her that she'd always have a home where she felt safe and loved. Just like you promised me and Darcie."

Gran June reached over and hugged her granddaughter. "Oh, honey. I'm glad you and Darcie felt secure living here with your grandfather and me. But don't you know it isn't the place that made you feel secure—it's the love you felt inside as a family."

She gripped Ali's hands. "It's the same love you give your daughter that makes her know she's wanted. You could move anywhere with Joanie and make her feel the same way, because you love her. I'm ashamed to say it, but your mother, for some reason, didn't want you and Darcie. I blame your father mostly. My son, God rest his soul, could never handle responsibility. At least he married Beth when she got pregnant with you and Darcie, but he never could manage to stay in one place long enough to make a home for his family. Your mother wasn't much better. She followed after him, then when he was killed…she began looking for another man to love. Your parents were selfish. That wasn't love, Ali. Not the kind of love you have for Joanie, or that Jake has for you."

Ali's chest tightened as her grandmother's words began to sink in.

"Look at the advantages Jake had growing up, but the house he lived in was never a home. It was never a place for him to feel safe. He's been neglected, too. He never had a real family until you and Joanie."

"Oh, God. I just took away Jake's family."

"Love is a rare gift. Jake stood by you when he found

out about Joanie. Even Darcie couldn't pry him away. I think he's proved how he feels.''

"But what about his hatred for his father? He can't get past it. It colors his whole life.''

"I doubt it's hate. Jake has to work through a lot of things. Isn't there a little resentment you still feel for your mother? Well, Jake's mother was drunk most of his childhood. Cliff used to work at the plant to avoid facing the problem. That left a small boy to deal with things he never should have had to face alone. He's had a lifetime of turmoil. If he and Cliff are to work things out, he needs time. Time, and you standing by him, letting him know that you love him.''

Ali felt her throat tighten. She didn't want to think about the lonely little boy left all by himself. Worse, she didn't want to think about the man she turned away from when he needed her. She jumped up from the table. "I've got to go find Jake.''

Gran smiled. "That's a good start.''

"Will you watch Joanie?'' She kissed her grandmother as the phone rang. Hoping it was Jake calling, Ali raced to answer it. "Hello.''

"Ali, it's Ray.''

Her heart sank. "Oh, God, Ray. Is something wrong?''

"No. But Deputy Hank Peters just called in. He saw Jake skid out on Highway 26 just south of town.''

She raised her trembling hand to her lips. "Is he okay?''

"Jake's okay, but he nearly hit a deer. His car went off the road. Hank thought for sure he was going to crash again, but Jake managed to get the car under control at the last minute.''

"Is he still out there?''

"No. He drove off right away. Ali, what's going on? Hank said Jake seemed upset.''

Ali closed her eyes. Jake was upset and she'd caused it.

"We had a fight." She didn't wait for Ray to say any more. "Did Hank know where Jake was headed?"

"Hank stayed behind him until he turned off at Hillcrest Road."

Jake had gone to see Cliff. "Thanks, Ray. I've got to go."

"If you need anything, call me."

"I will. Goodbye, Ray." She hung up the phone and ran upstairs to get dressed, fearing father and son were finally going to come to blows.

Jake pulled into the circular driveway of his father's house. He jerked open the car door, stepped out onto the concrete driveway and looked toward the imposing two-story brick structure. The house was dark, but the white shutters glistened in the cold night as Jake made his way up the walk, limping heavily. By the time he reached the porch, his ankle ached. He'd forgotten his damn cane.

He pressed the bell, and when no one answered, he began to pound on the door. Finally Harry appeared and let him inside.

"I need to talk to my...Cliff."

"I believe Mr. Hawkins has retired for the night."

"Well, get him up." Jake pushed past the man. "Tell him that his son needs to see him. Oh wait, that doesn't work with my father. You see, Harry, Cliff has never come when I needed him. He always promised, but then he never shows. Never."

"That's enough, Jake," his father's voice rang out.

Jake walked around the eighteenth-century table in the middle of the huge entry, and went to the spiral staircase, watching as his father descended.

"Sorry. I forgot," Jake snapped. "I shouldn't be airing the family secret."

Cliff glanced over Jake's head to Harry. "You may leave us alone, Harry. I can handle this."

The middle-aged man nodded and left the room, but not before giving Jake a threatening look.

Cliff was now face-to-face with his son. "Come into the den," he ordered as he walked past. Jake followed.

Once inside the paneled room, Cliff strode across the slate gray carpeting to the desk, then sat on the edge, motioning his son to a chair.

Jake shook his head and began to pace. He could feel his hands trembling, and he didn't want his father to know how upset he was. "I remembered the day of the accident."

Cliff didn't even blink. "I knew you would. It was only a matter of time. What triggered it?"

Jake made a snorting sound. "I nearly had another wreck."

"My God, Jake." Cliff stood and came to his son.

For the first time since he'd woken from the coma, Jake saw terror in the man's eyes.

"Were you hurt?" Cliff asked.

Jake shook his head. "No. But like I said, I remember that we were together on the day of my accident." He studied his father closely. How the hell did Cliff Hawkins pull off looking so cool and collected? "We argued. We argued about Mother, and the fact that she and I caught you with another woman."

Cliff's mask of reserve finally fell as he rubbed his temples, then he raised his eyes to met his son's. "Would it make any difference if I told you it didn't mean anything to me?"

"What didn't mean anything? Mom and me?" Jake yelled. "I already knew that. But I believe your wife lived in an alcohol fog of hope."

"No. The affair."

"Which affair?"

"I know you won't believe this, Jake, but I was unfaithful just that once. It only lasted a few weeks."

Jake tossed out a few expletives. "Next thing you'll try to tell me is that work kept you busy all those nights at the plant."

Cliff paused, then finally shook his head. "No, not always. But when your mother's drinking had gotten so bad that she was incoherent, I did use the plant as an excuse to stay away."

Anger welled inside Jake, and he felt his gut twist. "What about me, Dad? I was home. Waiting. But you never showed up. Instead, you abandoned me to deal with a drunken mother." Jake pointed at his chest. "I was the child, yet I'm the one who put her to bed, cleaned up her messes, reassured her that you loved us. Not you. No, you didn't give a damn about us. Just your precious plant. And you wonder why I hate it so much."

Jake walked up to his father. He saw the remorse and sadness in his old man's eyes, but he didn't care. "That night at the plant, when Mom and I found you with your secretary, we hid behind the door and I had to watch you fondle that woman. For God's sake, I was eight years old. When I needed a father at home, you were out screwing another woman."

Cliff flinched. "Jake, I know what I did was wrong. I'm sorry. I'm so sorry for the times I left you to handle everything. Your mother was sick. I tried several times to get her into a rehab program, but she refused to go. At the time, there was no way to force her to get help." He sighed. "Her family was pretty influential, and they threatened to close down the plant if I ruined their good name in this town."

"So you left me to deal with her? Why didn't you just get a divorce if you didn't love her?"

Cliff tensed. "Because I couldn't."

"Why, because you'd lose your precious Hawk Industries?"

"No, because I would lose you."

Jake stepped back as if he'd been struck.

Cliff's eyes narrowed. "Your grandparents threatened to take you away if I divorced your mother."

Jake didn't want to believe him. Cliff Hawkins had never shown any interest in being a father. "The courts wouldn't give an alcoholic custody of a child."

"Carol tried very hard to hide her problem. You were the one who suffered the most. I know I handled things wrong, son. I ran away from the problems your mother and I had. It was easier. After she died, I wanted to rebuild our relationship, but whenever I tried to get close, you pulled away."

"Because everything had to be your way. You never took the time to listen to me or to ask what I wanted. All you wanted was for your son to follow in your footsteps at Hawk Industries. You never got to know me at all."

"I've always been proud of you, Jake. And everything you've accomplished in your life."

"You hated me going into ROTC, and my army career."

"I hated that we couldn't be close, but I was so proud when you made captain."

Jake felt a rush go through him. "I never knew."

Cliff looked embarrassed and he walked back to the desk. "I know I should have told you, but where I came from, Jake, men never showed affection." He turned around, and there were tears in his eyes. "I've watched you with Joanie and I envy what you two share. I'm sorry that things weren't the same between us. I know I can't be the father you want, but I hope, in time, maybe we can be friends."

Jake combed his hand through his hair, trying to hold his own emotions in check. So many things had happened in the past few months. He'd been given a second chance at life, he'd discovered he had a daughter…and he'd found love.

"Sometimes we need a second chance." He saw his father relax. "Maybe I didn't reach out for you, either, Dad."

"Son, I wish I could turn back the clock—"

"No, Dad," Jake interrupted. "We've both made mistakes. We need to start here and now." He looked at his father, and saw the pain leave his face and a smile appeared. It felt good to have a father again. "But before we do, you need to know that I'm never going to feel about the plant like you do. I'll help start up the new electronics operation, but I have other ideas about a new career. Ray Benson isn't running for reelection next fall."

"So you're not leaving town?"

"No, Webster is the perfect place to raise a child, and Joanie needs to be near her grandparents."

Cliff gave him a broad smile. "Then I'll have plenty of time to teach my granddaughter the family business. That is, with yours and Ali's approval."

"I have to warn you, she's a pretty independent little girl."

"An excellent quality." Cliff grew serious. "I'm going to do everything differently, Jake. I'm going to take time off for family."

Jake scribbled something on paper. "Will you give this note to Ali, Dad?" Jake started out the door as his father called him back.

"Aren't you going to wait for her?"

Jake smiled. "I've been waiting for Ali all my life. I just have to prove it to her. Just give that note to her."

It was midnight when Ali parked in front of the cottage. She got out of her car and looked around. The moonlight illuminated the snow blanketing the edge of the now frozen water. The trees along the slope were stripped of leaves, creating eerie shadows.

Shivering against the cold air, Ali pulled her jacket closer to her body and headed to the steps. She had to find Jake.

When she made it to the deck, memories of the last time she'd been here rushed into her head. Darcie's wedding. Jake had disappeared from the church that day, too, and she'd come here hoping to find him. She'd never dreamed that they'd end up in each other's arms....

Ali closed her eyes as a warm tingling ran through her at the memory of Jake Hawkins making love to her the first time. Tears soon replaced her joy. She had driven him away tonight.

"Oh, Jake, where are you?" she whispered. "Please, give me another chance. I love you."

She went to the French doors and saw a dim light inside. There was a fire in the hearth. Trembling, she opened the door and walked in.

"Jake?" What if he didn't want to listen to her? All his note had said was to meet him here, that they needed to talk.

"Ali-cat."

Hearing her nickname, she jumped and looked up to see Jake standing in the doorway across the room.

"Jake, I've been worried about you."

He had on jeans and a flannel shirt. He was minus his cane, and she barely noticed his limp as he made his way across the room. She heard only the loud pounding of her heart.

"I was worried about myself, too," he said. "I needed some time to sort things out."

Ali swallowed back the lump in her throat. "Did you?"

He stood in front of her, so close she could feel the heat of his body.

His dark eyes searched her face. "I'm not sure. I think

I need a little help.'' He reached out and began gently tugging off her jacket. Ali didn't protest as the nylon jacket slid easily from her arms. Jake laid it on the back of the sofa, then took her hand and led her to the fireplace. He tossed a couple of pillows on the floor and motioned for her to sit down.

"I was hoping we could talk this through together,'' he said.

"I want that, too,'' she managed to say as they both sank to the floor.

"Good.''

He squeezed her hand in his, and her pulse raced. "I went to my dad's tonight. We talked. I guess I should say we had a long argument.''

He gave her a sexy smile, and Ali had to fight to keep herself from jumping into his arms.

"But I think we finally cleared the air. There's a lot of our past to resolve. A lot of secrets. I don't know if we'll ever have a good father-son relationship, but we're working on a friendship.''

Hope surged through Ali.

"I know now that I've blamed my father for a lot of things he had no control over. My mother's drinking, for one. I know now she was the one who refused professional help for her problem. I've kept a lot of anger bottled up for years.'' He gave Ali a sheepish look. "Maybe some counseling might not be a bad idea.''

Ali smiled. "I think that's a good idea. You and your father need to work through this.'' Her gaze moved to his muscular chest covered by soft flannel. She couldn't help but wonder if she'd ever again lay her head against his broad shoulders. She looked up at his face and caught his smile.

"I have other issues to resolve, too.'' His ebony gaze locked with hers. "Ali, the first time we made love, I

should have stayed with you. I knew we didn't take pre-
cautions.''

Embarrassed, Ali glanced away, not wanting to listen to
his regrets.

Jake touched her chin and made her turn back to him.
''No, it's not what you think. That night was so special.
I'd never felt so close to anyone as I did with you. You
reached inside me and took hold of my heart. I'd never let
anyone get that close before and I panicked.'' He rubbed a
hand over his face. ''But damn it, Ali, I used you. You
should have hated me.''

''Oh, Jake. I could never hate you. I love you. Even way
back then, I loved you.'' She swallowed. ''I thought you
were ashamed of what happened between us. I thought you
wanted to forget about me and that night.''

Jake tugged on Ali's hand and brought her into his arms.
''Oh, Ali-cat. I was never ashamed of you. That night was
so special to me. We created a child together. Our daughter.''

Tears blurred her vision. ''Oh, Jake...'' She couldn't get
any words out. For a long time, they just held each other,
forgiving themselves for the mistakes they'd made in the
past.

Finally Jake pulled back. ''Ali, I want us to build on
what we have. I want to be a family—you, me and Joanie.
I've stopped running. Wherever you and Joanie are is
where I want to be. Even right here in Webster.''

Ali raised her head, and looked at him through her tears.
''No, Jake. I was wrong to ask you to stay here. Gran June
made me realize that it isn't this town or the house that
made me feel secure all these years. It was the love. You
give me all the love I need. I feel at home with you, Jake.
Anywhere. I love you.''

''Oh, God, Ali. I love you, too.'' He cupped her cheeks,

and his gaze bored into hers. "I need you and Joanie more than I need to breathe."

Ali's trembling hands went to his chest, feeling his racing heart. "We need you, too, Jake."

She nuzzled the curve of his neck, savoring the joy of being in his arms, inhaling his familiar masculine scent that always drove her crazy.

"You're like an angel," he groaned. "I can't live without you."

Her arms tightened around his neck as she placed tiny kisses along his jaw. "I can't live without you, either.

"I love you," he repeated. "I want us to have forever." He lowered her to the carpet in front of the fire. Then his mouth took hers, and he kissed her until she writhed in hunger under him.

"I want forever, too, Jake, but can we talk about this later?" she asked as he continued his sensual assault on her body. "I'm going to die if you don't make love to me soon."

A cocky smile appeared across his handsome face. "Aren't you the one who's always saying we need to talk?"

"There are all kinds of ways to communicate." Ali's breath caught as Jake's hands moved over her, then stopped under her breasts.

"Please, Jake," she pleaded.

"I thought I lost you tonight," he said. "Marry me."

"Yes, I'll marry you," she breathed.

The crackling sound of the wood hid the loud drumming of her heart as his hands moved under her sweater, then raised it over her head, leaving her with just her lacy bra. He unfastened the front clasp, and his eyes burned with raw hunger.

"You are beautiful."

A rush surged through her as he bent his head and covered her mouth. He traced her lips with his tongue, then he plunged deep inside her mouth, again and again, until she moaned. Anxious, she tore at the buttons on his shirt, until he was bare chested. Then, in a flurry of need, the rest of their clothing came off.

Jake raised his head, feeling his head spin. He looked down at Ali's satiny cheek, her full breasts rising and falling with her rapid breathing. The pulsing desire that took hold of Jake almost frightened him. He fought for control. He wanted Ali desperately, but he also needed to show her how much he loved her.

His gaze drifted to her sightly parted mouth. He leaned down and kissed her, but when Ali's warm searching hands roamed over his body, all his good intentions disappeared. He couldn't stand the torture anymore. He moved over Ali and tested her readiness. Again he lowered his mouth to hers, massaging her with a slow, consuming kiss as he entered her. He swallowed her gasp as she took him deep into her warmth. Her breasts pushed up against him as he moved inside where there was no more thinking as their bodies moved fervently, finding a rhythm that took them closer and closer to the edge.

Suddenly she tensed and cried out his name, triggering his own release. They entered paradise, together.

Ali savored the wonderful sensation as she lay in Jake's arms. He'd pulled the blanket off the sofa and covered them with it.

"Hey, you're not going to fall asleep on me, are you?" he asked.

She sighed. "No, reliving what just happened."

He rose up on his elbow and smiled at her. "No need. I can give you more memories any time you want." He raised his hand to her face and began tracing her jaw. When his finger reached her mouth, she kissed it.

''Pretty sure of yourself, aren't you?'' Ali teased. ''Sure you can keep up with my needs?''

Jake drew her against his body, letting her feel that he was definitely ready for whatever she desired. ''I think I can handle it.''

Suddenly feeling giddy, Ali laughed. ''You're everything I need.''

Jake grew serious and brushed her hair away from her face. ''Tell me you'll marry me soon.''

Ali blinked. ''Anywhere, any time, any place.''

Jake cocked an eyebrow. ''I think soon is a good idea, since we didn't use any protection when we made love.''

''Oh, gosh,'' Ali gasped. ''I forgot.''

''We seem to do a lot of that,'' Jake said. His fingers moved under the blanket, and he began tracing her nipple, causing the tip to harden. Ali sucked in a breath.

''Yeah, we better have the wedding real soon.'' He reached behind him and grabbed his jeans. Going into the pocket, he dug out the sparkling diamond ring that Ali had returned to him earlier that night.

''I believe this belongs to you,'' he said.

''Oh, Jake.'' Tears flooded her eyes.

''Or maybe I should get you another ring. It seems this one doesn't want to stay put.''

''Don't you dare, Jake Hawkins.'' She grabbed his hand. ''I want this one, and I promise it will never leave my finger again.''

''Just so long as you don't leave me. I need you, Ali. You and Joanie are my life.''

''As you are mine.''

She held out her hand as Jake slipped the ring on her finger. He kissed the precious stone, then her.

Jake's kiss was a promise of love, forever.

Epilogue

It was a sunny April afternoon, and Jake stood at the cottage railing that had been decorated with fresh flowers for today's wedding ceremony.

He glanced down at the lake about fifty yards away. The trees and shrubs were rich with green, and colorful wildflowers covered the slope to the water's edge. Everything had come alive. Just like his life.

In about fifteen minutes, he and Ali were going to exchange their vows right here on the deck, where it had all begun.

"How you holding up?"

He turned to see his father.

Jake smiled. "Anxious. I want it over with. Seems like it's taken forever to get to this day."

"You've crossed a lot of bridges in the past six months."

"Yeah. A lot of good things have happened." He gripped his dad's shoulder. They had spent some time together the past few months. For the first time, they were getting to know one another. Cliff had even managed to keep regular hours at the plant, and let his supervisors handle the running of things while he took time for a personal life. After all, he was only fifty-six years old. And as part of their father-and-son reconciliation, Cliff had been acting as Jake's campaign manager for the upcoming sheriff's race.

In June, Jake would start his new job as deputy to learn the ropes. The people in town had taken a liking to him, and seemed happy that if Ray Benson had to retire, then Jake "The Hawk" Hawkins was a good man for the job.

"I just hope I can live up to Ali's expectations."

"You know, son, love is a funny thing. It can forgive a lot of shortcomings. If you take time to talk...and listen."

Jake saw the flash of sadness in his dad's eyes. The man had been lonely for a lot of years. Hopefully Jake and his new family would change that.

Gran June came through the French doors. "We're ready to start."

Jake nodded as excitement raced through him. The minister stood at the railing, as did Jake and his best man, Cliff. The soft music that had been playing shifted to the bridal march, and all heads turned to the doors.

First came Margo. She was dressed in a pink lace dress that came to her ankles, and in her hands she carried a bouquet of spring flowers. Next came the maid of honor, Darcie, who was dressed in a mint green dress, and who also carried a bouquet. Ali's sister had made the trip from New York. Darcie was happy with her career, and the two sisters had made peace, proving that love was indeed an unbreakable bond.

The small group of guests turned and watched as little Joanie came next. She toddled out, wearing a sunny yellow dress, her short black hair adorned with ribbons and flow-

ers. Her concentration was on the miniature basket of rose
petals she carried in her tiny hands. She looked frightened
seeing the people, then spotted her daddy and took off running in her new Mary Jane shoes. The wedding guests
chuckled.

Jake scooped his daughter up in his arms, then turned to
see Ali as she stepped through the doors. Suddenly his
breath locked in his chest.

His bride was dressed in an antique dress that had been
her grandmother's. The high collar was made of lace, and
a beautiful cameo was pinned at her throat. The skirt gathered at her waist, and draped to midcalf. Her auburn curls
were done up, and a circle of flowers sat like a crown on
her head. His gaze met hers, and she gave him a trembling
smile as she walked toward him.

When she stopped at his side, he ached to lean over and
kiss her. But instead, he whispered, "You're beautiful."

She blushed. "You're pretty handsome yourself."

"Mommy, Mommy," Joanie said, and held out her
hands.

Jake held her back. "Oh, sweetie, remember our promise. You go to Grandpa."

Joanie stopped fussing when Cliff took her in his arms.
Jake turned back and gave his full attention to his bride.
He took Ali's hand.

Most of the ceremony was a blur, but Jake did hear the
minister say, "You may kiss your bride."

Without hesitation, Jake pulled Ali into his arms. Her
emerald eyes sparkled with love as he lowered his head and
took her mouth in a heated kiss that should have been saved
for private. Finally when applause and whistles erupted, he
broke off the kiss. "I'll finish that later."

"Ladies and gentlemen, Mr. and Mrs. Jake Hawkins."

For the next thirty minutes, they took their congratulations from the guests, then Jake pulled Ali aside, wanting to have some time alone with his bride.

Ali resisted. "Jake, we can't leave."

"Just for a minute," he promised as he took her down to the lake. He helped her over the stone-covered path until they made it to the water's edge. He gathered Ali in his arms and looked out at the lake. "I always loved it here. It's so peaceful." He glanced down at Ali. "You sure you don't mind having our honeymoon out here?"

She shook her head. "No. This place will always have special meaning for me. Our daughter was conceived here."

Jake smiled. "Maybe we'll luck out again. What do you think?"

"Maybe we should give *us* a little time," Ali suggested.

"I could go for that. I'll be getting used to a new job. But I want you to cut your hours down at the sheriff's office. Besides taking care of Joanie, you have a house to redecorate."

Just a month ago, they'd found a beautiful old house. It hadn't been in the best shape, but they both fell in love with it and knew it was perfect for their home.

"Wait until you see the bank account after we finish decorating. You'll send me back to work." She turned in his arms.

He kissed her, then they remained silent for a long time. Finally Jake whispered, "Thank you, Ali. Thank you for bringing me back."

She looked confused. "What did I do?"

"My life didn't mean anything until I heard your voice when I was in the hospital. Your voice brought me back. Then your kiss saved me."

Ali had tears in her eyes. "That's because we needed you. We need you to complete our family." She wrapped her hands around her husband's neck and bent his head toward her and kissed him.

With the touch of her lips to his, Jake knew he was truly home…at last.

* * * * * *

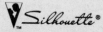

If you enjoyed what you just read,
then we've got an offer you can't resist!

Take 2 bestselling
love stories FREE!

Plus get a FREE surprise gift!

Based on the bestselling miniseries

A FORTUNE'S CHILDREN *Wedding:*
THE HOODWINKED BRIDE

by BARBARA BOSWELL

This March, the Fortune family discovers a twenty-six-year-old secret—beautiful Angelica Carroll *Fortune!* Kate Fortune hires Flynt Corrigan to protect the newest Fortune, and this jaded investigator soon finds this his most tantalizing—and tormenting—assignment to date....

Barbara Boswell's single title is just one of the captivating romances in Silhouette's exciting new miniseries, **Fortune's Children: The Brides,** featuring six special women who perpetuate a family legacy that is greater than mere riches!

Look for *The Honor Bound Groom,* by Jennifer Greene, when **Fortune's Children: The Brides** launches in Silhouette Desire in January 1999!

Available at your favorite retail outlet.

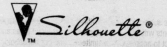

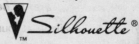

#1231 DREAM BRIDE—Susan Mallery

That Special Woman!/Brides of Bradley House

According to family legend, Chloe Wright was destined to dream of her future husband on her twenty-fifth birthday. The self-proclaimed pragmatist didn't believe in fairy tales...until enigmatic Arizona Smith mysteriously entered Chloe's life—and passionately swept her off her feet.

#1232 THE PERFECT NEIGHBOR—Nora Roberts

The MacGregors

Brooding loner Preston McQuinn was determined never to love again. But he could hardly resist his vivacious neighbor Cybil Campbell, who was determined to win his stubborn heart. Would the matchmaking Daniel MacGregor see his granddaughter happily married to the man she adored?

#1233 HUSBAND IN TRAINING—Christine Rimmer

Nick DeSalvo wanted to trade in his bachelor ways for his very own family. And who better than Jenny Brown—his best friend's nurturing widow—to give him lessons on how to be a model husband? But how long would it take the smitten, reformed heartbreaker to realize he wanted *Jenny* as his wife?

#1234 THE COWBOY AND HIS WAYWARD BRIDE—Sherryl Woods

And Baby Makes Three: The Next Generation

Rancher Harlan Patrick Adams was fit to be tied! The only woman who'd ever mattered to him had secretly given birth to *his* baby girl. And he couldn't bear to be apart from his family for another second. Could the driven father convince fiercely independent Laurie Jensen to be his bride?

#1235 MARRYING AN OLDER MAN—Arlene James

She was young, innocent and madly in love with her much older boss. Trouble was, no matter how much Caroline Moncton enticed him, gorgeous cowboy Jesse Wagner insisted she'd set her sights on the wrong guy. But she refused to quit tempting this hardheaded man down the wedding aisle!

#1236 A HERO AT HEART—Ann Howard White

When Nathan Garner returned to Thunder Ridge, Georgia, he was enveloped in bittersweet memories of Rachel Holcomb. Walking away from her gentle tenderness hadn't been easy, but it had been necessary. Could he reclaim Rachel's wary heart—and bring his beloved back into his waiting arms?